DEATH BY DEMON

LAURA PRIOR

LAURA PRIOR

ISBN: ISBN-13: 978-1492217053

LAURA PRIOR

Dedication

A huge thank you to all of my friends who have supported me on this exciting adventure! Special thanks to Sheree and Tanya who have spent hours proof reading. Dedicated to my Mam and to my Nana who reads my books but skips the 'naughty' bits.

1

A pessimist is a man who thinks all women are bad. An optimist is a man who hopes they are.

Chauncey Mitchell Depew

I reached down and placed three fingers on the concrete beneath me. I pressed down and shifted the weight on my aching feet. My calves were beginning to cramp, crouched down as I was and my eyes were stinging from staring so intensely into the darkness. Enough moaning. I sucked in a long silent breath and focused, pushing aside my aches and pains.

I was crouched behind a large dumpster in the back alleyway of a department store. Excess boxes that hadn't been put in the bin were stacked up beside me haphazardly. Between the smell of the rubbish, the broken glass surrounding me and the light rain falling, it wasn't the most comfortable of places to hide. I had spotted an angel – the bad kind - a few blocks back and I had had to make a quick dash for a safe hiding spot. I was regretting my choice.

A flutter of movement in my peripheral vision caught my attention. I stiffened and leaned forward, trying to pierce the blackness surrounding me. Nothing moved. I was sure there was something there. I had seen it. My nerve endings were tingling, alarming me, telling me something dangerous was out there. The prickly swirl of power was churning inside my chest, eager, ready to be unleashed.

Instinct told me to move. I sprinted forward away from the dumpster just as it exploded into a fiery bomb. The impact hurled me against a chain gate divide, separating the alley way. The metal dug into my back as I landed heavily against it, before dropping to the floor. I landed on my feet and kept moving. I rolled across the gate, narrowly missing being crushed by a metal bar. I jumped onto a dumpster and ran up the brick wall of a store, before somersaulting backwards and landing in a crouch in the middle of the alley. I turned side on to my attacker and raised my sword.

The man before me narrowed his black eyes; wrinkles around his face crinkling, almost hiding his eyes from view. He scowled at me and lifted his hands. Whereas normally in a fight one would clench their fists, he straightened his fingers out, revealing thick black claws. I knew from past experience that those claws would be able to rip me to shreds. The man was dressed all in black – typical. You would have thought they would get sick of wearing black, but no, almost every single one of them was dressed head to toe in black, with or without the leather accessories and chain mail. It was as if they had specifically picked the darkest colour possible to rebel against their angelic roots.

When you heard their story, you felt sorry for them. You would think they were to be pitied, forgiven even. But ninety nine percent of them were evil, in every sense of the word, and could not be redeemed. Most humans were safe from them, but for those like me, well, they would rip out your throat, feast on your blood, and laugh while doing it.

This monster before me, like the rest of his kin, was pure evil: demons of the night who reveled in pain and torture. It hadn't always been so. They had once been true angels, made up of goodness, light and courage until they had been caught up in the battle that had swept through the heavens thousands of years ago. An angel named Lucifer had caused their fall from grace. He had rebelled against Heaven and all it stood for. He plotted and schemed until a war broke out among the angels in the Heavenly realm in which they lived. The war was so damaging, so great, that many other realms were obliterated in its wake. It lasted years; the amount of beings lost, incredible. In the end the price paid was even greater. Lucifer had lost the war and the angels who had sided with him and fought in his army fell will him into Tartarus – a Hell dimension guarded by the Warriors of Death. Those who landed there would be tortured for all eternity in punishment. Only some did not fall there. Some angels who had been powerful in angel magic created portals as they fell, and were then able to conjure them from inside Hell. Those angels fled to other realms and hid, plotting their revenge.

It is thought that Lucifer is one of those who remained free. In retaliation for his loss his army has preyed on the Nephilim, half angel - half human beings, who are weak and unable to protect themselves. They have hunted down and killed thousands upon thousands of them. Some angels protected the Nephilim. The angel's aura covered their scent so that they couldn't be tracked. Other angels attempted to hide their Nephilim offspring, abandoning them to the human world in the hope that they would be safe, but that didn't always work out. Strong emotions left a scent for the Fallen, and though in many cases the angels managed to intervene in time, the Fallen destroyed more. The Fallen did not understand love or forgiveness, only anger and hatred, and the need for revenge. They were formidable enemies.

It wasn't only the Fallen who were out to kill the Nephilim. Other demons were always looking for a way to upset the balance between good and evil. Angels of light will always serve God, and the demons will always serve their own masters. The Nephilim can be swayed either way: good or bad. So Nephilim were monitored and either protected or destroyed accordingly.

The power swirling in my chest warned me the Fallen Angel was about to move. He swept out with his claws trying to slit my throat. I threw myself backwards, flipping away from him. As I landed on my feet I swept my blade out in front of me slicing the black clothing on his chest. He paused and touched his chest before looking up at me, alarmed.

He spun, his leg trailing out and I jumped, higher than he could have imagined, landing on the side of the building. I caught hold of the metal staircase at the fire exit and stood on the metal overhang. As the Fallen jumped at me, scrambling up the side of the wall I jumped off, landing on the roof of an abandoned car in the alleyway. I continued running as I heard the whoosh of a fireball land behind me. The car exploded, hurtling me into the brick wall opposite. I smashed through it, landing on my back.

I coughed, hacking up blood from my cut throat and mouth. I was scrambling to my feet as I was dragged up by my hair. I could smell the stench of the Fallen Angel as he leaned close to bite. I ducked and spun under his arm, twisting to be free. I grabbed hold of his arm, tearing my hair out of his grasp. I sent my power through it, burning and sizzling the flesh anywhere it could. The angel screamed and dropped his hand. He backed away, snarling at me.

A cunning look passed across his eyes and he dived for me. I rolled across the floor, picking up my sword and slashing out at him, catching his face. He howled in anger and grabbed me by my arms, throwing me through a wall. I landed back in the alleyway, in the light rain. I had fallen onto a pile of cardboard boxes. The rain had made them slippery and as I was struggling to regain my feet, the angel descended upon me. I rolled backwards, back-flipping my way over the boxes.

He jumped, landing just in front of me. I punched out with my right arm. He ducked and kneed me in the stomach. Nausea hurtled through me as I coughed and choked. Bent over as I was I bared my teeth and bit into the flesh of his leg. I focused and spread my power through my mouth into his flesh. I grinned wickedly in my mind as I envisioned a poison, burning, and devouring his flesh. I imagined it being sucked into his blood stream, scorching its way through his body. I wanted this, I wanted him to suffer. I wanted him to be writhing in agony as his organs popped, as his blood boiled.

He kicked me away. I slid to the side and stood slightly crouched, ready to attack him again. He fell to his knees screaming. Saliva pooled from his mouth, pouring down his chest. Blood streamed from his eyes. The black of his pupils began to turn red, and ran out in a thick cream down his cheeks. He snarled, and growled, the tortured sound of an animal. He fell to all fours and tried to crawl towards me, reaching out with his claws, wanting to rip me apart for what I had done. I held on to the thought of my glittery, swirling power devouring him from the inside, encouraging it, forcing it to burn quicker and hotter.

A pain shot through my head and I found myself lying on the floor in a pool of water. I fought against unconsciousness, struggled through the fog in my head to clamber to my feet. I was knocked down again to my knees. I turned and through hazy eyes visualized this new attacker.

A woman, white blonde hair to her shoulders gazed down at me. Her face was sweet, her eyes crystal blue. An angel, you would have thought. Only an angel would never help one of the Fallen. Before she had time to attack me again, I pushed up off my knees and barreled into her, knocking her against the burned out remains of the car. Grasping her by her shoulders I smashed her head through the passenger window - the only window left intact. She screamed and slashed at my face with her claws. I felt blood splatter out from me but ignored the scream of pain from my tingling nerves. I battled against her, trying to gain ground. I kicked out at her heel and heard it snap. Taking the chance I reached down and whipped a dagger out from the strap inside my left boot. I sliced it up, cutting the Fallen Angel from the stomach to the throat. Blood poured out, saturating me, covering me head to toe.

I wiped the blood from my face and swiped at my eyes, trying to keep my enemy in sight. She screeched and leapt at me knocking me back. I slipped on the cardboard, sliding backwards from her. I punched out, connecting with her jaw. Her head snapped back and she fell to her knee. Hearing a noise behind me I turned. The male Fallen Angel on the ground had almost crawled within reach. Thick blood had coated his face and steam rose from his burning body. He snarled; his sharp, yellow teeth snapping at my ankles. I kicked out, connecting with his face. His cheek bones cracked loudly. Thick claws dug into my shoulders and I was wrenched back. I screamed as the fetid breath of the Fallen Angel stung my face.

I sucked in my power and screamed as it exploded through my veins, speeding through my muscles, pumping around my entire body. I leapt back, spinning through the air above her. I landed on her back and quickly placed my hands around her neck. I wrenched to the side, snapping her neck. She fell to the ground with a thump. I knew that wouldn't stop her. Fallen Angels were almost impossible to kill. I needed to decapitate them both or they would keep coming at me. I reached behind me and retrieved my second sword from the clip on my shoulder. I swung it round cleanly, narrowly missing my mark.

The Fallen Angel screamed her rage and leaped away, running up the brick building as though gravity were no issue. Which for angels, it wasn't. I let my power escape through me. A large glittering mass absorbed me in its midst, sparkling, dazzling. I pushed my power through my limbs and sprinted after her. I jumped onto the top of a dumpster and vaulted up the side of the wall. I clung onto the cracks in the old brick work and forced my body to pull itself up onto the roof where I had seen the Fallen Angel disappear.

Standing on the flat roof, stories up over the city, I spun around. The yellow and red lights from near and far shops and offices glimmered, highlighting my fighting zone as though it was a stage and I was the star attraction. It felt like that, and I knew it to be true. I could almost feel the eyes of the others out there watching me, judging me.

I was kicked from behind. As I flew forwards I rolled and came up in a fighting crouch. I still had my sword clenched tightly. As I steadied myself I began to wonder about this evil being before me. Why had she chosen to side with Lucifer? With her white blonde hair and beautiful face she must have been loved when she was among the angels. Why had she given it all up? I couldn't ever imagine giving up the light, all goodness, and embracing a wicked life killing and torturing. What had made her think that this life would be so much better than following the orders of God?

The angel ran for me and swung her fist, catching me in the face. I felt a tooth dislodge in my mouth, the pain shooting up my jaw. I spat out the blood that instantly filled my mouth and spun back punching my clenched fist just under her jaw. With that punch I felt myself wobble off balance. The Fallen Angel pushed me backwards with an unrecognizable force, driving us over the edge of the building. Just before I fell I grabbed hold of her arm, digging my nails in as far as they would go into the flesh. Within seconds we had landed in the alley below. Pain screamed up my side. I quickly tested my limbs and though in agony, they were firstly still attached, and secondly able to pull me to my feet.

I reached behind me and pulled out another blade from the belt at my waist. As the angel struggled to her feet before me, I brought it down and around and sliced her head clean off. It span in the air and disintegrated into thick sludge as it fell to the floor. The rest of the body began to collapse in on itself slowly.

I spun around to face the first Fallen Angel who remained on the ground groaning. I stepped closer to him. I stepped over his body, one foot on either side of him. I swung the sword back, steadying it.

“Who are you?” the angel rasped out. He turned his head to face me, spluttering blood out of his mouth with each word.

I paused and smiled at him. “I haven’t quite worked that out yet. But for now, you can call me Jasmine the Angel Slayer.”

I swung my sword down slicing through his throat cleanly.

2

Never underestimate the power of a girl who knows what she wants.

Unknown.

"Jasmine the Angel Slayer?" Trev called to me sarcastically. He jogged up the alley towards me, flagged by the others.

I laughed. "It was a spur of the moment thing. You don't like it?"

"It sounds shit," he replied. He stopped beside me and looked down at the two piles of bloody sludge that signified the Fallen Angel's remains. "Dude, that's gross. I think I'm gonna vom."

A hand on my shoulder turned me. I looked up into Sam's soft brown eyes. "Are you okay? That looked pretty intense. I was really scared for you for a moment," he said, concern etched on his face.

I shrugged then winced. "I'm fine." At his look, I conceded, "A few scratches, a few broken bones, but nothing I can't heal."

Sam grimaced in reply. A shadow of movement caught my eye. I looked up quickly as a dark shape dropped from the four story building onto the concrete in front of me. The tall man sauntered up to me sullenly. His dark black eyes stared into mine before his hands traced my shoulders where they had been sliced by the female angel's claws. *Zacharael. Zach*. The man of my dreams. Or more accurately, my very own Guardian Angel. My first and only love. According to some - my *One True Love*. How accurate that was I didn't know, but if he was supposed to be my soul mate, I'd definitely been stiffed somehow.

He was jaw droppingly gorgeous. Incredibly tall and not gangly like most tall guys, he was *built*. He had this kick ass warrior physique. Muscles upon muscles rippled beneath his clothing as he walked. You could see the definition of his chest and abdomen even when he was standing still. A dark swirling tattoo covered the left side of his torso and ran up his neck and down his arm. I had traced every inch of that tattoo with my tongue. His body was a machine, made to love and to kill.

Angels were born into classes. There were loads of different groups of them, each having particular talents, abilities and duties. Zacharael was from the Warrior class of angels which meant that he had a duty to keep the peace between humans and those of other realms. He had been chosen as my Guardian Angel, by whom, I wasn't sure, but I had my suspicions.

Zach stepped closer and lifted my chin to stare down at me from his height. I know people say that the eyes are the windows to the soul, but his really were. It was impossible to explain fully to anyone, but his eyes were so black you could see for miles inside them. He had the whites, like everyone, but his Iris's and pupils were coal black. He had long black eyelashes framing them perfectly. When I looked into them I felt myself sucked in, almost *falling* into them.

He had high cheek bones, and a long straight nose. His full, juicy, kissable lips topped off his physical perfection. His left eyebrow was pierced with a thick silver bolt. From the bolt to his dark hair shaved close to his skull, you would begin to think *criminal* if you were looking at him. Then you would begin to realize that he was loaded to the max and deadly as sin. Two swords were crossed at his back, the handles jutting over his shoulders, daggers were strapped to his thighs and ankles. He wore knee length black leather boots and tight black trousers. Today he had the decency to wear a black t-shirt, but usually he would be quite happy topless, which would reveal the strange silver chain and pendant he wore.

I knew others saw how attractive he was. I had firsthand experience of girls drooling over him while I was in his presence, but I knew that no matter how hot other girls found him, his attraction was multiplied by a million when it came to me. I *knew* what he could do. I knew what he had done. He was every bit as dangerous as he looked. Dangerous physically to everyone but me, but emotionally he had killed me over and over again. And yet my heart still pounded when I saw him, and thrills raced through me at his nearness, at his touch.

“Are you injured?” he asked softly. His low voice rumbled through my senses.

I swallowed hard and stepped back away from him, removing the temptation to touch him. “I’m fine.”

“You’re lying,” he replied, scowling.

“You were amazing!” Gwen ran up to me and hugged me. Thankful for the distraction, I hugged her back. I was secretly pleased that Gwen, Trev and Sam had accompanied me here. It was nice to show off a little, to be able to show your friends what you could do, but at the same time it was incredibly dangerous for them and I didn’t want them to get in the habit of going looking for Fallen Angels like we had done this evening. This time I had allowed it, as Haamiah, Maion and Zach had also been attending, so I knew they would be safe.

"Thanks!" I smiled at her, shaking my head slightly at what she had chosen to wear to a Fallen Angel hunt. I was sure she only ever wore designer clothing, taking advantage of her Father's guilt. Not that I didn't think he deserved it. Gwen's father had known that her mother was an angel and had given her over to the angels when she was a toddler. She had been moved around the Nephilim care homes throughout her childhood but had stayed in contact with her father who sent huge sums of money – and credit card details. I wasn't sure if she would ever forgive him, but that was her business.

She always looked amazing, dressed in the most beautiful, if not entirely practical clothes. Currently dressed in fitted black leggings and a leopard print tunic, she looked like a model. Light cocoa skin gave her a beautiful complexion and her curled hair was pulled back into a soft clip.

I looked over at Trev, smiling at how completely and utterly different he was to Gwen. He had the grungy look down. Brown dreadlocks streamed down his back, and his face was pierced again and again. His nose, ears, eyes, lips and chin were all decorated with studs and rings. At the moment I was fascinated with a silver chain that ran from his ear to his lower lip. I wouldn't say that Trev was really my type, but that chain was *sexy*!

Sam, to the other side of me was different again. With short blonde hair and a thick, stocky frame he was gorgeous in a boy-next-door kind of way. He was my best friend, and the one who I had the most in common with. Like me, he had never known his real parents. Sam had grown up in foster care and had eventually run away after being passed around from home to home.

Trev was the only one of us who had experienced a loving home, but his story was also the most tragic. Trev had grown up with his father who had passed away from lung cancer when Trev was just finishing school. He had no other family, and had been found by the angels and put into a Nephilim safe house. There, he discovered his true heritage, and finally contacted his mother. When he had found out she was an angel he blamed her bitterly for not saving his father's life. I had recently discovered that his Nephilim ability was to be able to contact the angels, including his mother, and I knew he was confused by the gift.

Sam was a telepath, meaning he could hear the thoughts of others. Most people, including the majority of the other Nephilim at the safe house resented that he was able to hear their private thoughts, and I admit I had thought it was a little intrusive at first. I had constantly worried that I would think something and he would be offended by it, or that he would tell my secrets to someone else, but I had learned to trust him. And he stayed out of my head as much as possible. He had once confessed that it was difficult for him, hearing voices all day long, but he dealt with it with minimal complaints. In fact since he never mentioned it, it was easy to forget he could hear my every thought.

Gwen had the gift of wings. We had recently been attacked by a Witch in another realm, and there to our shock she had unleashed these huge, beautiful, white angel wings. She could fly, though she said she wasn't very good at it.

My ability was undetermined. I was definitely able to open portals to other realms – a skill I didn't particularly enjoy, as it had sent me into trouble a number of times, but recently I had developed a multitude of other skills. I could heal and I was physically stronger and faster than any other Nephilim. The revelation of my talents had been disturbing to say the least, and the other angels were confused and worried about my abilities, and what they meant.

Tonight was a test of sorts. I had sparred with the angels in the safe house but they had wanted to know what I could do outside. I had been tracked and cornered a number of times by Fallen Angels so I had known what they wanted me to do. Whereas before my Guardian Angel had stepped in each time a Fallen Angel had been near me, I had known that this time it was up to me. And I had been pleased to show off what I could do.

Last year I had been so lost, unable to find peace anywhere. I didn't have a clue who I really was. I had been abandoned by the love of my life, and was left a broken shell. A recent quest in another realm had unleashed a world of possibilities upon me. I had been given the gift of a future. I'd had a tiny glimpse of who I could really be, of what my destiny could hold for me, and I had grasped on tightly. I was new, I was strong and I needed no one to protect me.

Another angel stepped out of the shadows. A tall, dark skinned man with black dreadlocks to his waist sauntered up to me. *Haamiah*. The most senior angel in our safe house. He was of the Principality class of angels and his purpose was to guide humans, Nephilim and angels in decision making. I was sure that it had been he who had ordered Zach to protect me in the first place, but he had refused to answer when I had asked him directly. I had begrudgingly accepted, along with most of the other Nephilim and angels to follow his lead as he tended to nudge people into a direction that made no sense at the time, but ultimately it would all work out for the best. I had considered if he were able to predict the future or if he was an oracle, but when Sam had 'listened in' he had said his thought process simply worked quicker than any he had come across. It was as if he analyzed every single possible outcome and was able to choose from them which path to follow.

Haamiah was wearing his usual dad-style beige trousers and a white button down shirt. Like most of the angels, he wore thick black leather boots and weapons were strapped in various places. He frowned down at the two piles of gunge on the floor and nodded his head.

"Very good," he said calmly. He turned to walk away.

"Was I good enough?" I called out, my hands on my hips.

He slowly turned back. Without turning fully, he paused, his profile highlighted by the streetlights further down the end of the alleyway. "Almost," he said.

"Bullshit!" I shouted, angry. "I've been at this for two months! You told me if I was strong enough to defend myself then you would tell me where my brother was!" I gestured around me. "I've killed two of the Fallen in one go tonight. I'm strong enough. I'm ready."

Haamiah turned fully to me and frowned. "You are not ready."

I launched myself at him. He spun at the last second and knocked me away. I ran up the wall and flipped backwards over the top of him. I punched out at him repeatedly, but he knocked each blow away with an insane speed. Before I knew it I was lying on the floor in the alleyway, my windpipe being crushed, my back in agony from the slam. Haamiah kneeled on me, his dark eyes boring into mine.

"I will tell you when you are ready. That time is not now," he said.

Rage covered my eyes in the form of silver film. I reached up and placed my hand on his knee. I smiled as I allowed the tingling glitter mist to pour through my arm and I shoved him backwards. He sailed backwards and with the speed and force I had used he would have smashed through the wall in the alleyway if it hadn't been for his wings that slowed his speed and brought him back to the ground. I sprang up to my feet and lifted my fists, ready for him.

"I'm ready!" I snarled. "You're going to tell my where my brother is or I'll find him myself!"

Haamiah smirked at me and nodded his head. Zach appeared before him and smashed his fist into his face. Haamiah dropped to his knee, the concrete giving way beneath the force. I gasped. Zach and Haamiah had been friends for centuries. I knew their friendship was a little tense now because of a disagreement they'd had recently but I never would have thought they would fight.

Zach's body was heaving, shaking. I could see him trying to rein in his rage. The urge to attack Haamiah was too strong for him to control. I stepped forward to run to him.

"Don't Jasmine," Sam warned me. He grabbed my arm, trying to hold me back. I knocked him off and continued on to Zach.

I stepped between the two angels. Haamiah was no threat now, not with Zach by my side. I turned to face Zach and placed my palm on his chest. Instantly an ache ran through my chest, down through my abdomen to my legs. A flush followed, then a pulsating sting. I could feel my soul pull outwards from my body, wanting to touch his. That one touch left me panting.

I lifted my face up higher and higher until I met his black eyes. I groaned as I felt his burning gaze touch mine. I could feel his eyes caressing my face, my neck, my collarbone. With angel speed he grabbed my around my waist and pulled me up to his chest. He bent his knees and launched us into the air. His beautiful white wings thundered as they unfolded behind him. They caught the air and hurled us both through the night sky above the city.

3

Being called weird is like being called limited edition, meaning you're something people don't see that often. Remember that.

Unknown

My stomach sunk as we made the initial climb above the city. I was pressed up to Zach's chest, my face resting on the hard muscles there. My arms were loosely draped on his shoulders. I didn't even need to hold onto him, I knew he would never drop me. Flying like this seemed so natural to me. Though we hadn't done this in so long it felt like second nature. I trusted him implicitly to keep me safe. I could feel the warmth from him sinking through my skin, reaching my core.

I felt a thrill when he spun me in his arms so that I was facing away from him. His arms remained in place, one wrapped around my pelvis, one around my chest under my arms. I let my head fall back onto his shoulder as we rose higher and higher in the sky. I turned my face to his neck, breathing in his scent. He was so masculine, so wild and animalistic. The dangerous aura surrounding him was part of my initial and continuing attraction. He had the bad boy persona down pat. I couldn't help but tingle with pleasure when I thought that he had defied and attacked Haamiah on my behalf. I was still pissed off that Haamiah had refused to allow Zach to travel through a portal to rescue me a couple of months ago. I knew it had turned out well in the end, and Zach had found his own way to that realm without Haamiah's help, but I'd like to think if anyone I knew was in trouble that I would do everything possible to assist. Haamiah was strange, maybe because of his duties, but he was firmly on the 'good' side so I had decided to forgive him for that. But this? Holding the information about my brother hostage like this made me really mad. And getting me mad wasn't a good idea.

I had grown up with an alcoholic mother and a vile man for a step-father. It turned out that that woman wasn't even related to me. Thankfully Zach had been waiting in the wings to swoop in and take care of me after being kicked out of home the moment I left school. I had never had the opportunity to question her about it because by the time I found out Zach and I had been miles away living on a remote island in the pacific.

Zach hadn't been thrilled about playing Guardian Angel at first, but we had grown on each other and eventually became friends, then lovers. Besides Zach, I had thought I was completely alone in this world. He had taken me to the Nephilim safe house, and there I had met Trev, Sam and Gwen, who I felt like I'd known all my life, but something was still missing. Haamiah had just informed me that I had a brother out there somewhere but was refusing to tell me exactly where.

Instead, he had told me that I needed to train harder than I ever had before if I was going to meet him. I had worked my arse off for the past two months learning everything the angels could teach me. Zach was my main teacher, though Haamiah would spar with me on occasion. Even Maion, an angel I despised, took his turn in taking me out to hunt the Fallen. I had explored my abilities and talents, learning to heal with my angel power, to fight, track and hide. I was stronger than I had ever been before.

What was Haamiah's problem? I knew that I should listen to him but the thought that I had one person who was actually related to me out there was too much to handle. I had to see him. I had to *know* him.

I sighed and closed my eyes, allowing the tension to seep from my body. Flying with Zach was magical. When we evened out, flying laterally, I felt the rush of excitement of flying with him, the adrenaline coursing through my veins. The lights below from the city sparkled and twinkled; cars, streetlights, offices, bars and shops. I spread out my arms to the side, pretending I was flying. The wind whipped through my hair, chilling my skin. Zach swooped and dived, causing thrills to race through me. I laughed, feeling as though I didn't have a care in the world as he did a full loop in the air and dived through a soft grey cloud.

We continued to fly over the city, high enough up that if anyone saw us they would think we were just a large bird flying overhead. I tilted my head to glimpse Zach behind me. I couldn't see his expression, but just knowing he was there, feeling his arms wrapped around me, made me feel safe.

Eventually we landed in a park I recognized. It wasn't too far from the safe house. This area had been purposely chosen as the houses were large and spaced out. Each had large gated gardens, and each block of land had lots of trees and bushes to afford privacy. You didn't want your neighbors peeking over your fence and seeing someone walking around with wings or calling a hundred birds to come and sit down around them, or even of someone walking around talking to the spirits or invisible angels, let alone the daily sparring sessions held out in the gardens. Haamiah had chosen well in situating the safe house here; we rarely saw anybody as the area was so remote that the houses were mainly used as holiday homes and rarely visited.

The park we landed in was only a few minutes' walk from the house. There was a large pond in the middle, otherwise it was pretty plain. As Zach let my feet touch the floor I spun around and raised up on my tip toes. His lips descended on mine. His lips caressed mine. His tongue darted out to lick my bottom lip, sucking it into his mouth. I groaned and pulled him closer, my hands forcing his head to mine. I could feel the scrape of stubble on his jaw. It made me even wilder. I panted as I kissed my way down his neck.

He stepped away and I felt the loss of him immediately. He reached behind and quickly discarded the braces holding his swords behind his shoulders, chucking them on the floor carelessly. He reached for me again, yanking me into his chest. I stumbled, falling against him.

He lifted me and I immediately wrapped my legs around his waist, my hands caressing his jaw. I could feel him pressed up against my core, hard and stiff. Shivers shot through me, making me burn. His lips reclaimed mine, biting and licking, becoming more forceful, more aggressive. He walked forwards into the cover of the trees. I felt him press me up against a tree, grinding against me. I dropped my head back, breathless, as he bit down my throat. His hands caressed my body, massaging and pinching every inch of me.

He laid me down on the floor, continuing his loving of my body. I reached down and pulled the remainder of his shredded black t-shirt up over his head. He balled it up in one hand and placed it under my head. In the second I had to think about it, my heart melted. I was quickly distracted as he ran his hand between my legs, pressing and rubbing. I was on the edge, on the very verge and I needed Zach to come over with me.

He leaned back and pulled my own t-shirt off and instantly laid me flat, exploring my significant chest with his mouth. He nibbled and licked, lathing me with his tongue. He rolled me over onto my stomach and caressed my breasts with his hands. He leaned over me, biting and kissing my neck.

He ran his hands down my sides and peeled my trousers down to my thighs. Parting me, he slid his fingers into my core, rubbing and delving. The pleasure was extreme and violent. I had needed this for so long...needed *him*. I could feel my juices running out as I reached my climax. As I began to feel more comfortable I felt him mount me, his thick knob sliding into me, slippery. He slowly forced me to lie flat, raising my bottom for his attentions. He began to slide more fully, filling me to the brim, forcing me to accept more. The burning began again, the ache spreading through my abdomen to my chest. I could feel the lust and need pump around my veins with each pulse of my heart.

I groaned loudly and reached back, needing more. He began to pound into me again and again, harder and harder. The pleasure-pain too much to bear. I screamed as I came again, but he still continued. I could hear him panting in my ear. His breaths came hard and fast just like his knob. He pushed me again, I was on the edge. I screamed again as I fell over the precipice again. My body going into spasms, clenching his tightly, never wanting to let go.

Zach fell over me, burying his face into my shoulders, breathless. I lay my head on his t-shirt, unable to move. I closed my eyes, needing to rest and regain my strength. I felt Zach's hands cup my breasts again, toying with my hard nipples.

"Well that was quite a show," a cold voice called out.

Zach and I jumped to our feet. As I turned around, Zach was already between me and the intruder, his trousers unbuttoned, a sword in his hand. The intruder was not human. I knew that immediately. Neither was he one of the Fallen. Ice blonde hair and piercing blue eyes, tall and muscular, he was definitely something 'other'. As he walked closer to us, I noticed the gun in his hand. That was unusual. Most mystical creatures had their own methods of killing, and stuck their nose up at primitive human methods.

Zach began to circle him. The man held up his hands, including the one with the gun.

"Easy now, I only came to talk," he said. "Don't you even want to know who I am?"

"I know *what* you are; I don't need to know *who* you are," Zach growled.

My temper got the best of me. "Well I don't know who you are, and I'd like to know!" I snarled, annoyed again at Zach for making decisions for me. If this peeping tom had something to say I wanted to hear it.

"Now that's more like it," the stranger praised.

"Cut the crap and tell me what you want," I replied.

He smirked at me. "Asmodeus sent me with a message."

I paled. My heart sank, the very fiber of my being shrank away, hiding inside of me. I felt faint. I could already sense my power beginning to take control, swirling around my chest higher and higher, wanting to be set free, wanting to open a portal so I could escape.

Then I got angry.

In one second I had sucked in my power and absorbed it into my muscles and bones. I forced myself around Zach and before he had even noticed I had hold of the second sword he had dropped on the floor. I was behind the blonde man in an instant and was able to enjoy the look of shock as I swung the sword decapitating him. I couldn't help but watch as the head flew to the side and rolled among the trees. The rest of the body before me collapsed sideways to the floor.

I had killed a number of things before. Fallen Angels turned into gunk – this thick disgusting stick mess, Fury Demons stayed whole, or at least how you left them, similar to humans, but this being – whatever it was – disintegrated into a fine dust like powder, grey in color. The breeze began to sweep it across the ground.

I turned to face Zach, now standing next to me. He was angry.

"Don't look at me like that!" I said, unable to take my eyes away from the pile of dust.

"You should have let *me* deal with him!" he retorted angrily, his eyes flashing.

I turned to him fully. "And why is that exactly? If I'm supposed to just stand back and let someone else look after me then what's the point in learning to fight? What's the point in any of this?"

He frowned, thinking. "You killed him before we could find out what the message was."

"I didn't want to know what the message was. And you know what, while you get all high and mighty, you were going to kill him anyway." I jabbed him with my finger, scowling at him.

"I know, but we should have heard what he was going to say first."

"I didn't want to know!" I bit out.

"Well it's not just your decision to make, is it?" he snapped.

"I don't care. And you can talk! You said you knew what he was so you didn't need to know *who* he was, so what the hell was he?"

"A vampire!" he shouted. "You've got a fucking vampire on your trail now!"

I marched away from him, sick of his ranting. "It's not a problem anymore, he's dead isn't he!" I called back to him.

With a whoosh of air Zach stood before me, making me stop. "We'll have to hide you somewhere else. Haamiah has links to the other safe houses."

I had just begun to storm off again when it sunk in. "Hide me? I'm not hiding anywhere! Haamiah promised me I could go and see my brother!"

"Are you crazy? There's no way he'll let you go so far away from the safe house when you have vampires coming for you!"

I whirled around. "That's why we're not telling him!"

"What? Have you got a death wish? He needs to know about this!" he said.

"No. You're right. He won't let me go if he knows a vampire came here tonight, so we're not going to tell him. I'll be safe when I've gone because they won't know where I am, and everyone here will be safe because they're coming after *me*, not them."

"No way. Its suicide! You're insane if you think I'm going to agree to that!"

"You owe me!" I said, a dangerous edge to my voice. *No one* was keeping me from finding my brother. Not Zach, not Haamiah and certainly not Asmodeus. "If you ever expect me to forgive you, you're going to have to earn it!"

Zach froze. I could tell he was trying to find a way out of it. There *was* no way out of it. Haamiah was not finding out about this, if he did he would never tell me where my brother was. And Zach *did* owe me. After we had escaped months of torture in another realm, he had abandoned me. He had broken my heart so completely I had thought I would never find myself again. Then, when I had finally thought I was getting over him and was just beginning a relationship with someone else he had the nerve to show up unannounced and expected me to forgive him. I couldn't deny that I loved him still, or that I yearned for him every minute of the day, but I was nowhere near to forgiving him.

"You know they'll come after you," he said grimly.

"They won't know where I am," I replied sternly.

He nodded his head, looking at the ground. "If I do this..." My heart sped up, relief beginning to ease my tension. "If I do this, I'm coming with you."

I scowled. "I'll be fine on my own!"

"It's a deal breaker. Either you make sure Haamiah agrees to me coming with you, or I'll tell him you're being hunted by vampires and Asmodeus wants to get a message to you."

I paused, trying to find another solution. There was no way I wanted Zach trailing me to another continent. More than likely he would ruin the moment, just like he ruined everything else. I couldn't see another way. If I didn't agree to it then he'd tell Haamiah. Maybe once we were in Australia I could ditch him. Plus, he did have certain talents that might come in handy.

"Fine," I replied quickly. "It's a deal."

I held out my hand and breathed a sigh of relief when Zach reluctantly shook it.

I stared him down. "So you're not going to mention this to Haamiah."

"And you're going to tell him that I'm coming with you," he replied, smirking.

"Fine," I answered. I turned away from him and began to march stiffly back to the house.

4

There's nothing more badass than being who you are.

Darren Criss

I walked through the front door and meandered down towards the kitchen where I knew Trev, Sam and Gwen would be. Annoyingly Zach appeared before me, halting me.

I sighed and pursed my lips. "What do you want?"

"Are you going to tell them?"

"I don't know. I haven't decided," I replied. I stepped around him, only to find that he had blocked me again. I glared up at him.

"You know they'll want to come with you to find your brother. They should know all the facts before you put them in danger."

Guilt seeped through my stomach. Admittedly I hadn't actually thought about that. I had known they would want to come – they were my best friends and I couldn't imagine going without them. But if I was going to be followed by vampires and Fallen Angel's, would it be fair to let them? Another thought occurred. What about my brother? It was enough that I was going to suddenly jump feet first into his life, but what if it resulted in him being injured, or killed? What if he didn't know about any of this?

"Does he know about our heritage? Does he know any of this?" I demanded.

Zach lifted his hands in surrender. "Woah! I have no idea – you're better off asking Haamiah."

I pushed him aside and stormed past into the kitchen. The kitchen was a huge room, and the main gathering place for the Nephilim. There was also a living room adjacent, but wasn't large enough to hold all of the Nephilim in one go. As one walked into the room the entire right side was lined with cupboards and benches topped with black, sparkly granite. A large island with cooking apparatus and a breakfast bar was in the middle. The far end of the kitchen was a whole glass wall with doors opening into the garden. Stools and seats were dotted around and back towards the middle of the room was the largest kitchen table you've ever seen. The large wooden table, with wooden benches either side long enough to fit 30 people, was currently occupied by a throng of Nephilim surrounding Trev and Gwen. They looked up guiltily as I entered the room. I rolled my eyes, imagining the story they were weaving of my fight with Haamiah and the Fallen Angels.

I ignored them. "Where's Haamiah?"

Sam came up behind me holding a beer. "In his office."

I turned on my heel and marched out of the kitchen and back down the corridor, past a bemused Zach, to the other end of the house. I paused outside the white door then knocked loudly. Within seconds a voice ordered me to enter. I took a deep breath and opened the door.

Haamiah was standing beside a book case near the door. "Come in." He stepped back and allowed me to pass by him.

I hesitated in the doorway for a moment before determinedly walking to the green high backed chair facing his desk and sitting down. I listened to the door close, and watched as Haamiah walked around the desk to sit in his own chair. He leaned forward on the desk and gazed intently at me.

Haamiah's office almost looked like the office of my high school guidance counselor. All pine furniture, not a single piece of clutter, light and airy, it was as none-threatening as you could get. Even Haamiah himself appeared on the outside to be a kind and gentle 'Head Master', as the authorities thought of him.

Many of the Nephilim here were still children or teenagers. Like me, they had struggled at normal schools due to their abilities and had been labeled problem children. Haamiah and Elijah had tracked them down and offered to place them within his 'boarding school' for troubled children. Unbeknown to their parents, here they were told about their angelic heritage, and taught to develop their abilities and fight off demons. Whenever there were inspections the Nephilim played along, they sat exams like normal children, and had parent-teacher meetings just like any other school. Parents thought that Haamiah was a miracle worker...we knew that he was an angel who had existed since the beginning of time.

Haamiah leaned forward onto his clasped hands. His thick black dread-locked hair was held behind his head with a metal clip. Angels had no need to physically change their clothes as they could simply think them clean, so whereas I was bedraggled, with mud and probably grass stains covering my clothes, he sat in a crisp white shirt and beige trousers looking clean and fresh.

I took a deep breath, trying to contain my temper. “Look, I’m sorry about before, but you need to understand-”

“None of that matters,” he interrupted.

I scowled, my anger raging through me. Here I was attempting to apologize and he just cut me off as if what I had to say was of no importance!

“You want to know if your brother is aware of his Nephilim state,” he continued.

I paused, biting my tongue. I narrowed my eyes and waited for him to continue.

Haamiah sighed and sat back in his chair. “The truth is, I don’t know. I was not assigned to his care, only yours.”

“I knew it was you all along,” I muttered. I felt pleased that I had guessed his secret. Since the moment I had first met Zach I had wondered who had sent him to be my Guardian Angel. Haamiah being an angel of the Principality Class, was an obvious choice, but neither he nor Zach had ever confirmed my suspicions. Angels would never lie outright, but they were very good at evading questions they didn’t want to answer.

I regarded Haamiah in silence. He seemed to be waiting for me.

“Was someone else sent to look after him?” I asked.

Haamiah shrugged. “I don’t know.”

“Then how do you know he even exists?” I demanded, leaning forward in my chair.

Haamiah sat back and clasped his palms together. "A long time ago, a Seer told me of his existence, and of yours. I waited for my assignation and only received you into my care." He unclasped his hands in a gesture of surrender.

"But you know where he is?"

Haamiah nodded. "I know *where* he is, but I do not know *who* he is."

"Where is he?" I whispered. I prayed that he would answer me.

A silence ensued. As I waited, determined to sit here until he answered me, I began to wonder what he meant when he said he didn't know *who* he was. Did he mean his name? Or his moral fiber? His spiritual identity? I couldn't care less what religion or culture he belonged to. He belonged to *me*.

I glared at him and lifted my chin. I wouldn't back down.

"What will you do when you know his location?" Haamiah asked eventually.

"I'll go there and find him," I replied calmly.

"And if he is unaware of his angelic abilities?"

"I...I don't know. It all depends on what I find. I can't tell you what I'll do because I don't *know* him. I just know that I have to find him. I need to make sure he's safe, that the Fallen haven't found him."

"What if they have?"

"Then I'll rip them apart for even thinking about touching my brother," I answered sweetly.

He nodded his head thoughtfully. “Apart from keeping him safe, why else are you so desperate to find him?”

I bit my lip and frowned at him. Hesitantly I said, “I have to know that he’s had a better life than I had.”

“And if he didn’t?”

“Then I’ll make it better. I swear it. I grew up not knowing who I was, not knowing that I wasn’t even the person I was supposed to be. I didn’t even think that I was worth more. It never even occurred to me to want more than I had, I didn’t know there was anything else to want.” I paused and looked at my clenched hands before meeting his gaze once more. “I didn’t know for certain that it was you who sent Zach to me…thank you. Zach completely changed my life. He saved my life before I even knew what he was or what I was. If you hadn’t sent him to me when you did, I’d probably be dead now.”

Haamiah stared at me for a moment then inclined his head briefly. “My actions are only the wishes of the Almighty. He must see something special in you. I believe you have an interesting future waiting for you.”

I raised my eyebrows. “My *present* is already pretty interesting.”

Haamiah smiled. “Indeed. What will you do if you encounter the Fallen on your journey there? Which, as you are aware, you will undoubtedly do.” He tilted his head at me.

“I’ve proven to you that I can fight. I took them down tonight, and I’ve done it before. You know I can do it.” There was silence as Haamiah gazed at me, his black eyes boring into my soul. I took a deep breath. “And…I’ll take Zach with me. I know he would just follow me in any case, so he might as well travel with me.”

Haamiah nodded. "He's in Victoria, Australia, in a small town called Meadowbrook. He's in high school there."

Relief surged through me. The dead weight that had been lodged in the pit of my soul for weeks was finally eased. I felt myself smile up at the angel before me. I knew I should have felt annoyed that the only reason he surrendered the information was because I had told him I would travel with Zach, but I couldn't help but feel ecstatic at the thought that I would soon find him.

Haamiah interrupted my thoughts. "When will you leave?"

"Tomorrow," I answered quickly, anticipating a rejection.

He nodded. "Very well."

Surprised, I jumped up to my feet and quickly exited the room. I closed the door behind me and turned to walk up the corridor towards the staircase. I passed a couple of other Nephilim in the corridor who greeted me, and I ran up the stairs to my room.

My room was pretty ordinary; pale blue walls, wooden floor boards, white trimmings. All of our bedrooms were decorated the same – as though the angels wanted us to remember we were supposed to be angelic. It hadn't worked. Most of the other Nephilim had plastered their walls with posters, some had even re-painted their rooms, new furniture had been bought, and some Nephilim that were now together were even sharing bedrooms. I had been surprised that it was allowed, but the angels hadn't said a word about it.

Though this had been my room for over a year I had made absolutely no changes, though the furniture had had to be replaced after I had trashed the room in a fit of fury and stress after returning from our capture in Castle Dantanian, it had been replaced with equally boring and unimaginative accessories.

As I closed the door behind me I turned and promptly jumped out of my skin.

“What are you doing here?” I growled.

Zach lay on my bed, his hands behind his head, and his ankles crossed. He smirked at me.

“You better get packing if we’re leaving tomorrow,” he smirked.

“Ugh!” I grunted at him. I turned away and began to rummage through my wardrobe. There was nothing particularly interesting in there. Everything I owned was made for fighting; I practically lived in cargo pants and t-shirts, I owned one decent pair of jeans, and a couple of dresses that Gwen hadn’t liked enough to keep for herself, and a couple of jumpers. I sadly gazed at the pathetic pile of shoes in the bottom of the wardrobe. Not even a single pair of heels was there, only trainers, boots and pair of flip-flops. Before I had left home I had had a decent variety of heels, pumps and wedges but I had left in such a rage I had barely taken anything with me. It was lucky really that I’d spent more time out of this realm than in it, or I would have been sorely underdressed for the majority of the time.

As I was stuffing rolled up socks and underwear into my trainers someone knocked on the door.

“Come in!” I shouted.

Sam tentatively poked his head around the door. It was pushed open further and Gwen marched past him, sitting on the white swirly chair at the white desk. Trev was the last one to enter my room.

Sam nodded his head to Zach. "He said you wanted to see us about a trip?"

I sighed and glared and Zach. "Big mouth," I muttered. I glanced around at them all. Did I really want to do this? If I told them where I was going, they'd want to come with me, and if I let them then I could be putting them in danger. Then again, if they stayed here they might also be in danger. I glared hatefully once more at Zach who seemed to be watching my unease with glee.

"Jasmine?" Sam asked, looking between Zach and I.

I huffed out my breath. "Okay, so I'm leaving tomorrow for Australia to find my brother. Haamiah told me where he is."

"We're coming with you!" Gwen warned immediately.

"I know, I mean, I knew you'd say that, but there's something you need to know." I glanced at Zach once more. "When we were on our way back here tonight we saw a vampire. He warned me that Asmodeus was looking for me."

"Actually-" Zach interrupted. "He came to us with a message from Asmodeus, only we didn't get to hear it because she killed him before he actually told us what it was."

"The point is, the Fallen Angels and vampires are now working together for some reason, and Asmodeus knew where to send him," I finished.

Sam frowned. “So if we come with you then we’re probably going to run into more vampires as well as the Fallen, and if we stay then they’ll probably come here anyway.”

I shrugged.

“Does Haamiah know? Is that why he told you where your brother is?” Gwen asked.

I shot Zach a guilty look. “Haamiah doesn’t exactly know. Like, obviously he knows that Asmodeus is after me, but not specifically about the vampire tonight.”

Sam stood up. “Because if you told him, he wouldn't let you go.”

I paced the floor then turned to them. “Exactly. Look guys, I know it’s selfish not to tell him, but I’m *going* to find my brother. *No one* is stopping me.”

Trev turned to Zach. “You’re on board with her going?”

He smiled. “I’m going with her.”

“I’m in,” Sam said immediately. “Wherever you go I’m going anyway, but there’s actually someone I haven’t seen in a long time there.”

Gwen narrowed her eyes at him. “A girl?”

Sam shrugged and tried to conceal his smile. “Yeah.”

Gwen raised her eyebrows then looked across the room at me. “Honey, you took down two Fallen Angels and a vampire in *one night*! I reckon the safest place to be is with you. And I could do with a vacation!”

Trev laughed. "I'm coming. I always wanted to go to Australia. Never reckoned I'd ever get there, but now I guess I will. And of course I need to check out this girl of Sam's...who *none* of us have heard of before now."

I smiled at them, feeling relieved that they were coming with me. At least I wouldn't have to deal with Zach on my own. I didn't give myself even a moment to think about Sam's mysterious history with a girl over there, for me this trip was all about my brother.

"Well we're leaving tomorrow, so you'd better get packing," I told them.

"How are we getting there? Portal?" Trev asked.

Everyone looked at me. I winced. "Better not. I am getting better but I've never been there before so maybe we should just fly, you know, just to be on the safe side."

"Angel or plane?" Gwen asked.

I looked at Zach. "If it had just been me and Zach then it would have been angel," I said ignoring his raised eyebrows. "But with it being all of us, we should definitely go by plane. The least amount of angels that know about this the better."

"Haamiah knows we're leaving tomorrow?" Sam questioned.

I swallowed. "Well, he knows I'm going tomorrow, but I'm sure he'll have guessed that you're coming with me."

Trev, Sam and Gwen exchanged glances. Trev stood up and ambled towards the door.

"It's nearly midnight, and I take it we're leaving early so I'm going to go and get packing," He called over his shoulder.

"Crap! He has a point!" Gwen jumped up and headed towards the door. "What time are we leaving?"

Caught out on the spot I turned to Zach. We hadn't thought that far ahead. "Umm, like five?"

He nodded.

"Jeez! Talk about short notice! Okay, I'm gone, I'll meet you here at five!" Gwen ran out of the room behind Trev and was shortly followed by Sam.

Now that my room was almost empty, I turned to Zach. "Don't you have packing to do?" I shook my head mentally, remembering that it was unlikely he had to pack anything at all. "Or somewhere else to be, besides here, annoying me?"

He laughed. "Nope! I'm all yours baby."

"No you're not! And get out! I'd like some privacy."

I turned back to my wardrobe, determined to ignore him until he left. I felt a sudden rush of air and a presence behind me. I whirled around and found myself centimeters from Zach's bare, muscular chest. I swallowed deeply and looked up, following the contours and lines all the way up his body to his soulful, black eyes.

"What are you doing?" I whispered.

"You're pulling away from me. I can tell."

"I'm not! I mean...I'm not yours! Zach..." I gulped, my words falling out of my mouth. "Tonight was a one off. We're not back together."

I felt his hand trail up my back to my shoulder. Goosebumps followed. Every hair on my body stood up. Every nerve was at attention, waiting for something more. His fingers feathered their way through my hair and touched my jaw, holding me tilted to him, our eyes locked.

"That's what you've been saying for weeks. Yet I'm still here." Zach released my jaw and stepped back. He backed away to the huge bay window and slid it open with the slightest of noises. I was still locked in position in front of the wardrobe. "Make no mistake Jasmine; I'll fight for you for as long as it takes."

In a fraction of a second he had launched himself out of the window and flown away. I breathed deeply trying to calm my racing heart. I hoped he'd flown into a tree. God, he was so infuriating! And so infuriatingly hot. His body, his eyes, his smirk when he thought he was being clever...I groaned in frustration and sank to the bottom of the wardrobe. I truly hoped that he had to go and dunk himself under a cold shower after that.

I sighed and turned towards the backpack that I had just begun to fill. It was going to be a long five hours.

5

If I find in myself desires in which nothing in this world can satisfy, the only logical explanation is that I was made for another world.

C.S. Lewis

As I neatly folded a pair of jeans I wondered how I would break the news to Valentina. Valentina was a good werewolf friend of mine I had met in another realm while running from Zach and Aidan. She had been betrayed by her brother and her pack and had been grievously injured as we made our escape together. She had recovered well in the care of Elijah and Samantha.

Elijah was the Guardian Angel of new born children and the young. In the past he had fought alongside other angels in protecting young Nephilim. He was a master healer and possessed great angel magic, a talent I had somehow acquired. Elijah had healed both Zach and I after our capture by the Fallen Angel King, and he had healed Valentina and Sam after our most recent betrayal. He was a nice guy, but quite elitist, not truly believing that I had a talent at healing, he acknowledged the ability but refused to teach me more.

Samantha was a 'close' friend of Valentina. We had had a tryst, Valentina and I, but I had discovered much to my dismay that I was still in love with Zach – not that he was fully aware of that fact even now. Valentina had met Samantha in the Nephilim safe house while she was recovering and it had been plainly obvious that they were enamored with each other from the beginning. I was glad for her, I couldn't help but be pleased that her life was moving forward, even if mine was messy and chaotic.

I felt bad that I was going to leave Valentina behind – we were good friends and I trusted her with my life but she was only beginning to adjust to this World and it would be stupid of me to uproot her and then risk the likely chance that she would slip up and reveal our identity.

In the realm Valentina had come from werewolves, angels and witches were the norm. If someone sprouted wings and took off flying or turned into a Wolf in front of you and loped off, you wouldn't think twice about it. Here, we were closeted with secret identities. Valentina had never experienced the need to hide her true self before and was still struggling with it in the safe house. In fact, just the other day she had terrified a new addition to the house by turning up for breakfast in her Wolf form.

I smiled to myself as I remembered the commotion and screams that had ensued.

No, Valentina had to stay here. If, by chance, my brother was still unaware of all of this, I needed to be able to decide if I was going to tell him. A girl turning into a wolf in front of him would make things even more difficult to explain. Would I have preferred not to know? What would my life have been like if I hadn't met Zach?

I frowned to myself, stuffing a pair of shoes into the bottom of the bag. Really, I didn't think I could use myself as an example; my terrible childhood and teenage years had made me yearn for *anything* other than what I had. But perhaps my brother had been adopted by wonderful people – would I really want to change his life forever?

But then what if he did know? What if he had been taken in by people 'in the know', and cared for and protected all these years?

I shrugged to myself. I guess I would be happy in that instance. He was my brother, of course I wanted him to be safe. But that would have meant that he had been looked after, and I had just been left to fend for myself. Hell, I didn't even know if that had happened and I could already feel jealousy rise up, gnawing at my insides. If I was being completely honest with myself, a small part of me wanted to charge in there like the big sister I was and save him from whatever horridness life had given him. I wanted him to be thrilled and excited that I was his family, and for us to bond instantly...I knew that would be a long shot. After all, just going off the examples in my life to date, how often did things really go to plan?

I turned and sat down on the edge of the bed, gazing out of the window, my deepest fear freeing itself and swirling around my head. What if he didn't need me? What if he didn't want me? There was no one in my life who needed me. Valentina had been the first person and we had needed each other in equal amounts really so that cancelled it out. My friends loved me, I knew, and I loved them back. But they didn't *need* me. The same with Zach. If anything, I needed him. Or I *had* needed him to constantly save my ass.

A knock on the door saved me from my depressing train of thoughts and as though I had conjured her up, Valentina strolled in with an inquisitive look on her face. Glancing at my half-filled bag she raised her eyebrows and smiled at me impishly.

"Hi!" I greeted her sheepishly.

She leaned down and kissed my cheek. "Hi." After a pause she continued. "You're travelling once more?"

As she sat beside me on the bed I turned my face towards her, smiling. She was beautiful, ethereal looking. If you had to guess which not so mythical creature she was you would have guessed fey or eleven maybe. You would never have guessed that this gorgeous creature beside me could turn into a ferocious Wolf with sharp teeth and a grip strong enough to wrench an arm free. I had always thought that if one of us was to be an angel it would be Valentina with her beautiful tanned skin and glowing amber eyes. She had long black hair that flowed behind her, loose and wavy. Next to her I looked completely ordinary.

"I am," I confirmed. "Apparently somewhere out there I have family! Who would have guessed it?" I shrugged, raising my arms dramatically.

Valentina smiled widely at me. "I knew there was a reason for all of your hard work these past few months. I'm so pleased for you Jasmine. When did you find out?"

"Mmm...when we got back here Haamiah told me. I haven't really told anyone and I don't want to make a big deal out of it. I mean it might not work out. And the only reason I didn't tell you was because you were going through your own stuff."

She nodded solemnly. "I know." We sat in silence for a moment.

"So who is it? The family you found?"

"A brother...and I haven't exactly found him yet. Haamiah said he exists and he's given me an initial place to search. So I'm headed there."

"I wish you luck with your quest then." Valentina stared at me with solemn eyes.

I fidgeted uneasily. "You'll be okay here won't you? I mean, I'd take you with me but..."

"...I'm better off staying here," Valentina finished with a smile.

I laughed awkwardly.

"Don't worry. I'm happy staying here."

I breathed a sigh of relief and grinned across at her.

"You need some help packing?" she offered, peering into my bag.

I declined. "No I'm pretty much done. I'm going to get some sleep. We're heading off pretty early."

Valentina nodded, standing up. She smiled at me, her eyes glowing, her hair swinging around her in a black curtain. She blew me a kiss and left the room, pulling the door closed with a soft click.

I zipped up the backpack and threw it in the corner by the door. I'd pack my toiletries in the morning once I'd showered. If I was going to be in Zach's arms for hours then I at least wanted to smell good. I frowned and tutted at myself for even thinking it and climbed into bed.

Remembering I hadn't brushed my teeth I groaned as I padded across the floor to the bathroom. Most of the rooms in the Nephilim safe house had ensuite bathrooms. There was a dormitory for the younger children and they had a shared bathroom, but the rest of us had our own thankfully.

I loaded up my toothbrush and began scrubbing while staring at my reflection in the mirror. I turned my face this way and that, thinking again of how Valentina looked more angelic than I, even with her dark colouring. I had very non-descript grey-green eyes and long straight blonde hair that hung just above my waist. I had a few light freckles across my nose, and thankfully I was one of the fortunate ones, who apart from a few hormone related spots in high school, had never been a sufferer of acne. Saying that, I loved makeup. Smokey eyes, lashings of mascara and cat-like eye-liner were my signature look. I rarely wore lipstick, though I had quite plump lips that suited it.

I wasn't, and would never be skinny; I had large enough breasts that *always* required a bra, and a round, pert bottom. I was pleased enough with my slim waist as the effect gave me an hour-glass figure. I had never been a fan of my thighs or calves but all the training I had been doing at the Nephilim house had dramatically toned them.

As I listed off my attributes to myself I was still resigned to the fact that I would never be a great beauty. I would never be jaw-droppingly beautiful like Gwen, or ethereal like Valentina, but I did have a few things I was pleased with.

As I scrubbed, I realised I could hear voices. I was surprised as it was late and wondered if I was having another late night visitor.

"Zach is that you?" I called through the open door. I stepped out into the bedroom with my toothbrush in hand. The room was empty. I frowned and shook my head turning back to the sink to rinse my mouth. Once again I heard voices.

I stomped back into the bedroom and opened the door leading into the corridor. The lights were now off and the corridor was empty. I pursed my lips and shook it off as one of the many weird things that happened around here, and clambered back into bed.

6

Holding onto anger is like drinking poison and expecting the other person to die.

Unknown.

I felt groggy when I opened my eyes. I had had one of those sleeps when you close your eyes for just a second then wake up with your alarm. I groaned and rolled over, snuggling into the cool pillow beside me. Only the pillow wasn't soft like the others.

I jumped up and shot out of bed, whirling around. I would have blasted my power through me only I knew who the intruder was.

"Sleep well, babe?" Zach asked, grinning at me.

I scowled at him, even as my body began a slow melt. He was sitting up against the headboard with his arms crossed behind his head. His legs were stretched out in front of him. As always he was topless, shadows shaping his pectoral and abdominal muscles as though they had been drawn on, decorated with swirling black tattoos. Black trousers were tucked into thick black leather knee high boots. The silver bolt through his eyebrow glinted in the light from my phone on the bedside table.

At my scowl he ran his hand down the stubble on his face to hide his smile.

I glanced across at where he'd thrown his weapons; two large swords encased in leather sheaths with straps that looped over his shoulders were placed neatly on top of my hastily packed bag.

"How long have you been here?" I demanded. I was alarmed that I hadn't heard him come in, or take his swords off, or climb into bed with me.

"A little while," he laughed. "I didn't want to wake you up. You looked cute."

"Ugh!" I grumbled, escaping into the bathroom.

I quickly showered and brushed my teeth. Annoyed he had sneaked into my room I stuck my fingers up through the wall in his direction. I stomped back into the bedroom where he remained as relaxed as ever in my bed. Not even pretending modesty, I dropped my towel and walked nude across to the dressing table where I had stacked black, fitted pants and a black t-shirt. After a moment of hesitation I pulled on a black G-string before sliding into my clothes. I smiled to myself, smug that the sight would surely torture him for the entire flight, even while I was sure that I would be regretting my underwear choice at some point. I pulled on a red hoodie and slipped into my black leather boots. My hair was quickly pulled into a pony tail, and I slapped on some makeup. I skipped the mascara and eyeliner as I had learned from experience that the moisture up there in the sky mixed with the speed Zach flew at equaled runny makeup. Not a good look for me.

I glimpsed at him in the mirror and saw him staring at my back hungrily. I smiled, satisfied with myself and turned to my bag.

Purposely ignoring him, I strapped on my sword. The belt ran diagonal across my back and over my shoulder, and a second strap ran across my stomach, holding it in place. A dagger was strapped to the inside of my boot, and second to my thigh. I pulled on my back pack and stomped out of the room.

Zach was already outside leaning against the wall with his weapons strapped to his body.

I growled at him, and pulled the door closed softly so as not to disturb anyone sleeping in the rooms near mine. After all it was almost five in the morning. I slunk down the stairs and into the kitchen to find Gwen, Trev and Sam waiting with their bags. Unfortunately Maion was also there. My eyes narrowed on their own accord, my lips setting in a grim line.

He returned my glare and stomped over to the open French windows leading from the kitchen to the back garden, staring out with his back to us all.

Maion, a Warrior Angel like Zach had never liked me. In fact he had once suggested that I be killed in order to prevent Asmodeus from using me to open a portal to the Heavenly realm. I had made no secret of the fact that he thought I would be much less hassle dead. *That* was the kind of angel he was.

Maion was tall and thickly built with a shaved head and the air of arrogance. He looked the epitome of the thug he was. If you were unfortunate enough to be in his presence you'd see that his eyes were solid black. No light twinkled in them like in Zach's, no humor or expression of love ever made them shine, only anger, rage and disgust.

He rarely wore anything other than typical 'Warrior' attire – metal armor over black leather trousers, metal cuffs to his forearms with swords crossed over his back like Zach's.

I twirled around to face Zach.

"He's not coming," I hissed.

Zach sighed. "How else are you planning on getting everyone there?"

"We were going to go by plane." I retorted.

"And where will you get the five thousand dollars or so that you will need for the airfare?" He asked smugly.

I glowered at him. "Fine. Then we'll fly."

Zach grinned. "So who gets left behind?"

I frowned and looked around. That was something I hadn't thought about. Zach would fly with me, Jasmine would fly with either Trev or Sam, which left one of them without transport. I hissed out my breath and glared up at Zach.

"There must be someone else who can come? If not, you know we can always borrow the money from someone and take a plane!" I suggested angrily.

Maion swirled around to face me, his arms crossed over his chest. "Perhaps you should just stay here. If you think we will allow you to leave unescorted when the Fallen Angel King is hunting you, you are very much mistaken," he growled out with his thick Russian accent.

"Don't you talk to me like that," I snarled, turning to Zach. "You *told* him?"

"Jasmine think about it for a second." Sam stepped up to me, his soft brown eyes gazing at me knowingly. "Maion's on our side. We need someone else to come with us not just for flying but you know it's better to have another angel with us. We're going *expecting* trouble. I think we should be prepared."

I turned my glare on him. It lasted only a second before I sighed and turned away. I could never stay mad at Sam.

"Fine," I said simply. I turned and marched out of the kitchen, pissed off.

Zach followed and spun me around. "Jasmine," he whispered. "Come on. I had to tell him. Your life is at risk here and I'm going to do whatever I have to do to protect you. Stop being stubborn."

"He doesn't like me," I heard myself whine. I winced. Could I have sounded any more needy?

Zach leaned closer. "He doesn't know you. But he's a good guy. I promise," he whispered.

"Ugh!" I exclaimed and walked back into the kitchen, followed by Zach. "Let's get going."

I watched as Trev, Sam and Gwen gathered up their backpacks and we all slid out of the French windows. I waited for Zach to slide them closed silently then together we stepped carefully down the stone steps onto the large rectangular lawn.

I smiled as I looked around. The garden was beautiful. Some of the Nephilim had abilities in working with plants and with the very nutritious soil the flowers were blooming. Sweet scents enveloped me whenever I sat out here, which was often. I was also reminded of Aidan, a sweet, kind man who had taught me much about the garden.

Guiltily I looked up at Zach then away towards my friends. I cringed as I saw the embarrassed look on Sam's face. He'd heard what I was thinking. And he'd heard that I knew he'd heard. Telepathy was tricky. I grimaced at him and he smiled meekly in response.

"So who's going with whom?" Sam asked, halting our uncomfortable silent exchange.

"I'm going with Zach," I said immediately.

I rolled my eyes as he grinned proudly. "I only picked you so that I won't get dropped," I muttered.

He leaned down. "As long as you know there was never an option of you going with anyone else. If you think I would allow anyone else to have their hands on you when you're wearing that thong, you don't know me very well." His whispered words tickled my senses, sending heat pooling into my lower abdomen. I *had* gotten to him with my underwear. I smiled to myself and shrugged him off.

Oblivious to our whispering Gwen had already stated she would fly with Trev. I had missed her reasoning but I was just thankful she hadn't asked me to fly with her. I would have been the obvious choice, being lighter than Trev and Sam, but when training she had already dropped me numerous times. I knew she had been practicing with the boys so I could only presume she'd improved enough to fly the distance without killing one of our mutual best friends.

That left Sam with Maion. I didn't like it but as Zach had pointed out there wasn't much choice if we were all going. And one of us had to fly with the obnoxious Russian.

I watched, my stomach twisted in nerves, as Gwen spread her wings. Huge white billowing wings shot up majestically above her. I had touched them before and they were softer than they looked and the light breeze tousled them gently. The more she had practiced with them the more they had begun to take on a violet hue. It was very subtle but you could definitely see the streaks of colour between the snowy white feathers. She forced them down once and in the split second it took to shoot through the air she had wrapped her arms and legs around Trev and hoisted him up with her.

It looked uncomfortable and incredibly unsafe to me, but Trev seemed happy enough with their flying arrangement. They must have been practicing more than I had realised.

I turned to Sam and watched as Maion grabbed him roughly, wrapping his thick arms around his waist and shot up into the sky like a bullet.

I turned to Zach and rolled my eyes as he gazed down at me, a look of adoration in his expression.

"Let's just get on with it okay?" I chastised.

Zach stepped closer and closer until his right leg was wedged between mine. I was sure he had done it on purpose. I could feel the hard thickness of his thigh on my sex, the pressure and friction causing heat to begin to swell. I kept my facial expression free and tilted my chin up to him.

Standing at well over a foot taller than me I felt surrounded by his body. I closed my eyes as he leaned down and looped his arms around my waist. He squeezed me tightly and lifted slowly so that I was slid up his body until he stood straight again. The friction was unbearable. My sex pulsed, feeling tender and hot.

Holding me, he turned his face and nuzzled into my neck. He bit sharply at the flesh between my neck and shoulder. I exclaimed and dropped my head to the side, allowing him complete power over me. I knew I shouldn't allow him this control, but he was exquisite. As though we had been designed for each other every place he touched tingled. Though we had had sex last night I felt starved for his cock. I could feel it against me now and all I wanted was for it to be buried inside of me to the hilt.

Zach laughed softly and jumped, his wings catching the air, sending us soaring into the deep blue sky.

7

Why wish upon a star when you can pray to the one who created it?

Unknown

We took off after Maion and Gwen, catching them up quickly. Trev seemed quite content in Gwen's grip and she looked as though she was flying with ease. Her wings were truly beautiful to watch move through the air and I was surprised to find that I was quite envious of her. To be able to fly seemed a truly miraculous gift, one that I hadn't realized I coveted. With each sweep of her wings a purple hue seemed to swirl around both her and Trev, almost like my silvery mist did me when I used my power.

As I looked closer I wondered at the look of content on Trev's face. There was almost a smug, satisfied air about him. Perhaps it was the joy of flying. I too felt the exhilaration of soaring high above the clouds, and I remembered flying with Zach back when I had first met him. The experience had changed me forever, to know that there was someone so powerful in the world. To know that that person was *my* Guardian...it was surreal.

I turned my head to catch a glimpse of Maion. I frowned immediately. It wasn't that there was anything wrong with him flying with Sam. In fact, Sam seemed in a much more comfortable position than Trev, but still, just the thought of *Maion* touching my best friend. It was almost more than I could stand. I simply couldn't abide him. Whenever he spoke I felt as though I was a cat who'd had its fur rubbed the wrong way. He just...*irritated* me. Aesthetically he was as beautiful as the other angels. He had a magnetic quality that drew your eyes to him. His body was magnificent, his eyes dark and dangerous...though he was nothing compared to Zach.

It had occurred to me numerous times that he could be a Fallen Angel. He had the right temperament for it. He was rude, obnoxious, conceited, had the opinion that if anything was complicated it should just be destroyed to avoid the inconvenience. In fact, I would even go as far to say it was a possibility he had no feelings at all.

I had a moment of guilt at that thought. As much as I disliked him, I had a suspicion that he was Zach's best friend. If angels even *had* best friends.

A long time ago at my pestering Zach had confided that there were four angels he was closest to; Elijah, Haamiah, Machidiel and Maion. Elijah, Machidiel, Maion and Zach had trained together as Warriors while Haamiah had had separate training - being from the Principality Class. Maion was a hunter of Fallen Angels like Zach.

He had told me a sad story of how they had been separated by their duties for hundreds of years until they came together to protect a group of Nephilim children. Machidiel had collected the Nephilim at a temple they were using to hide them from the Fallen. Elijah and Haamiah had guarded them, while Maion and Zach were drafted in, then the temple was attacked by a large force of Fallen Angels.

Apparently a huge amount of angels were killed in the attempt to defend the Nephilim as were some of the Nephilim. The four angels had been heart broken, struggling to make it through the aftermath. They built a house on a tiny island called Ujelang Atoll in the Pacific Ocean. The angels had stayed there, recuperating for months until they were sent out on other tasks.

The way Zach had told the story had made my heart and soul ache for all of the angels, until I had met them. I had yet to meet Machidiel but the others were all stoic Warriors. Every angel I had met besides Aidan had been obnoxious, full of self-importance and so sure that they were above all other creatures in all terms – intelligence, importance and strength. As though we were all sheep and they were our Shepherd, there to insure our safety because we couldn't look after ourselves sufficiently. Had we proved them wrong yet? I had escaped and rescued Zach from being tortured by Asmodeus. I had rescued two angels from imprisonment by an evil witch, albeit unintentionally. I had even trained with the angels and shown them my talent at killing the Fallen, yet still it was deemed unsafe for me to travel alone. Was I really unsafe or was it just that the angels couldn't stand the thought of not being needed? What would they do if all the Nephilim were trained to use their abilities and could fight back at the Fallen who came for us?

The flicker of a voice distracted me from my train of thought. Had Zach said something? I looked up but he was looking ahead, concentrating on the flight. I turned my head and caught Sam looking at me. I knew immediately he had been listening to my thoughts. He smiled grimly as though I had given him food for thought. Perhaps I had.

I smiled apologetically. It must be frustrating hearing everyone else's thoughts. All the good and the bad, the desires, the secret longings.

I turned my face away from Sam, cringing into Zach's chest. I tried to think of something else but my own desires had well and truly kicked in, following on from my previous train of thought. I closed my eyes and concentrated on the feeling of flying. It lasted a couple of seconds then I was very much aware of the throbbing between my legs again.

I tilted my head to look up at Zach, gauging his mood. Could I somehow convince him to land and have a quickie without losing all power in this bizarre relationship we were now in? I had planned on teasing him the whole way there; tormenting him and enflaming him until he couldn't bear it anymore. Unfortunately wearing the thong hadn't helped matters at all as I was acutely aware of the thin piece of material snug in between my buttocks.

Zach seemed oblivious. He was staring straight ahead with a look of intense concentration on his face. I supposed that was a good thing, after all I wouldn't have liked to by flying thousands of feet up in the air with an easily distracted angel.

But how to ease the ache that was now tormenting me? I turned my face away from Zach's and let go of his shoulders with one arm. I didn't actually have to hold onto him; I knew he would never let me fall, but holding on to him came naturally. I reached back with my hand and discreetly slid it down over the soft skin of my bottom, aiming to remove the material from between my cheeks. I figured that that would be one less thing turning me on.

Unfortunately Zach surprised me. He caught my hand and removed it, bringing it up to his chest. My cheeks flamed in embarrassment; after all it was hardly a lady-like thing to do. As Zach stared at me he slid his hand down to where my own had just been. His fingers trailed down right between my buttocks right to my anus. My breath caught and my heart pounded erratically. In that instant I lost all power. I would do anything for him. I would let him do anything to me. There was no thought of anger, mistrust or even annoyance that he had turned my own game back on me. I ached, and only Zach could appease it.

I felt the tips of his fingers catch something. He began to remove his hand quickly. Though I was lost in the moment I soon realized the tormenting had turned to an inferno between my lips. I looked up as Zach winked at me and grinned a self-satisfied smirk. He pulled, wedging my thong unbelievable tight against my clit, between my lips, and so tight between my buttocks my anus was touched with the material.

I groaned and dropped my head back, relinquishing all control to him. I closed my eyes as he dropped his head to my throat and nuzzled until my head fell to the side. He licked and bit and kissed until I was panting. My thong was now soaked through, I could feel the cold wetness wedged up against me. My bottom tingled with pleasure at the tightness of the material. I felt when my nipples budded, sending shoots of need through me, needing to be bitten, needing to be squeezed and caressed.

Now, I needed his cock inside of me. I reached around him, trying to rub my sex against him, wanting to encourage him and urge him to fuck me immediately.

The opposite happened. In an instant Zach spun me round so that I was facing down, seeing the glow of streetlights below me. My arms were caught by my side so that I could do nothing other than wiggle my fingers pointlessly. I groaned and tried not to struggle in his arms. Being confined and dominated in this way was torture and bliss rolled up into one. I could feel every muscle on his chest and abdomen pressed tightly into my back and ass. I swear his body would rival that of the hottest guy I had ever seen in a magazine or on television. He was the ultimate tall, dark and handsome guy. Sculpted muscles, ridges so deep I could trace them with my tongue, thick, hard thighs with the strength to piston his cock deep inside me. Throw in the fact that he was an angel and he *was* the definition of an erotic fantasy.

I smiled as he reached around, still holding me close, to slip his fingers down the front of my trousers. His searching fingers ran through my naked mound until they reached what they were looking for – my throbbing, aching clit. He pressed hard, refusing to move his fingers to give me the friction I needed to come. The pleasure was so intense it bordered on cruelty. His free arm held me clamped to his body so I couldn't rock my hips against his hand. I needed his fingers lower; I needed them inside of me.

My stomach gave way as we suddenly plummeted from the sky, a ginormous black shadow covering my vision.

I screamed as we fell from the sky, unable to suppress the urge. We twisted and zoomed out from under the shadow, zipping around like there was no tomorrow. Though the wind would take my words, I knew if I spoke to Zach, he would hear me. I had to know what was happening, after all, if he let go of me I would plummet to my death – not having wings and all. That just reaffirmed my inclination to think that out of us all Gwen's ability was by far the best.

As I opened my mouth to form the words, something knocked Zach sideways with a force that would have blown me apart. We rocketed off to the side, spinning and rolling through the air. The adrenaline rushing through me was useless. I couldn't do a thing to help – and I didn't appreciate that at all. I had learned the hard way to rely on myself and I didn't enjoy feeling helpless again. Saying that, I didn't have long to ponder the unwelcome feeling as we dropped from the air again then soared back up.

The G-force was immeasurable. I was pressed back into Zach's body with such force that I was surprised we hadn't melded into one. In fact the pressure was so extreme it was incredibly painful. My ribs hurt the most, followed by my neck. It was too difficult to keep my head straight with the constant change of direction so when the opportunity came, I turned my face to the side and allowed my cheek to be pressed into his chest. At least I wasn't likely to accidentally snap my neck in this position.

It seemed to me that we were dodging, more than fighting. As we dipped again I had the misfortune to look up and see what it was that was causing the chaos.

A Dragon. Or what I can only presume was a Dragon as to my mind they were still categorized as 'Mythical Creature' and the thought to confirm their existence with any of my angel teachers had never occurred to me. It was difficult to accurately register their appearance in my mind, due to the constant moving, but from what I could see they checked all the right boxes for 'Dragon'. Giant, bat shaped wings – check. Reptile like body – check. Scaled exterior and glinting, gigantic teeth – check.

And just to make matters worse, sailing through the air beside the Dragon were a small contingency of Fallen Angels. I was now pretty adept at identifying them on sight, though other Nephilim still confused them with the angels. The Fallen had a certain quality to them. A light, transparent feel to them as though their lacking a soul made them have less substance. When I touched them with my magic they had a slimy texture to them. It was weird to describe, but I was positive that the black dots flying around above me were Fallen Angels.

And they were coming in fast. Zach dived instantly, avoiding the swing of a blade. He swooped low and came up beside Gwen.

"Go! Now! Fly as fast as you can!" he shouted to her.

She looked absolutely terrified. Fighting had never been her strong point, and though Trev was great in training there wasn't a whole lot he could do to help hundreds of feet up in the air. She nodded in reply and pushed her wings harder, gaining speed. Zach turned to face Maion and Sam who were fending off an attack to our left.

The dragon returned, plunging us into darkness. I could sense something strange about it. Almost like a muttering sound coming from it. My eye widened. It was being controlled! The sound was clearer now, like a chant, a spell perhaps.

I clenched my teeth together as Zach spun in a dizzying speed towards Maion. My eyes met Sam, he looked as though he was barely hanging on to his bravery, his expression similar to mine I would imagine. Maion had Sam clutched between his legs and had a sword in each hand.

Blood splattered across my face, hot and wet. I froze, my heart erupting into a frenzied patter. I dared to look up at Zach, expecting the worst but instead saw a grim smile as he shook his sword in the air, red droplets spraying off in every direction. The body of the Fallen Angel to our side fell from the air instantly, beginning to dissipate slowly.

Another angel instantly took his place. The clash of metal rang out, deafening me. I needed my sword desperately, but in the position I was being held I didn't have a chance in Hell of reaching it. I could reach down and take the dagger that was strapped to my thigh but that meant maneuvering myself around Zach and I didn't want to distract him while he was fighting.

I felt him pull me closer to him.

"Trust me babe," he whispered.

In the next instant I was free falling through the air. I refused to scream, though in my head I was raging. How dare he drop me? I was so furious I would gut him when he caught me. I felt sick, my stomach somewhere around my throat, my adrenaline on an insane high.

I was caught. Thank God. We began moving at a slower pace, almost a crawl compared to what we had been doing. Something didn't feel right. I could hear muttering again. An annoying, incessant chatter. I looked around praying the Dragon wasn't swooping in on us again and realised to my horror that it wasn't Zach who had caught me.

A Fallen Angel grinned down at me. Or at least he bared his rotten teeth at me. White hair hanging over his green eyes, he started to laugh, an evil cackle I had thought reserved only for witches.

I screamed. It wasn't in fear though. Admittedly I should have been utterly terrified, but I hadn't counted on my power being so quick in taking over. I could feel its viscosity up to my jaw, trying to take me over completely.

In a haze that I wasn't entirely sure I was in control of, I turned in my captor's hold and stared into his eyes, allowing my sparkling mist to begin to dissolve them. I hadn't realised I could do that, and I was both repulsed and captivated by the sight of his eye balls crumbling in their sockets.

"Asmodeus is going to rip you apart and feast on your entrails!" he ground out, the pain debilitating.

"No dear," I whispered softly. I knew he could hear me. "I'm going to rip *you* apart."

With that I buried the dagger I had retrieved from the strap on my thigh into his neck, embedding it to the hilt. As blood splurted from his mouth I sliced sideways, cleanly decapitating him, and then began to fall.

"Zach!" I hollered as loud as I could. "Catch me...NOW!"

Uncoordinated arms caught hold of mine. I looked up expecting another Fallen Angel but instead saw Trev's face scrunched up with effort as he strived desperately to hold on to me. Above him, Gwen struggled to keep us all in the air, her wings flapping manically.

We descended rapidly to the ground, falling into a tangled heap together. I made sure to keep the dagger pointed away from my friends as they landed on top of me. We had landed in a grassy field, a couple of boulders nearby. There didn't seem to be any houses around that I could see, so no inherent danger of someone running out to see how people could just fall out of the sky.

"I'm sorry! I couldn't keep us up any longer! The weight was too much!" Gwen panted.

I rolled my eyes. "Oh great! *That* makes me feel like a fat heifer!"

Trev was already standing, staring up at the sky. "I can't make out what's happening."

Grumbling to myself, I stood cautiously, testing out my legs and arms to see if anything was broken. I looked up. It was impossible to work out what was going on. I couldn't make out the Dragon's shape any longer, but the black figures above us were spinning, diving and quite clearly trying hard to kill each other.

"I hope Sam's okay!" Gwen worried, chewing on her nails.

I knelt beside her, moving her hand away from her mouth. "Sam will be fine! Come on, he's got that lunatic Maion keeping him safe!"

She nodded and smiled grimly. I hadn't thought I'd ever find myself defending the arrogant prick of a Russian, but to give him his dues – he *was* a ferocious fighter.

"Problem!" Trev screamed.

I spun around, already hearing the chanting. I reached back, swinging my sword out in front of me, my feet apart, knees bent. I powered my mist into my veins, pushing the magic into my muscles and bones.

"Fuck! Fuck! Fuck!" Gwen shrieked louder and louder.

"It's okay! It's okay!" I chanted, unsure if I was trying to calm Gwen or myself.

The beast was huge. On all fours, I barely grazed the top of its leg. I had to do this. There wasn't any other option. And if I was going to even attempt anything, I couldn't stay here thinking about it, I had to just act.

I darted to the side, rolling as I heard the snap of teeth coming at me. Leaping up I managed to slice it's hide with my sword. At least, I thought I'd sliced it - no blood seemed to come from it. I back flipped again and again to move out of its way as it charged at me and I threw myself to the floor around its back, regretting that decision when it kicked out with one hind leg, sending me flying into a boulder. The boulder cracked behind me, or my spine did.

I crumbled onto my bottom in front of it, gaping as the Dragon loomed over me.

A spark of lightening illuminated the sky. The flash so bright I was blinded for a second. To my distress it faded slowly, my eyes desperately seeking to see where this new danger was coming from.

The Dragon was gone, and where it stood was a large singed area of grass – black tinged with brown, smoke trailing upwards in little tendrils.

I gaped open mouthed at Trev as he stood in front of Gwen, his sword still held up, shaking.

It took a second before I could speak. "Was that you?" I gasped.

He shook his head. "I…um…not really, but kind of," he stammered.

I gulped. "What?"

His breath heaved in and out as he bent over, leaning on his knees. Gwen leaned over him, patting his back as he dry reached. I remained where I was, still unsure if I could walk, or if it was even safe to. When he stood up I raised my eyebrows at him in question.

He lifted his finger and pointed to the sky. “My mother was watching,” he whispered.

I released the breath I hadn’t realised I was holding. His mother. Of course! I’d never thought Trev’s ability to be particularly helpful in the physical sense until this actual moment. Emotionally, yes. I mean who wouldn’t want to speak to their long lost parent whenever they wanted to, but physically, I had thought it was an entirely unhelpful gift.

I hadn’t realised I was saying this out loud until I saw Trev bend over laughing. Gwen, who had been staring at me in shock while I had been rambling on, had also burst into hysterical laughter. Falling to her knees, gripping at her stomach, the tears poured down her face as she choked on her giggles. Trev leaned a hand on her shoulder, unable to contain himself. I remained silent until they had finished. It took a while.

“Who knew Dragon’s existed man?” Trev sighed, shaking his head.

Trev said Dragon. I was going with Dragon. “Haamiah could have been a little more helpful!” I said.

“What do you mean?” Gwen asked.

“Come on! We keep coming up against stuff that we didn’t know existed! What the fuck? It would have been helpful if we’d *known* that Dragons could be killed by lightening!”

“Actually that was heavenly fire,” Trev corrected. At my look, he shrugged. “Apparently someone broke it out of its...cell...and the fire transported it back there. Wherever *there* is.”

"Yeah. 'Wherever *there* is,'" I mocked.

"I know what you mean though," he continued. "I didn't even know those things existed! It was a bit of a shock to see it barreling towards us!"

"*You* can say!" Gwen confirmed.

Zach chose that instant to drop to the ground – scaring the crap out of us.

"Is everyone okay?" he asked, staring at me with his intense eyes.

"Oh we're just peachy. No thanks to you," I replied, standing up gingerly.

"No thanks to me? I just killed six of the Fallen trying to defend you!" he growled.

"You dropped me – letting me plummet to earth, to my death!" I growled back.

"They were coming at me, what was I supposed to do? And you're clearly fine!" he replied, scowling at me.

"Yeah...*no thanks to you*!" I reiterated.

He growled under his breath and turned as Maion and Sam also dropped out of the sky. Sam looked ill, his face was actually green. As Maion let go of him, he stumbled towards Trev, puking on the grass in front of him.

"Dude, that's gross," Trev muttered, helping him stand.

Zach and Maion then had the nerve to jabber away at each other in Russian.

"Quit it!" I demanded, stomping into the middle of them. "Quit that *right now* and tell me what you're saying!"

Maion turned to me, glowering. It was then that I noticed the blood coating his sword, and the splatters of blood across his face. He had gone all sorts of kick ass up there.

"We were discussing where the Dragon had gone," he bit out slowly.

I scowled. "Well if you had included us in the conversation, we could have told you." I felt smug as they frowned at me in surprise. "We killed it."

"*You* killed a Dragon?" Zach asked sarcastically.

"Not exactly. Trev's mother killed it," I replied.

The angels turned to face Trev.

He shrugged, "She didn't technically kill it. I think she said something about transporting it back to its cell? It had been broken out apparently."

"Heavenly fire?" Zach questioned.

I frowned at him as Trev nodded.

"Good," Maion said. "Let's keep going."

Sam groaned, falling to his knees.

"He can't travel like this!" Gwen argued.

"I might be able to help," I said, trotting over to him. "I can't promise, but I'll try."

I lay my hand on his shoulder and called on my power, feeling it swirl up and around my stomach, flowing down my arm to my fingertips. Sparkles appeared in my skin, a mist beginning to surround me. I could feel their cooling presence begin to flow into Sam, healing and soothing.

When I thought I had done enough I let go of him and stepped away, waiting anxiously.

He stood up and smiled at me, nodding. "I feel better, thank you."

I smiled back. I took a deep breath and turned to an impatient Zach and Maion. Sheathing my sword, I lifted my chin and stood beside Zach refusing to be intimidated by his glare. He was such an arrogant bastard, but God he was hot when he was angry.

I waited expectantly for him to pick me up and felt a jolt of need as he did so, face to face, letting me feel his arousal at the junction of my legs. Without another second he had leapt and the wind took us higher and higher until we were once again above the clouds, on our way to Australia.

8

There is more to sex appeal than just measurements. I don't need a bedroom to prove my womanliness. I can convey just as much sex appeal, picking apples off a tree or standing in the rain.

Audrey Hepburn

We flew with the speed of light through the day and night and into the next day again. The original plan had been to stop somewhere to rest but after the attack it was agreed to keep going until we reached a safe place. By the time Maion agreed we were in safer territory we were over water and couldn't land. I worried for Gwen but she seemed to be holding her own with the angels. She was quick and fearless as she swooped, her wings shooting off sparks with her speed. Trev seemed to be comfortable enough and Sam seemed to have recovered well enough to travel.

Occassionally we ran into bad weather, but Zach simply rose higher than before, sailing above the thundering clouds and aggressive winds, descending when the sea was calm again. He pointed out breaching whales and the occasional dolphin as we passed over. If I hadn't felt so uncomfortably wound up and anxious I might have enjoyed it, but as it stood, I was desperate for it to be over.

When we began to descend, the lights of a huge city coming into view in the darkness, my heart sped up. Zach landed softly on a flat rooftop, in what appeared to be the middle of a city.

"Are we here?" I asked eagerly.

He shook his head. "Almost, but not quite. This is Melbourne. We have allies here. We need to speak to them first before we continue."

"What? That wasn't the plan!" I growled. I was *desperate* to get there. What if he was in trouble *now*? "I don't want to wait, I want to keep going."

The others landed with a thump next to us. Gwen released Trev gently, whereas Maion just let Sam fall to the ground. Maion tilted his head in question at Zach.

"We need to find the Sorceress of Ice. She's the only one that can help us here," Zach said.

"I don't want to find a Sorceress! I want to find my brother!" I yelled, anger taking over.

"God, you're a pain in my ass Jasmine! Yes your brother is in Meadowbrook but you don't even know his name! You don't know what he looks like! And while we're here in the Sorceress' territory – we need to pay our respects. She can also offer protection if she is willing!" Zach snarled.

My eyes blazed holes in his face. God, I hated him right now. I hated that he was right even more. I couldn't think of a single argument to throw at him. It *would* be handy having a Sorceress on our side with Asmodeus tracking me. He was also right about not knowing my brother's name, though I had a feeling that I would just *know* him when I saw him. It made sense, but that didn't mean I had to like it.

"Fine," I conceded ungraciously.

"The Sorceress of Ice?" Sam questioned; a quivering excitement in his voice.

Zach nodded in reply. He and Maion marched over to the fire exit and the side of the building and began to climb down the ladder.

Gwen, Trev and I looked at Sam expectantly.

"My friend is there, she's a Sorceress," he smiled.

"Your secret girlfriend is a Sorceress?" Gwen mocked.

"I didn't say she was my girlfriend. And she's only a minor Sorceress," he chuckled.

"You're kidding me right?" Gwen persisted. "How on earth would *you* meet a Sorceress?"

"I'm well-travelled remember. Haamiah brought me here a long time ago, before we relocated to the current safe house. The reason we left in the first place was because Melbourne was becoming a hotbed for the supernatural! You name it, and it's here! There's a witches coven not far out of the city, you've got a nest of vampires further north."

"Come!" Maion's voice bellowed.

We scampered to the ladder and began climbing down hurriedly.

"Somehow I just can't picture Haamiah being friends with a Sorceress!" I called down to him.

"He's quite a mellow guy when you get to know him," Sam shouted up.

I snorted. As if the word 'mellow' could ever be used to describe Haamiah. The serious angel-chief was anything but mellow.

At the bottom of the fire escape we jogged to catch up with Zach and Maion who were already at the bottom of the alleyway and onto the main street. Though it was late evening, the city was bustling. Trams and buses running down the street, yellow taxis beeping and dodging traffic and people ran across the road and loitered outside bars and restaurants smoking. The streets were lit brightly by streetlights and music and chatter drifted out from the busy bars and restaurants.

As we pushed passed the slow walkers, almost running to keep up with the angels, we continued our interrogation of Sam.

"And how exactly did you meet this Sorceress?" Gwen demanded to know.

Sam laughed, not bothered by her intrusive questions in the slightest. "I went with Haamiah once to a meeting with them. He was providing them with information about their enemies and liaising with their allies. She-"

"Her name?" Gwen asked.

"Lilura." He pressed on. "She was at a lot of the meetings and we got talking. She's quite young compared to the other Sorceress' so she was really interested in talking to me and finding out about the Nephilim and our way of life. She was so interested in hearing about the safe house and how we live here. It was really different for her growing up as a Sorceress. You know, she never even went to school? Her whole life she's been surrounded by her family.

She would sneak out and I'd take her places. I'd take her to the safe house I lived in then and introduce her to other Nephilim. And she had heaps of knowledge about other creatures too. The Sorceress' are allies with Werewolves and Nymph's as well as the angels. And they have this ongoing feud with the Lycan's of Abernon – they've been killing each other off for years," he blushed. "We dated and we were really good friends, the best, until I had to leave. We tried to do the whole long distance thing but it didn't work out. We stayed in touch though."

I was intrigued. I had never thought of Sam as a particularly sexual person before. I mean, sure he was good looking, in fact he was incredibly handsome but he was my best friend. He was too sweet and good to think of like that. I was also a little annoyed that he hadn't confided in me before. Though, I had to admit it wasn't as if I told him a lot about my life before I had come to the safe house. Still, I felt a little bit cheated. I was looking at him in a slightly different way now, and I didn't like it.

"Did you tell her we were coming?" Trev asked.

Sam nodded. "Yeah I text her before we left. I didn't think we'd be going straight there though, I thought I'd have to make some time while we were in Meadowbrook to travel into the city."

Further ahead I saw Zach pause with an annoyed look on his face. I rolled my eyes and jogged forward. He gestured with his hand into a bar entrance. It was pretty non-descript, just a small open doorway, pink neon lights illuminating the entrance, no sign or name plate. It appeared Maion was already inside, so I entered, followed by Zach, Gwen, Sam and Trev trailing behind.

Inside it was pretty average. There was a small corner bar, made from a dark wood, with spirits hanging upside down behind, and the beer taps protruding highly. The few tables that there were, were already filled by laughing groups of people. The pink neon lights extended from the entrance through into the bar and cast everyone in an eerie glow. The walls were bare, painted white.

Maion was already at the counter talking to the bar tender – a young and very exotic looking girl. Painted flowers decorated the skin on her face, her long black hair trailing behind her, interwoven with pink and blue flowers. She was scowling however, not seeming pleased in the slightest with whatever Maion had said to her. That was unsurprising.

As Zach and I approached the counter we were quickly surrounded by women. I could sense Zach beginning to get angry.

“We come from the House of Haamiah. You owe us allegiance,” he hissed.

The women seemed taken aback by this and paused, glancing at each other. One particularly burly woman stepped forward and gestured for us to follow her. We were led through behind the bar, through another doorway into another room, this one much larger than the first, but much much weirder.

I felt as though I had stepped into a brothel. Red, carpeted floors ran through and thick sofas with gold and red throws covering them were dotted with the light spun from the giant chandeliers hanging from the high ceiling. I could see that the room led through to another similarly decorated room.

The room was packed with Sorceresses', and they were...*incredible*. They all wore similar clothing – or lack of it. Most of them were in hot pants or leather skirts, with exquisite corsets made from gold with jewels embedded in them. They all wore thick gold collars to protect their throats and intricate masks covering their faces.

One, with black hair swept up in braids behind her head marched up to Maion and prodded him in the chest with thick gold spikes protruding from the end of her fingers.

"What do you want angel?" she snarled.

"We seek counsel with the Sorceress of Ice," he replied calmly.

"She won't see anyone," the black-haired woman spat.

"She will see me," he replied, glaring at her.

We glanced at each other. This was awkward. It didn't look as though she was going to back down and we all knew how aggressive Maion was. I wanted to get this over with, but a little part of me really hoped that this Sorceress would kick his arse.

Unfortunately after a pause, she waved her hand and someone behind her scuttled off out of the room. A few seconds later she scurried back up and whispered in her ear.

She glared at us all. "Fine. Be my guest." She stepped aside and pointed through the archway into the next room with her talons.

The six of us cautiously moved passed her, unsure whether it was wise to turn our back on her. As I had glimpsed, the next room was decorated exactly the same, only in the corner on the floor sat a woman with a huge gold headdress. She wore an even more magnificent bodice and a mask that glinted like a thousand stars. Her black hair was swept up on top of her head with the ends hanging down in ringlets decorated with gold and jewels. She was sitting in a meditating pose, with her legs crossed and her wrists resting upturned on her knees.

Maion stood before her. “Sorceress, we have come for information.”

“Why should I waste my time on you?” she asked quietly.

Within seconds Maion had her held against the wall by her throat. Though she wore the impressive gold choker that the others wore, I could see it crumple beneath Maion’s crushing grip. With a cry the other Sorceress’ began to chant. Zach swung his sword around to face them, his eyes blazing.

“Stop! Stop!” someone cried out.

A beautiful girl who looked a lot younger than the others pushed past a particularly vicious looking Sorceress. She had blond braids and a purple mask decorated with gold flecks. She too, wore a thick gold choker and wore what appeared to be a top and skirt made of black leather. She ran forward to the front of those chanting, shoving them aside. She stomped up to Maion and prodded him in the chest. He let out a low growl.

“Put my grandmother down now!” she bellowed.

Maion frowned but did as she demanded, scowling at her. The woman was released to her feet and quickly reached back to remove the crushed gold plate around her neck, flinging it on the ground.

“Lilura?” I heard Sam’s voice call softly.

She spun around to peer behind me. “Sam?” She grinned when she saw him and ran past me to him, jumping into his arms.

Gwen, Trev and I exchanged a look. Talk about have dodgy in-laws! Could he have picked a girl with a *worse* family? Though the timing and circumstance of the reunion could have been better, it served well to soften the hostile environment. The other women had stopped chanting and were now staring at Sam and Lilura curiously and at us with less hatred than before. Maion continued to scowl but no one was paying him attention anymore.

The Sorceress of Ice smacked her hands together to return everyone's attention to her. "Let's get to business so you can leave. Follow me." She pushed past Maion and stormed out of the room into yet another, this one empty.

We filed in after her, leaving Sam to his reunion. She closed the door behind us and moved to sit on the carpeted floor.

"What do you have in exchange for information?" she asked in a cold voice.

"Our allegiance," Maion growled.

She tilted her head. "I already have that. What else can you offer?"

"You will obey me or I will take the head from your shoulders," He loomed over her threateningly.

Suddenly she was on her feet, the floor beginning to freeze over as frost spread to each wall. I shivered as the very air froze, my breath coming out in fog. Gwen rubbed her arms as Trev blew into his hands to warm them.

"Do not threaten me! I will freeze you to the bone then chop pieces off as you begin to melt," she whispered, malice dripping from every word.

Maion frowned. “What do you want in return?”

She smiled. “It is not something that *you* have that I want.” She turned to me. “I want *your* allegiance.”

Zach hissed and pushed me behind him. The Sorceress laughed and began to circle him slowly.

“Why do you want *my* allegiance? You have the allegiance of the angels and I’m with them,” I said.

She tutted. “This is what I ask for.”

Maion glared at me. I glanced at him then at Zach.

“Fine,” I said. “You have my allegiance.” I couldn’t see any problem with that. It wasn’t as if the angels would be allies with a faction of evil.

“Ah ah ah!” she wagged her finger at me. “Think carefully.”

I frowned at her. She reminded me of a nagging school teacher. “I said it’s fine.”

She smiled broadly at me and flounced across the room to sit on the floor. She waved her hand in front of her and a glittery gold tray appeared on the floor.

“Ask what you will,” she said in a bored tone.

“I want to know what my brother’s name is,” I stepped forward. I wasn’t interested in what Maion was going to ask, I had my own questions and I *would* be told the answers.

The woman smiled grimly. “Stare into the reflection and it will be known to you.”

Ignoring Zach's warning look I knelt in front of the plate and leaned forward. The moment my eyes met their own I felt as though I was falling through the tray. The feeling was horrific. It was as though something was sucking my brain through the gold tray to get at the answers. My mind hammered at me, screaming to pull away, but in that moment I couldn't have pulled my gaze away if my life depended on it.

Abruptly I fell back, my hands shooting out behind me to catch me. I swallowed a gulp and panted, trying to catch my breath. I looked up at the worried gazes as I scrambled away from the Sorceress.

"Did you get it?" Zach asked.

I nodded, unsure if I could actually speak yet.

"Are you sure there isn't anything else you want to know?" she asked suggestively.

I pursed my lips. I'm sure she was implying that there was something else I should know. After all, why else would she ask for my allegiance. Was there something I was supposed to do? I shook my head after a moment's thought. There was plenty I'd like to ask but I couldn't quite face looking into the mirror just yet. I could always come back.

Maion knelt before her. "Have our enemies beaten us here?" he growled.

The Sorceress placed her hand into the tray, deep up to her elbow, as though it were hollow. Drawing her arm back out she allowed drops of gold to roll off her finger tips and drop onto the now solid tray in frozen drops, with a *ping*. "Your enemies are all around you," she whispered. She raised herself off the floor. "You bring your enemies to us. We are allies, but that is not an infinite state of being. You must leave."

"Wait. One more thing." Maion grabbed her arm and swung her round to face him as she turned to leave. "You must have a safe house we can use, one protected from our enemies."

The Sorceress took in a deep, angry breath and scowled at him. She held out her hand and a thick gold key appeared in her palm. "*This* is what you're looking for. It will guide you to the house." She turned away and pulled open the door, marching through.

We quickly followed her into the main room. Sam was locked mouth to mouth with Lilura. Her legs were wrapped around his waist, her hands in his hair. I scowled, that was a tad too much PDA than I needed to see right now. Besides the fact that I wasn't entirely sure I was happy with Sam being locked at the lips with the Sorceress after the show of power we had just seen, I was feeling entirely too unsatisfied and this was the last thing I needed in my current state. I glared over at Zach, even more annoyed when I realized he was smirking at me, fully aware of my need.

I huffed out a breath and followed Maion out the door back into the bar. I paused as I heard Sam promise Lilura he'd call her as Gwen and Trev attempted to disentangle them.

I was pulled into an alcove. I turned and gasped as the Sorceress of Ice stood before me.

"The Wolves aren't finished with you!" she whispered quietly. She said it with such urgency and such warning that I froze and missed my chance to ask her what on earth she meant.

Zach appeared next to me and glowered at the Sorceress. She lifted one eyebrow and scowled as she backed away. Trev and Gwen barreled into me with Sam and we all left the bar together.

"Zach I could have handled that without your interference!" I hissed.

"They may be our allies but you should never trust them," he said quietly. "They will only ever look out for themselves. Ignore whatever she said."

"If you can't trust them then why are you allies with them?" I asked, completely exasperated.

"They are in deeper with other creatures in the mystical world. They often have information not accessible to us."

I scowled. "That sounds like a really healthy relationship. You know, plenty of trust and friendship!"

He frowned at me and pulled me to where Maion stood waiting impatiently. I waved Zach away and ignored his warnings. This night was getting more ridiculous by the second.

I looked at Maion expectantly. "*Now* are we going to Meadowbrook?"

9

I'm selfish, impatient, and insecure. I make mistakes. I am out of control and at times, hard to handle. But if you can't handle me at my worst, then you don't deserve me at my best.

Marilyn Monroe

Maion turned and glared at me. "We have other issues to resolve first."

I huffed out my breath impatiently. This was ridiculous! What now? What else could possibly be more important than getting to my brother? The Sorceress had just said that our enemies were all around us so surely it was more important than ever that we find him and protect him.

I took a deep breath and closed my eyes. It had taken months to get to this point so I knew that realistically a couple of hours more wouldn't make any difference, but I was so close now I could almost sense him. I could imagine his face, see his smile. I used to think that I would be alone forever, that life was just a hell I'd never escape alive but now I knew that my purpose was to protect my brother. Everything was coming together the way it was supposed to. Now I had friends and family, my life had purpose. How could I be expected to wait even a minute longer than necessary? I didn't even *want* Maion on this trip. This was none of his concern.

Gwen linked her arm through mine. "It'll be okay. I'm sure it'll only be a little longer."

I grimaced at her and let her pull me along after the angels as they began to walk away from the bar.

"I don't see why I can't just wait here if there's other things you need to attend to," Sam called, sounding drunk.

I scowled. He was probably drunk on lust. I knew that feeling and I wanted it now - anything other than walking around the city of Melbourne in the middle of the night. We traipsed the main streets, blending in to the crowds of tourists and locals chatting as they explored Melbourne's busy walkways. We followed the slow moving crowd, skipping past the drunken people as they stumbled from one bar to the next and ducking through the cigarette smoke.

As we walked I thought about what the Sorceress had said about the Wolves. Surely she had meant the Werewolves. Had she meant Valentina's Werewolves? They certainly weren't my favourite people. A Witch had manipulated their ancestors into betraying the angels they worshiped and then she had enslaved them. When I had appeared they had lied and cajoled to get me into the right place to fight with a Witch in the hopes I would magically release the angels and then when they were free they would take the credit for it and earn their forgiveness. It was such an ill thought out plan that only Wolves could have come up with it. As I had left that realm one of the Wolves had shot at Valentina, injuring her severely. For that alone I wanted to return and skin them all. Maybe this would be my chance.

As I brooded I realised that we had ended up near Flinders Street Station. I glared at everyone and everything as Maion and Zach entered the walkway leading underneath. The smell of urine and cigarette smoke hit me as we jogged down the steps trying to keep up with the angels. I could see Gwen wrinkling her nose in disgust at the smell while the guys dawdled past a busker, wanting to stay and listen. Previously white tiles were covered in a multitude of posters and stickers, while the floor was littered with rubbish and flyers. Green metal gates guarded by smartly dressed security personnel blocked the entrances to the platforms.

Zach stopped by one particularly mean looking guard and must have said something to him as we all swept past him unhindered. We skipped up the steps to platform four and stood silently as Maion checked out the timetable on the wall.

“Hope they’re planning on paying the fine if we get caught without a ticket,” Sam muttered quietly.

Trev laughed then coughed into his fist when Zach scowled in our direction. “Dude you’ve got to relax.”

I rolled my eyes at Gwen, who laughed.

I stiffened as a train guard stepped onto the platform and paced up towards us. I glanced at Sam nervously as he passed by us and paused, staring down the track. A low rumble alerted us to the oncoming train and it soon groaned to a stop in front of us.

We were forced to wait while hordes of people scrambled off the train and down to the platform. I decided not to bother finding a seat as it was still pretty packed so I edged closer to where Zach stood near the doorway. I hung on to the safety bar as the train began to move away while Zach stood perfectly still without any assistance. We received a few odd glances from the other passengers who had noticed the weapons strapped to Zach and

Maion, but no one said anything, leaving the entire carriage in an uncomfortable silence.

Thankfully within a few stops Maion left the train and we jumped down after him. I hadn't been paying enough attention to know where we were and I was alarmed by the platform he had chosen. The station appeared deserted. The entire platform consisted of two metal benches and one sole light flickering at the top of a post, illuminating us and casting moving shadows everywhere.

Maion obviously knew where he was going and marched off down the platform, entering the stairwell. We followed him and entered what appeared to be a warehouse district. Towering buildings loomed over us, surrounded in chain fences. 'Beware the Dog' signs appeared every few meters, accompanied by growls and snarls, warning us away. The whole area appeared to be completely empty – not a soul in sight, no lights on anywhere.

Maion took a running jump, his wings shooting out behind him as he sailed over the top of the chain fence, landing on the other side with a soft thump. I shook my head, irritated, and rolled my eyes at Gwen. Sam shrugged, grinning – he had expected it obviously.

Zach grabbed hold of me by my waist, grabbed Sam by his upper arm and launched us into the air. He dropped Sam to his feet then let me slide slowly down his body. I avoided his eyes and turned to face Gwen and Trev as they landed next to us.

I stepped away, lifting my chin up as I glared in the direction Maion had gone. Zach led the way around the scrap yard towards the grey building at the back. A security light flashed on as we passed the sensor, Maion glared at us as we were lit up.

Within seconds we were surrounded by Fallen Angels. I tensed, lifting my clenched fists as I prepared myself. I frowned as I began to feel a sense of sadness emanating from them. Some of them weren't Fallen Angels...some of them were *angels*. What was this? What the hell was Maion playing at?

A tall blonde angel stepped forward, "What do you want Brother?"

Maion snarled at him, "Who do you watch?"

A Fallen Angel dressed in black leather pushed forward, his head lowered as if for a fight. "Why do *you* care?"

"Silence!" the first angel thundered. He was forced back through the crowd as others struggled to control him. The angel turned to Maion. "Apologies Brother; we watch a vampire near here – he is turning large amounts of humans. Our order is to discover his purpose for this. There is also a female Nephilim in the city we are observing.

"Anyone else?" Maion growled.

The angels glanced at each other before seeming to consent. "A male Nephilim along the coast is also in our sights."

My brother, I thought. I was dying to ask them a thousand questions, but bit my tongue when Sam nudged me.

"And someone is watching him now?" Maion questioned.

At their unanimous nod, I sighed a relief. He was safe for now.

"Where is Asmodeus?" Maion growled in his thickly accented voice.

My heart froze. Asmodeus? Why was he talking about him now? I couldn't help but glance around nervously.

"I know he is in this realm," Maion continued.

The angel signed and gestured to a young looking Fallen Angel. He was short for an angel, with brown eyes and unremarkable short brown hair – very unlike the other angels I had known. He stepped forward at the angel's command.

"Asmodeus is currently in the Northern Hemisphere gathering recruits. We have had word of an army beginning to form in this realm, and of an intention of bringing the First over."

Zach hissed at that, glowering at the Fallen Angel. "And you didn't think to impart this information before now?"

The Fallen Angel took a step back, fear and uncertainty on his face. "Michael is aware. He has given us no further instructions on the matter."

I stared at Zach, desperately wishing I knew what he was thinking. Who was the First? The First what? I rubbed at my temples as they began to pound, my head feeling noisy all of a sudden. What was Asmodeus doing here? I knew he had sent the vampires and Fallen after me, but I had still felt relatively safe knowing he was in another realm.

"Does he know our current location?" Zach growled.

"No, not yet," the Fallen answered. "He has shown no sign of leaving the North."

I breathed out my relief. Gwen reached over and stroked my arm. I shook her off, not wanting to appear vulnerable in front of these angels. Maion seemed satisfied with their answers and exchanged a few more words with them, ordering them about before he led us away. I scowled at him, refusing to believe that he wasn't going to kill them. They were Fallen Angels and we were just going to walk away, leaving them alive? What on earth were they thinking?

When we had cleared the fence I pushed Zach away and stormed up to Maion.

"Why are you letting them live?" I snarled angrily.

He ignored me and turned to Zach. "Your Nephilim seems angry at me."

I hissed and was about to launch myself at him when Zach gripped me by the waist and shot into the sky. I desperately wanted to pummel him but resisted the urge knowing that if he dropped me, it was a long way down.

"They are Grigori!" Zach said into my ear.

Grigori? They were a class of angel. Their purpose was to watch and observe and if anything was amiss they would report to the Principalities who would then send the Warriors out in force. They were like the spies of the angel world – blending in and observing then reporting their findings. They were often tasked with following Nephilim while they were unaware of their angelic heritage. Even I had been watched by them...apparently. That some of them were actually *Fallen* Angels was news to me.

"How can a Fallen Angel be a Grigori?" I shouted. My stomach plummeted as Zach landed on the roof of a skyscraper in the city. He steadied me as I stumbled away from him.

"Grigori are watchers," he began.

"Yes I know!" I interrupted. "I want to know why Fallen Angels are watching *with* the Grigori!"

He shook his head, a look of exasperation crossing his face. "They *are* the Grigori! Some of the Fallen want redemption, they want forgiveness...God is all forgiving and has tasked them with the duties of the Grigori."

"How can you trust them?" I asked, amazed.

"They are earning their forgiveness."

"So? They're evil! You have *evil* angels watching over my brother!" I shrieked. Lightening forked in the sky behind me. I glanced at it then raised my eyes at Zach.

"They're not evil," he denied. "They made mistakes and now they are working to clear their names and restore their glory."

I snorted. "Well that's just great! You guys have been drilling into us how bad Fallen Angels are, when you've actually been trusting them to do your dirty work?"

He scowled at me. "That's not how is it, Jasmine!"

I threw my hands up. "Whatever! Look, I'm exhausted, I now know that Asmodeus is here in this realm, and you and Maion are seriously pissing me off with your lies and secrets. I want to go to Meadowbrook *now*!"

He growled under his breath and picked me up dropping us both fifty floors down to the pavement below us. The others were already there waiting for us.

After some silent communication between Maion and Zach, Sam eavesdropping of course, we readied ourselves to take off again just as a group of tourists wandered around the corner of the building.

Maion scowled at me and began to march up the street, taking a left at the nearest creepy alley. We ran after him, leaving the tourists staring after us in suspicion. Spinning around and grabbing hold of Sam he launched into the air. I turned to Zach about to state for the hundredth time how much I hated that arrogant dick-head of an angel, when he grabbed hold of me and flung us both into the air, Gwen and Trev following closely behind.

I held onto Zach tightly as the wind buffed us as we soared higher and higher until we were above the clouds. Thankfully we weren't flying for long before we landed on a narrow beach in a darkly lit town. Maion was already marching off ahead as he had been doing all night. I groaned and shoved away from Zach, forcing my exhausted limbs to jog after him. He jumped over a fence onto a wooden deck outside a pretty beach house. He stuck the gold key in the door there and walked in, switching on the light on the inside of the door.

I let out a sigh of relief. It looked like we were here and could finally rest. I'd slept in Zach's arms a little on the way, but it was hard to truly relax when you're flying a hundred meters over the top of shark infested waters, with your stomach sinking into your feet with every swoop. I'd been able to rally myself at the bar but now I just wanted to sleep. I didn't even want sex. Well, that was a lie, I pretty much *always* wanted sex but this time it could take a backseat to my priority need which was lying full stretch on a bed and zonking out.

Zach pushed past me into the house, a worried expression on his face. I waited as he searched every hidden corner for a trap then turned to me and nodded grimly. Without acknowledging him at all I stomped upstairs and entered the first room I found. It was plain – like holiday accommodation. There were two single beds on either side of the room, and big French windows leading onto a little balcony. Matching bedside tables with lamps and a tall wardrobe completed the room's bare necessities.

I threw my bag on the wooden floor and threw myself on the nearest bed, crawling up the hideous green and yellow bedspread to lie face down. My eyes closed instantly, my body sinking into the mattress as I floated into oblivion.

10

There are only two ways to live your life. One is as though nothing is a miracle. The other is as though everything is a miracle.

Albert Einstein

Opening my eyes, I groaned as my muscles told me they were unhappy with the previous day's activities. My thighs in particular ached like a bitch. I scooted up in the bed and glanced over across the room, pleased to see that Gwen occupied the second single bed. To be honest, I was pretty surprised Zach hadn't taken it.

With Gwen still fast asleep, I tiptoed out of the room into the hallway and located the bathroom. I rolled my eyes at the granny-style surrounding me. The wooden floors were great, but the yellow and green wallpaper was old fashioned *and* beginning to peel, and was faded where the sunshine through the window would fall on it. The toilet, sink and bath were made of a hideous green ceramic. And there wasn't even a separate shower – it was one of those old fashioned ones with the shower above the bath. I couldn't have been more surprised of our accommodation. This dingy old house was owned by a Sorceress! Wouldn't you have thought they would have marble floors, tricked out bedrooms, and judging by their bar – neon lights everywhere?

I quietly closed the door and locked it. I peeled off the clothes I had travelled and slept in and pulled my hair out of its lopsided ponytail, letting it fall stiffly down my back. Realizing belatedly that I had left my toothbrush and shampoo in my backpack I debated going back to the room. I could just wrap a towel around me and run back...but then I would probably wake up Gwen searching through my bag.

Screw it, I decided. I rummaged in the drawers for toiletries, sighing when all I could find were Lynx shower-gel and home brand shampoo. I grimaced. I hoped Gwen had some leave in conditioner with her. And I'd have to brush my teeth later.

Stepping into the bathtub and pulling the shower curtain around, I turned on the hot and cold taps, testing the temperature with my hand until it was hot enough. Plunging under the water was bliss; feeling the hot water wash away my old crusty make-up, and the heavy droplets pounding on my aching muscles. I groaned in pleasure.

Leaning against the shower wall – somewhat awkwardly because of the rim of the bath – I closed my eyes and tried to relax.

Though I tried to keep my mind blank, I found myself drawn back to the memory of Sam and Lilura the Sorceress and their over-the-top PDA. I couldn't help but feel a little annoyed, but I couldn't work out why. Why should I be irritated about my best friend getting it on with his lover? I grimaced again at the bitchy direction my thoughts were taking.

Truthfully there was absolutely no reason I should be annoyed. I should be the complete opposite of annoyed. I should be ecstatic that my wonderful friend had a girlfriend and that he had found some happiness in our chaotic world.

Sam *deserved* someone wonderful. Maybe that was it – I didn't know if she was good enough for him. I didn't know if she would take care of him or make him happy. For all I knew she could be using him.

I guess I was also a little annoyed that he had never mentioned her before. I was supposed to be his best friend and he's never confided in me. He knew all of my secrets, he knew *everyone's* secrets because he was a telepath, but still, did this mean he didn't trust me? Maybe it meant that he didn't class me as his best friend?

I wondered if Trev and Gwen had known. With all of their questions it had seemed that they were as clueless as me, but maybe I was wrong. Did he trust them more than me? It would make sense if he did, he'd known them both a lot longer than me, but then did it really matter how *long* you had known someone for if you could hear all their thoughts? Surely within a few minutes you'd be able to tell if you could trust them or not. Which came back around to Lilura. If she was thinking about screwing him over then he would know better than anyone else. He would know exactly how she felt about him; which meant that she couldn't be the evil bitch I thought she was.

Another thought occurred to me and I fought uselessly to ignore it. Was I jealous of him? They seemed so excited to see each other...beyond excited. They practically breathed each other in. I'm sure if they had been alone they would have ripped each other's clothes off and got busy right there and then. Why didn't I have that? What was really going on with me and Zach? I was attracted to him beyond belief, my soul and body yearned to be bathed in his presence constantly. I got chills when I saw him, butterflies raced up through my stomach when he touched me. When he looked at me with that oh-so-masculine look, I felt as though I could instantly combust. If I could fuck him all day long I would. At least, I corrected, if I could tape his arrogant mouth closed.

I smiled as I imagined it. Wouldn't that just be the best of both worlds? He had betrayed me yes, but now I realized that somehow I had begun to move past it. But was it possible that I found him more arrogant now than before?

I thought back to the first time I had met him. He had been so smug, so proud and self-righteous, thinking he was above me. He had been so pissed off that he had been sent to protect me, and even angrier when it turned out I wasn't a meek little girl ready to do everything he demanded.

I smiled, tipping my face up under the water. He *had* earned his rights to be smug though. The way he fought...god it made me wet just thinking about it. He had a boxers body – all thick muscles, huge arms, sculpted chest and abdomen. When he fought against the Fallen he was a true warrior – an avenging angel. He was both terrifying and mesmerizing. The way his black eyes could see into my soul was intoxicating, his very scent arousing.

The first time we had had sex had been ferocious. Weeks of pent up lust had exploded, taking over both of us. Our emotions had been sky-high. Hunted by the Fallen, learning about what I was, topped with Zach declaring he was my soul mate – it was lucky we didn't kill each other is all I'm saying.

I turned and pressed my forehead to the cool tiles, letting the water pound on my back. Hands slipped around my hips, descending between my legs. I wondered if he had somehow sensed I was thinking about him and come to assuage my ache.

My senses came screaming back to me. This wasn't Zach.

I grabbed the hands touching me and tore them away just as I felt teeth sink down into the curve of my shoulder and neck. Throwing my head back I cracked him in the face and spun round as he fell back. Lifting my fists, I turned to the side and kicked him through the shower curtain into the bathroom wall beside the sink. As he fell to the floor, I let my power seep over me, infusing my muscles and invigorating my soul. He had fallen onto his backside on the floor and he looked up seeming surprised...then angry. He was pretty non-descript, but with fangs sticking out of his mouth like lollypops I presumed him to be a vampire. He certainly wasn't the hottest vampire I had seen; average looking, short brown hair, brown eyes, insane look on his face...definitely not my type.

Seeing him scramble to his feet, I stepped out of the bath tub quickly and ducked as he charged me. Spinning around behind him I punched him in the kidneys, knocking aside his hands as he tried to grab my throat. I grabbed his head and brought it down as I slammed my knee up into his face. He howled and fell backwards, cracking the bathtub with his weight.

I began to hear noises in the hallway. Yep, I had definitely woken everyone up.

A blow to my face sent me flying to the floor. Damn, I had been distracted. My ears were ringing, and I could feel the blood pouring from my cut lip. I rolled on the floor to avoid the kick to my ribs and jumped up behind him, kicking him in the back. He sailed into the bathroom sink, smashing it and the mirror above it. I grimaced and hoped the bad luck coming from that would go the vampire not me.

He rushed me again and I ducked, sending him over my head and to the floor. As I was about to kick him he grabbed my leg and sunk his fangs into my calf. The pain was excruciating. Fire shot up my calf to my thigh, my foot rapidly going numb, as I screamed. I drew on all my power then and pulled him off my leg by his hair. I spun quickly and kicked him sideways through the bathroom door – splintering it in half. He landed on his back in the hallway. I ran out after him and kicked him between his legs as he tried to stand. As he growled at me I returned my own growl, reveling in the feeling my power afforded me – the otherworldly, invincible kick-ass female reveling in rage feeling. I head-butted him, letting him fall back against the wall.

As someone shouted my name I turned my head, catching the knife thrown to me. I turned and sliced the vampires head from his shoulders, not even flinching when the fairly blunt knife paused for a millisecond before hacking through his spinal cord.

I stood tall, breathing hard, wincing at the bruises beginning to form.

"Jasmine…" I turned and glared at Sam daring him to say something about the broken door. "It's not about the door…" he muttered.

I lifted my eyebrow and glared harder as he stared open mouthed at me. Trev had already disappeared down the corridor and Gwen reappeared with a towel in hand. As she quickly wrapped it around me, I felt the haze of rage slowly descend, allowing me to think clearly again. I quickly realised everyone's shock was the fact that I was standing completely naked in the hallway and clutched the towel to me, cringing that *everyone* had seen me naked. I felt my anger return.

"Can I not even take a shower without something attacking me? What the hell is the point of you two being here if it managed to get into the bathroom while I was naked?" I screamed at Zach and Maion. I felt my body shoot off sparkled little fireworks and desperately tried to reign it in.

Maion grunted and stormed off, but Zach was still looking at me dumbfounded.

"What?" I snapped. I heard the scuttle of feet as Sam and Gwen descended the stairs hurriedly, leaving me and Zach alone.

"Your back..." Zach trailed off.

Horror burned through my body. He had seen my back again...and so had everyone else. My eyes felt scalded with tears instantly. I felt humiliated and ashamed. My face flushed and my heart ached. My back had been savagely scarred and bitten by Asmodeus when I had been held captive. In fact most of my body had been covered in welts and scars but most had healed with time and magic. The first time Zach had seen my back he had left me, saying that he couldn't be with me. He had betrayed me. Betrayed my trust and betrayed my love. I had made certain he had never seen my back again.

"Great. Just great," I said bitterly, determined not to cry in front of him.

I turned and stormed back into the bathroom, turning on the water of the shower to wash off the blood coating my body. I felt Zach crowd behind me.

"Fuck off Zach! Just leave me alone!" I screeched.

He grabbed hold of me and turned me around. I knocked his hands away instantly and glared up at him with as much malice as I could muster.

"For fuck's sake Jasmine!" he swore. "Your back is healed! It's healed," he trailed off in wonder.

My mind clouded. Thoughts echoing through my head so quickly I struggled to make sense of them. They flew quicker and quicker, making me dizzy and nauseas. I spotted my ring on the floor and quickly picked it up, slipping it on my finger. I turned towards a large shard of mirror and turned to look over my shoulder.

It was true. I couldn't see a single blemish. Not one single mark marred my skin.

I turned my head to look at Zach. "How is that possible?"

He shook his head. "I have no idea. I've never heard of anything like it before."

I turned back again to look at myself. How was it possible? What did it mean? Had I healed myself? Had my angel father healed me? Was it just an illusion? I stroked my fingers over the skin. It was soft and smooth. There was nothing there.

I looked up at Zach, frowning. "I need to shower again, will you leave?"

He nodded slowly and backed out of the room.

11

Every morning you have two choices: continue to sleep with dreams or wake up and chase your dreams.

Unknown

After I had showered again I returned to my room to dress. Pulling on plain black jeans and a grey T-shirt, I scraped my hair up into a ponytail. I didn't know what to think or do about my newly minted back so I decided to put it away in a box to think about another time. For now, I needed to concentrate on the task at hand. I walked into the kitchen to find Gwen, Sam and Trev leaning over the kitchen table with coffees. My stomach churned as I realised how hungry I was. I scooted behind the bench and poured the still hot water from the kettle, mixing it with the instant coffee on the bench. I stirred in a sugar for good luck.

" Where's Zach?" I asked after my first sip.

"Here."

I looked up to find him standing just inside the doorway that led out to the decking. I nodded.

"So are we going to make a plan?" Trev suggested, breaking the awkward silence.

I nodded my agreement.

"What's his name?" Gwen asked.

I smiled. "James."

At my smile the others all smiled at me. I knew I had a goofy grin on my face but just the thought of having a brother made me feel ecstatic. Like all my troubles had been worth it. I had a *brother*!

"Don't suppose the Sorceress gave you any idea how to find him?" Trev asked.

I shook my head. "I figure we can ask around. It's a pretty small town."

"Or we could go to the Council and look up their records?" Gwen said.

I nodded. Her idea was best. I slurped down my coffee and scoffed some toast eager to get going.

Unfortunately it took a while for us to leave. Everyone had to shower and Gwen insisted on Trev and Sam clearing up the shattered mirror on the bathroom floor before she would go in. I restrained myself from telling them to hurry up and instead sat on the decking, looking out at the sea, trying to find my inner calm.

Eventually we were ready to go. Maion refused to come with us, simply scowling when I asked him. We left him sitting on the decking and loped off up to the main road. It took a while – and a Google search on Sam's phone – but eventually we found the Council office.

We walked up the main reception where a fat, bald man with skin that looked like wrinkled leather, sat eating a bag of crisps behind a small counter.

"Excuse me," I began.

He huffed out a breath. "Yes?"

I frowned at him. "Hi. Um...we're looking for a friend of ours who lives here and I wonder if you can help us find where he lives."

He rolled his eyes at me. "I'm not a private detective."

"Yes, well can you point us in the right direction? Isn't there an archive of the names of everyone who lives here? Like a census?"

He leaned forward over the desk and scowled at me. "I can't give out private information to just anyone. If this person is a friend of yours, then you must have *some way* of contacting him."

I scowled back, beginning to get angry. I couldn't believe this prick. What the hell was he being such an arse for?

Sam pushed in front of me. "Look, I'm sorry if we got off on the wrong foot, we're from out of town obviously. Our friend's name is James. We figured this is a pretty small town and there can only be a handful of people under twenty-five called James. If you have any suggestions of where we might begin looking for him that would be really helpful. We've got some news of his family."

An odd look crossed the man's face then he frowned at us. "You're wasting my time! Get out of here!"

Zach stepped up. His presence dominating the room. The man stepped back from the counter, knocking his crisps to the floor.

"Speak with respect, lest you want your tongue cut out," he said coldly.

The man's face paled. "I'm sorry sir...it's just there's nothing I can do to help you..." He reached the side of the glass and slid it across, frosted glass now separating us.

I looked up at Zach. "Great. Thanks for that."

He smirked. "Anytime."

"Let's go." Sam marched through the door.

"What are we going to do? We can't just go around asking everyone we meet for someone called James," Gwen said.

"We don't have to," Sam smiled.

"Did you get it?" Trev asked, slapping him on the back.

Sam laughed. "I got a lead. It might not be the right one though. When I said we're looking for someone called James and that he's under twenty-five I saw a couple of faces."

"Why did you say under twenty-five? What if he's *older* than that?" Gwen interrupted. I had been wondering that too.

Sam shrugged. "He has to be younger than Jasmine. If he was older than her then surely he wouldn't need her to save his ass."

"Huh!" I grunted. I hadn't even considered that. It was a good idea to narrow down the search, although there was still a possibility of him being older than me. I grinned again. I *probably* had a baby brother. I was a big sister.

"When I said we had news of his family, he thought 'that must be Wainwright's kid' and I got a flash of 'Meadowbrook Secondary College'.' Sam smiled proudly. "So we're looking for James Wainwright at Meadowbrook Secondary College."

Zach raised his eyebrows at me. I knew that look.

Sam laughed, looking from me to Zach. "I know it's a slim chance and it's presuming a lot...but it's a lead – we might as well look into it."

I smiled at the look of disapproval on Zach's face. "It's worth a shot."

Zach grunted. "Well while you look for this James Wainwright I will return to Maion and discuss other options. I believe there is an Oracle contactable from this area." He turned to me and leaned close. "If you are in danger I will know." He turned and disappeared around the corner of the Council office.

I turned to face Gwen who couldn't wipe the grin off her face.

"What?" I asked.

"He is one *fine* man," she sighed.

I rolled my eyes and pulled out my phone to Google the college. When I found the directions Gwen called Trev and Sam from where they were looking in the window of a surfing store.

We followed the directions leading us to the college. It was a bit of a walk, and if we had realised how far it was we probably would have driven.

"How are we going to actually find him?" I mused out loud.

"We could have a look at the year group photos in the school foyer?" Gwen suggested.

That was an idea. "That depends on if they *have* year group photos though."

"We could ask for him at reception," Sam said.

"They probably wouldn't give out information about him though," I countered.

"But Sam can pick it out of their head," Trev said grinning. He slapped Sam on the back again.

"That's true!" I exclaimed, smiling.

Gwen slipped her arm through mine. I had never really been a touchy-feely kind of person but she always ignored that and did what she wanted anyway. "What are you going to say to him?"

Nerves raced through me as I shook my head and grimaced. I looked at her. "I have *no* idea. It would be easier if I knew whether *he knew* about any of the angel stuff. I don't want to meet him and immediately scare the crap out of him, but then how else do I tell him I'm his sister and that there are Fallen Angels hunting him? He's going to think I'm crazy. Oh my God. He's going to think I'm crazy!" I stopped and turned wide-eyed to Gwen, Trev and Sam. "If he doesn't already know, he's going to call the police or something!"

As Trev stifled a laugh I glared at him.

"So just tell him that you're his sister, and see how he takes that first. Hopefully his response will give you a clue as to if he knows or not." Sam rested his hand on my shoulder.

I nodded, biting my lip. "What if he doesn't know he's adopted? What if he thinks his family is actually *his family*?"

"Girl, you're making *me* nervous!" Gwen argued. "You gotta say what you gotta say!"

“That doesn’t help me in the slightest!” I scowled.

We stood there on the pavement for a minute while I searched the faces of my friends, and searched my brain for answers. How could I even start the conversation? How would I meet him? It’s not as if I could just go up to him and start talking - he’d think I was some weirdo! What if I was about to ruin his life? What if I told him that he was fostered or adopted and he had no idea? He would *hate* me forever, and he didn’t even know me! I pressed my hand to my forehead as I began to feel dizzy. Was I hyperventilating?

“What’s this?” Trev muttered, distracting me from my thoughts.

A navy Subaru pulled up a little distance from us and two men got out. They began walking towards us. I immediately straightened and began to draw my knife from the band under my T-shirt.

“Jasmine!” Gwen hissed.

I gulped and replaced it. Of course. I hadn’t been thinking. These were clearly humans and I would definitely be in trouble if I beheaded one of them.

“What do they want?” Gwen muttered. I could feel the anxiety coming off her in waves.

I reached out with my power to them, trying to get a feel for their purpose. All I got was a mixture of anger and worry. If Sam heard anything he didn’t tell us.

We stepped back a little way to let them pass, watching them carefully as they approached. One was tall, in a shirt and trousers, maybe a business man. He had thick grey hair pulled back into a pony tail. The other was dressed much more casual, in T-shirt and cargo pants and a thick hoodie open at the front. They were both scowling.

We waited silently for them to walk past us. Only they didn't. Instead they stopped about a meter away and glared at us.

The grey-haired businessman spoke first. "Leave town, now!"

"We don't know you," Sam began.

"This isn't a discussion and it isn't a question. You will leave town *now*, or I will make you leave," he repeated.

His friend opened his jacket just slightly to show us the handle of a gun sticking out of a holster inside. Shivers ran through me.

The grey haired man smiled grimly. "Whoever you are...whatever you want...you're not wanted here. There's nothing here for you." He held his hands up and the two of them began to back away.

We remained still as they returned to their car and drove off.

"Oh my God," Gwen muttered. "Who the Hell were they?"

I took a deep breath as Sam met my eyes. "That was James' father."

12

Never be afraid to fall apart because it is an opportunity to rebuild yourself the way you wish you had been all along.

Rae Smith

"His father?" Trev echoed. He snorted. "He's not a pleasant man. I could feel the hostility coming off him in waves."

I nodded my agreement. Maybe *he* was the reason James needed my help. Was he a threat to him?

"I don't think so," Sam answered my thoughts. He shook his head. "He was afraid. The guy at the Council tipped him off that we were looking for your brother and he came looking for us to warn us off. I get the feeling he's trying to protect him."

I frowned, my heart sinking a little. "Then maybe he knows?" I turned to Sam, hoping he had heard something that would help us.

Sam nodded. "That's the feeling I got. Except... I don't think he knows everything." He glanced at me sideways before returning his gaze to the road. "He was warned someone was going to come looking for him, but he was told it was going to be Demonic. He doesn't know we're half angel. And I'm pretty sure he doesn't know what James is."

I blew out a long breath. I had no idea what to do. Maybe it would be better to find James right now and explain before he had a chance to turn him against me.

"I don't know Jas," Sam muttered. "I reckon he's gone straight to wherever James is right now and if we go there too there could be trouble."

"If we go there we can expect a fight," I said quietly.

"Or at least a bullet wound," Trev drawled.

"Damn!" I exclaimed. "What are we supposed to do now?"

Gwen rubbed my arm. "Maybe we should head back to the house and come up with another plan to meet him. At least one good thing came out of this - we know it's him now, right? I mean, that's pretty suspicious behavior on his father's part! If he had been hoping to hide him then he did a poor job!"

"That's true," I conceded.

"And all we really wanted to accomplish today was to *find* him. We haven't actually worked out what you should say to him yet anyway..." Gwen trailed off.

I sighed. "You're right. We know his name. We know where he goes to school and we know his father knows about us. Or at least he *thinks* he knows about us."

Gwen linked her fingers with mine as Sam put an arm around my shoulders. Together they tugged me back in the direction we had come. Trev and Gwen chatted lightly about what we could do for the rest of the day. Sam put in a few comments but I stayed silent. I was too busy in my head.

Half of me hated that guy for warning me off. He didn't know me, how dare he tell me what to do? He'd sure feel like an idiot when he found out I was here to save James. It made me so mad to have someone interfere like that. This was a huge deal for me. And that fat idiot in the Council office who snitched on us as soon as we left the building! Well, I just wanted to storm in there and rip his head off!

Then there was the other part of me who couldn't help but be envious. He obviously cared enough about James to try to protect him. I had never had that. No one had ever tried to protect me except Zach, and I had to wait eighteen years for that.

Another thought occurred. Was he protecting James or hiding him? What if he was actually a bad guy and James needed rescuing from him?

"I think you were right the first time," Sam whispered.

I glanced up at him. "About what?"

He shrugged and took a deep breath, kicking a stone out of his way. "I think he genuinely cares about him. I didn't get the *evil vibe* from him."

I snorted then sighed. We walked in silence a little further until I muttered, "Me neither."

As much as I hated to admit it I was jealous. Why did he get the loving, protective parent when I got the douche bag and drug addict? I hated to be all *poor me* but it was looking more and more like James was the favourite.

Once we were back on the main street Trev and Sam disappeared into the surfing shop they had been gazing at earlier. I wasn't in the mood to shop. I wasn't in the mood to do anything really.

"I'm going to head back to the house," I said to Gwen, trying to smile so she didn't worry.

"Oh, Jasmine! It's going to work out! I promise!" She gripped my hand tightly.

I pulled my hand away gently and smiled. "I know! I think I'm just going to go back and try to work out a plan, like we said. You guys should shop though, and have some fun and I'll tell you what I've come up with later."

She narrowed her eyes at me. "Okay..."

I smiled brightly and turned away, marching quickly down the road in the direction of the house. When I was out of distance I let the tears spill down my face. I was so annoyed at myself for crying that it made me cry even harder. I was so weak, so pathetic. The slightest hitch in my plans and here I go, running home crying like a little girl.

Only it wasn't the slightest hitch. It was a huge moral dilemma. Here was everything I had ever wished for right in front of me, yet I didn't have the courage to go for it. I was too worried about what would happen, what I would say, what *he* would say. I was too afraid.

"I should never have come here," I whispered to myself.

"If you hadn't come you would have regretted it," A low, gravelly voice whispered in my ear.

I jumped and spun around realizing belatedly Zach was standing next to me.

"How long have you been following me?" I wailed.

He dropped his eyes, his expression glum. "Since the men approached you."

"Why didn't you say something?"

"I didn't want you to think I was spying on you, or that I didn't trust you," he whispered.

His soft words made my soul ache. I turned away and marched off, wiping at the torrent of tears that flooded down my face. I couldn't really see where I was going and was relying on my angelic senses to avoid cracks and holes in the pavement.

Zach appeared in front of me, holding me by my shoulders. I wanted to knock his hands away, to tell him to leave me alone. I didn't want to appear weak in front of anyone, let alone him. But I also wanted him to hold me and tell me everything would be alright. Why did I have to always be alone?

His arms wrapped around my waist and I felt him lift me against his chest. I buried my face in his neck and let the tears flood out. I felt my stomach drop away, adrenaline trying to kick in, but I just ignored it and let him do what he wanted.

We flew for what seemed like hours through the afternoon sky. He took us up high enough so that anyone looking up would think we were a large bird, which were common in the area. The wind dried my tears as soon as they were shed, and soon I was able to concentrate on the feel of Zach's strong body holding me, not on the crushing sorrow. It was difficult trying not to think about anything, but the raw magnificence of Zach at least focused my thoughts a more pleasant topic. I nuzzled into his neck, kissing and nipping, needing something, needing to feel him respond to me. I had to know that I wasn't alone. While holding me he managed to unhook my bra, and trail one hand under my shirt across my breasts, which peaked instantly for him. Desire burned through me like a fire.

We quickly descended and I found myself on my feet in a thickly wooded area. He ripped my T-shirt from my body throwing it to the ground without a second thought. He ripped my jeans down below my cheeks and sat me on a trunk as he stripped them off completely, pulling my boots off with them.

Completely naked I stood before him. As he paused, his gaze devouring my body as he tensed his lips, I realised I had never felt more beautiful or more wanted. This man *wanted* me. He didn't need to say the words. He didn't need to do anything. Just with that look, the way he was looking at me now...I knew.

I didn't say a word as he pulled his T-shirt over his head and dropped it on the ground. I didn't even open my mouth to sigh as he peeled his black trousers open and lowered them a fraction to his buttocks. I just waited...needing, *burning*.

He flew at me, lifting me in a fraction of a second and pressed me back against a tree. I could feel the rough bark abrade my skin but it only heightened everything I was feeling. His mouth on my breast was exquisite. He suckled and bit and pulled while he held me prisoner. I closed my eyes and rested my head on the trunk as he lowered his mouth to my belly and further to my clit. He licked and bit and when I thought I could take no more he returned to my mouth, letting me taste his desire for me. His fingers replaced where his mouth had been and he poked and prodded, massaging, widening, preparing me for his thick length of cock.

I could feel myself on the edge...I couldn't wait any longer.

"Now," I whispered.

He plunged into me, stretching my legs around his waist, letting me ride him. With his strength he kept me pinned to the tree as he plowed into me again and again, his mouth eating mine, biting my lips, licking my tongue savagely. In those moments I didn't exist. I could only feel. Passion and lust mingled with my power and I could do nothing to stop the mist that enveloped us, coating us in glitter.

"Harder," I moaned. I didn't even recognize my own voice.

He began to pound into me, deeper and deeper until the pleasure bordered on pain. Still it wasn't enough. I dug my nails into his arse, dragging him into me with as much force as I could manage.

"I need more, Zach!" I screamed throatily.

He threw us to the ground at the base of the tree and withdrew from me with a sucking noise that sent sensual shivers through my body. As I was about to scream my frustration he threw me to my stomach and lifted me to my knees. Inserting a thick knee between mine he split my thighs apart sharply. I slid on the leaves, exposing myself completely to him. There was nowhere to hide, he could see all of me. I was completely at his mercy...and I had never felt more turned on in my life.

13

When you know yourself, you are empowered. When you accept yourself, you are invincible.

Tina Lifford

He grabbed my breasts and eased me up to lean against him. He covered them with his huge palms, stroking and caressing, using enough strength to keep me burning up. He then pushed me to all fours and ever so slowly ran his cock up and down my seam. I was so wet, so moist I could feel my juices beginning to trickle between my thighs. He was teasing me. I loved it but at the same time I needed more. I always needed more.

He inserted just the tip, moving his hips gradually so that little by little he filled me until his full length was inside me and I could feel his balls rubbing against my clit. I trembled with the effort not to move. It almost felt as though I had been skewered. He was so incredibly long and so thick I'm surprised he had never split me, as it was, it was sweet agony feeling him there, not moving.

And then it began. He pounded over and over, harder, faster with all of his strength. My breasts were knocked viciously against my chest, his balls smashed into my clit and squashed my lips with force again and again. And then I came. The strongest orgasm I had ever had rocketed through me. I actually felt the ground shift, our bodies vibrating with the power I let off. My skin electrically charged with the sparks that shot from me. He came with a blow inside me as he yelled his completion.

As I began to collapse to my stomach he turned and pulled me so that he lay on his back with me on top of him, our legs entangled. My head fell back against his chest and I panted for breath as the aftershocks sent earthquakes through my body. His hand trailed electricity down my stomach as the other cupped a breast, thumbing my nipple gently.

I turned my head just slightly to find a comfortable niche between his pecs. I closed my eyes and let myself drift, knowing that Zach would take care of me always.

A good few hours later Zach woke me with kisses to my hair.

"Are you awake?" he whispered.

"No," I murmured.

"You feel cold."

"No I don't." I replied, keeping my eyes closed. The truth was, I did feel pretty cool. My nipples were so hard they could have cut glass and our mixture of juices coating me had frozen against my inner lips. I moved slightly and realised he was still inside me. And still hard.

I tilted my head to look up at him. "You're still..."

He grinned. "When am I not?"

I blushed. "Seriously."

"Around you? All the time. Why do you think I swim in the sea so often? I need something to take the edge off."

I bit my lip and looked up again shyly. "You want me to take the edge off for you?"

He grinned. "What do you have in mind?"

I let him slip out of me and rolled onto my knees between his legs. I lay down a trail of kisses from his nipples down to his cock, lavishing him in my attention, sucking and squeezing and licking. It lasted only a few moments before he threw me to my back and lowered himself onto me again.

When we were completely exhausted he slipped out of me and pulled me to my feet. He glanced at my ripped clothing by our feet and gave me a sheepish look. I just smiled languidly. I couldn't have cared less about my clothes. I felt deliriously happy.

I stood still as he pulled his T-shirt over my head. It was a happy coincidence that it dropped to my knees as the flight back to the house was quite breezy.

We landed on the balcony outside my bedroom window and scooted inside quickly. As Zach disappeared, I grabbed my towel and toiletries and ran to the bathroom, hoping no one would see me. Unfortunately God saw an opportunity. All three of them had happened to return at that precise minute and were all standing in the hallway.

They stared open mouthed at me as I blushed furiously.

"Are you okay?" Trev asked. He instantly winced and blushed as I glared at him in utter mortification.

Mud coated my knees and hands, I was wearing Zach's white T-shirt with no bra and it wasn't as if I was *small* in that department. My hair was a mess, and I knew I had a heap of twigs and leaves still matted in it.

"Oh my God," Gwen whispered, trying not to laugh. She turned to face Trev and Sam and shoved them into the nearest room out of the hallway.

I scooted through the broken doorway and jumped into the shower immediately. I scrubbed and scrubbed, removing any evidence of our animal behavior in the forest...all the while glowing inside.

When I was clean and dressed I went down to the kitchen where Zach was preparing dinner for all of us. He grinned at me wickedly, setting a new flame. Gwen cleared her throat and I turned away from him and sat next to her, trying not to smile, but failing.

Trev coughed. "So what's the plan?"

I looked up. "The plan?"

"Your brother..." Gwen laughed.

"Oh. Right." I searched my mind. What was I going to do about him? "You know, let's just leave it for now, and we can decide tomorrow. We'll sense any of the Fallen that come into the area, so we don't need to make any hasty decisions."

All three grinned at me. At my glare they began talking about something else.

14

Imperfection is beauty. Madness is genius. It is better to be absolutely ridiculous than absolutely boring.

Marilyn Monroe

The next day I decided to spend the day relaxing on the beach just outside the house. The others had wanted to go exploring the coastline a little more so after a lot of persuading them that I would survive a day without them, I waved them off. Zach had been absent all morning and Maion had been his usual sulky self, sitting on the deck so I decided to take myself out of reach of his miserable aura and relax.

I sat on the beach for a few hours. I read a few pages of a book I found in the house before deciding that dreaming about Zach was much more interesting. I put in my headphones, cranked up my Alicia Keys playlist and began fantasizing. I couldn't help but wonder what he had been like when he was younger. I imagined him in various scenarios – saving people mostly. The way his muscles moved when he fought…he was just amazing. I also wondered if he had ever been in love before. I knew that before me he had only ever thought of Nephilim in the same context as duty, but I wondered if he had ever been in love with another angel? Or maybe not in love, maybe he had dated one? He *had* told me that each species normally stuck to their own kind, in matters of love and sex.

Not liking the turn my thoughts had taken, I returned to the house and dressed. I washed up the dishes from that morning and tidied my room then went out for a walk along the main street. Before I knew it, I found myself walking towards the college. I hadn't initially planned it, but the more I thought about it, the more right it seemed. This was it. I'd see my brother for the first time! I was racked with both apprehension and excitement.

I began to jog – I wasn't far away but my nerves were beginning to get the better of me. I slowed as the road curved up a hill. I could see the building in the distance surrounded by playing fields, high wire fences keeping out the wildlife.

I walked slowly up the road, not wanting to feel sweaty and out of breath when I met him for the first time. I stopped when I reached the open gates.

'Welcome to Meadowbrook Secondary College' it read. I shivered with nerves, questions shooting across my mind. Would he like me? Did he know about me? Would I look like him? Was he brainy, or was he like me – dragging my feet through school only just scraping through?

"Are you lost?" a female voice called out.

I jumped. I had been so engrossed in my thoughts I had been oblivious to the mauve Subaru driving up the road behind me. I chided myself.

When I didn't answer she spoke again. "Are you looking for the game? If you follow the road straight up you'll not miss it! It's almost over though!"

I nodded politely and gave a brief smile, turning to follow her instructions. I wasn't entirely sure if I was looking for the game. I had thought to find James inside the school, but maybe he was watching the game, or even playing.

She was right about not missing it. A crowd of spectators gathered at either side of the pitch some stood, some sitting on benches, cheering loudly as one young man tackled another to the ground. I flinched then berated myself. It wasn't long ago that I'd been trying to decapitate a dragon – who was I to flinch as the guys on the field rammed each other into the mud?

I milled around at the edge of the crowd uncertainly. I wanted to follow my instincts which were telling me he was here, but how could I tell who he was? Shouldn't I just know?

I bit the inside of my cheek and perused the crowd, rolling my eyes when I realised it mainly consisted of giggling girls. Most of them were dressed up in cute little outfits that had no place at a sports game, and probably cost more than my sword did.

I glanced away from the crowd feeling self-conscious. Dressed in my black knee high boots, black pants tucked in and a plain white t-shirt, I stood out like a sore thumb. I actually looked like some kind of weird ninja compared to these school kids. Would he take one look at me and laugh?

Ugh! I was annoyed at myself for even comparing myself to those girls. I was different in every way possible. Hunted, tortured, and honed into a fighter, could I be any more unlike these pretty girls in their tight jeans and Gucci tops, chatting on their iPhones and drooling over a bunch of hot guys? I would never be one of them. I have never *been* one of them. Was I jealous? You betcha!

I scowled and stomped over to the benches, choosing a seat at the back where I wouldn't have to sit next to anyone else. I was being completely ridiculous. The hottest guy in the entire world was in love with me, and I with him. I didn't need anyone else's approval. Not even my own brother's.

As I watched the guys on the field I realised I had no idea what he looked like. I had thought that my eyes would be magically drawn to him and I would just *know*, but looking at the players and at the crowd on either side, I was completely stumped. With his additional Nephilim strength it could be the captain of the team, surely he would be the strongest and most agile member of the team. Or would James hide his strengths, hoping to blend in? Was he actually sitting nearby wishing that it was *he* who was playing? Then again, I could have been right in the first place and he could be in the school – probably in detention if he was anything like me.

I was distracted from my musings by the row of girls in front of me. They were gushing over the players as you expect from a group of teenage girls. I rolled my eyes and tried my best to ignore them, continuing my perusal of the crowd opposite. With my excellent Nephilim eyesight I could see each person exceptionally well, and studied each one at length.

"Well James is taking me to *his* place tonight because his dad's out of town," one of the girls boasted in front of me.

I snapped to attention immediately. *My James*? I leaned forward trying to catch their words over the cheers and shouts.

"I thought you were sleeping with Brody?" one girl with thick black hair giggled.

The brunette in front of me tossed her hair back and laughed. "I *am*, but that doesn't mean I can't do him too. What he doesn't know won't hurt him," she sniggered.

I hoped that she wasn't talking about *my* James but a sinking feeling in the pit of my stomach made me nervous. I imagined kicking the shit out of my little brother's girlfriend wouldn't go down too well with anyone except me.

A whistle sounded then the crowd erupted into cheers. I hadn't been watching at all so I had no idea who had won. To be honest, I didn't even really know what I was watching, and I had been so distracted by the cheating bitch in front of me I hadn't had time to work out who James was. I scowled as the girls waved and blew kisses at their boyfriends on the field. *Pathetic.*

"What are you looking so angry for babe?" a low voice rasped in my ear.

I jumped and turned to face Zach. Typical! Just as I was wallowing in a pit of self-loathing Zach chose that exact moment to appear next to me. After yesterday *I* was the one who was pathetic to be feeling anything remotely close to self-pity.

"What are you doing here? I want to be alone when I do this!" I whispered, even as my eyes raked over his body. The longings began to stir in the pit of my stomach.

He smirked and snaked an arm around me, pulling me close. Too close. I felt my body begin to melt for him. He leaned closer, wisps of my hair catching in the stubble on his jaw.

"I didn't want you to be alone," he whispered in my ear. He stepped back and turned me so that I was facing the field with him standing behind me, holding me to his chest. I felt my eyes fill with tears of joy and my soul began to burn.

15

Whatever you want to do, do it now. There are only so many tomorrows.

Michael London

As the players ran off the field and the crowd began to file out I pulled away from Zach, lifting my shield and blocking him out. I couldn't afford to get emotional right now. Yes I loved him, blah blah blah. But now I needed to concentrate. I needed to be sensible.

I ignored Zach and located the brunette girl following her as she sauntered towards the sports building, her friends in tow. Following at a discreet distance I walked up the paved entrance and pulled open the old red door, paint flicking off in patches. Once in the corridor I saw them up ahead waiting outside the mens' changing room. I stopped a little distance away and pretended to be interested in the pictures lining the walls of past sports teams holding trophies and medals, all of them grinning proudly. Zach had stopped beside me and was smirking at me as I tried to ignore him.

Within a couple of minutes the changing room door began to bang open, the hinges creaking loudly as the players traipsed out, laughing and shouting at each other. Three boys stopped by the group of girls and indulged on what can only be described as a disgusting show of animal lust, while the other girls looked on, giggling.

I glanced up at Zach to see him trying to hold back a laugh. I sucked in my breath slowly, irritated. I scowled as the brunette girl grabbed the boy by his balls so indiscreetly, pushing him against the wall as she sucked on his face. I could only be pleased that the boy wasn't my brother. I guess I had been wrong thinking she was talking about him.

Only I hadn't been wrong. As I stared, now open mouthed, the brunette slut untangled herself from him and stepped away, sashaying back up the corridor past me with a satisfied look on her face. The boy she left was tall and broad shouldered. He was a little on the slim side, but definitely good looking, with an upturned nose, brown eyes and short brown hair. He grinned and laughed as his friends slapped him on the back and congratulated him for having a slut for a girlfriend.

It was him. I knew it. My whole body and soul told me that this boy was my brother, that he was connected to me somehow. My breath was taken away completely. I was completely frozen in shock. So frozen in fact that I belatedly realised one of the slut's friends was hitting on Zach.

I turned, my mouth still open, to face Zach. "Did she just ask you to meet her tonight?"

He laughed. "Yeah, think so."

"That fucking..." I trailed off as I took in Zach's expression. It could only be described as pleased. He was loving that I was feeling possessive of him. I scowled at him, turning back to James as he trudged past me with his friends. If I had thought the connection I felt would be shared I was wrong. Without a single look, he moved past and left the building.

Disappointment bloomed in my chest. He didn't know me. He didn't recognize me at all. I pushed my hair behind my ear and stomped out of the building, marching quickly down the road away from the school. Cars zoomed past as parents took their kids home after the game. Zach remained silent, my constant shadow.

My mind in turmoil, I didn't say a word until we had reached the house. Zach grabbed my arm and swung me around before I could enter.

"Jasmine," he said softly. "What are you going to do?"

I shook my head. "I have *no* idea. He didn't...he didn't know me."

Zach sighed. "That doesn't mean anything."

"I know! I just...I just thought that he would *know* me." I glared at him. "And you know what? It certainly didn't seem as though he was in trouble like Haamiah said! He's obviously got terrible taste in women, and is clearly dating a two-timing whore, but that's hardly reason for me to come here and jump into his life!"

Zach pursed his lips, thinking. "Maybe the trouble hasn't come yet. Maybe you need to be *in* his life before it happens."

I groaned, rubbing my face with my hands. "What was I thinking, coming here?"

"Haamiah wouldn't have told you where he was if he didn't think this was the right thing to do."

"Oh, and *Haamiah's* never wrong!" I grumbled. "How do I actually meet him? What am I supposed to do – just walk up to him and say 'Hi! I'm your long-lost half angel sister, you're in terrible danger and I've come to rescue you!' Do you realize how insane that sounds? I've played this over and over in my mind for days and I can't come up with a better intro!"

Zach chuckled. "How about we just work on *where* to meet him? They're going to a club called River tonight. We'll go there and maybe an opportunity will present itself."

I frowned. "How do *you* know where they're going tonight?"

He smirked. "I was invited remember."

I growled an incoherent sound and shoved past him into the house. Stomping through the kitchen I decided to go sulk upstairs where I couldn't be pestered. Pulling on my hoodie I pulled the hood up over my hair and slid the balcony doors open, taking a seat on one of the metal chairs.

"Hey girl, what's happenin'?" Gwen's silky voice called out from behind me a little while later. When I didn't answer she took it as an invitation to join me, and pulled another chair up, studying my face. "Your relaxing day didn't go as planned?"

I shook my head. "Not in the slightest. I went to see James."

"Oh my God! Why didn't you tell me? What happened?" she exclaimed.

I turned fully to face her, sitting up straight. "He didn't know me. Am I crazy to think he should have?"

She shrugged. "Are you sure you had the right guy?"

"I'm positive. I know it was him," I replied sullenly.

"What did he look like?"

I shrugged. As If that even mattered! “He was fairly tall I guess, brown hair and eyes. He looked nice. *Normal.*” I rubbed a hand down my face. “He’s going out with a skanky whore who’s two-timing him with someone called Brody.”

Gwen clicked her fingers. “Well it sounds as though someone needs to teach the bitch a lesson.”

I raised my eyebrows. I wasn’t stupid. “You really think he’s going to *thank* me, and be grateful for me randomly appearing here after I tell him his girlfriend is cheating on him?”

“Maybe not,” Gwen frowned.

“Zach said they’re going to be at a club tonight,” I continued. “He thinks we should go.”

She laughed. “Now *that* sounds like a plan!”

“That is *not* a plan!” I denied. “It’s not even part of a plan! I can’t just show up there and say ‘Ta da! Here I am!’ Seriously Gwen, what the hell was I thinking coming here?”

Gwen stood up. “Haamiah said he’s in danger, right? So you can either sneak around following him without him knowing, or be upfront and just tell him who you are? What have you got to lose?”

I didn’t reply as she skipped back into the house, probably to start getting ready for tonight. The thing was; *none* of them got it. None of them *would* get it. They all had at least one person to call family. Except Sam, but he’d lived in the safe house for so long he thought of it as his home. James was a flesh and blood relative, and not even a distant one! He was my brother! He was my last chance to have a family. If I screwed this up I’d have no one. Okay, that wasn't entirely true. I had Zach. But he was my lover, not a relative.

They all thought that I should just go for it. They thought that I should take a chance and throw myself out there. They didn't realize that I would prefer to not know him, and just know that he was out there *somewhere*, rather than for him to meet me and hate me.

"Alright! I hear we're going on the drink?" Trev startled me. He and Sam appeared beside me, grinning.

"I don't know if I want to go," I replied, irritated. Why were they all pushing me?

"Because no matter what happens we've got your back," Sam answered my silent question. I *hated* when he did that. He held his hands up in apology. "If you leave without talking to him you'll regret it, that's all I'm saying."

I sighed and gave in. "Then I guess we're going out." I rolled my eyes as Sam and Trev high-fived. "Gwen, I hope you're up to the task of making me look *amazing* because if that whore looks at me the wrong way even once, I'm going to bitch-slap her into next year."

16

A girl should be two things: who and what she wants.

Coco Chanel

Gwen lived up to her promise and by the time we were all ready to go out, I was feeling pretty good about myself. I hadn't exactly packed for clubbing, so I wore a dress of Gwen's – a red strapless bondage-type, it fitted snugly, perhaps a little *too* snug around my boobs but I could still breath in it...just. Gwen had gone all out doing my hair and makeup. My hair was braided around the front and pulled back into a clip, and the rest hung loose. My eyes had been made up in shades of gold and bronze, with a hint of metallic green, making my eyes stand out. Unfortunately Gwen and I were a different shoe size and the only footwear I had were black and white trainers or my knee high boots.

"There's no way you're wearing those boots!" she told me, handing over a pair of bronze strappy heels. I forced my feet into them and found that they weren't as crippling as I thought they would be. They would do.

Gwen wore a stunning knee length black dress with her hair pulled up and back away from her face. Smokey eyes completed her. She looked stunning, but then she always did.

Together we descended into the living room. I hid a smile when the guys stared at us, completely speechless, but my breath hitched when I glanced at Zach. He looked shell shocked. His mouth was slightly open, his face in awe as he stared at me, dumbfounded. Pride heated my blood, making me blush.

"Let's go!" Gwen hollered, pushing open the door.

We filed out one by one. Maion refused to come and advised Zach to stay behind with him. As I expected, Zach just lifted his eyebrow in response. Sam, Trev and Gwen led the way, saying they had Googled the club and knew which way to go. Zach and I trailed behind.

Sam, Trev and Gwen chatted about the last time they had sneaked out of the safe house and I laughed along with their stories all the while feeling distracted by Zach glowering beside me. We dropped back a little. I tried not to ask, berating myself for even thinking it, but eventually blurted the words out. "Do you think I look nice?"

Zach looked down at me, scowling just a little. "You look...you look-"

I scowled up at him. "Jesus! You could at least lie." I felt tears creep up into my eyes. I had thought his expression in the house had meant that he thought I looked good, not the opposite. Just when I thought we were getting somewhere he had to go and say something to make me doubt him.

I looked at the houses we passed, determined not to cry, trying desperately to control my emotions. What did it matter if he didn't like the way I looked? It wasn't as if he was my boyfriend or anything, so he could take his opinions and shove it up his arse.

I walked faster, catching up with Gwen. Noticing I was upset she glared at Zach, correctly guessing he had something to do with it and dropped back to walk beside me. We crossed a road and headed for the path on the opposite side which led down a road filled with shops and cafes. They were mostly closed now as it was getting late. A couple of small restaurants were open though, and the smell of the food wafting out made my stomach grumble.

At the end of the row we turned left and walked up a quieter street that seemed to consist mainly of tourist gift shops. The further we walked the dimmer the light got – the street lights only went as far as the cafes then ceased. Just as I was about to question our direction the distant sound of thumping music reached my ears. A little further on we reached the club, which to be honest wasn't at all what I had expected.

When the one bouncer on the door didn't bother to I.D. us, that should have been my first clue, but as we passed through the door and entered the club I rolled my eyes as I realised that just about *everyone* in this place was underage. It was like being at a kiddie party.

Sam turned and looked at me in amazement as a young boy who I swear couldn't have been more than 16 walked past me with a pint of larger in his hand. I shook my head in shock and followed as he lead the way to the bar. Ordering Budweiser's for himself and Trev and the house cocktail for Gwen and I he lifted his eyebrows in question at Zach. Zach shook his head in reply.

I didn't bother explaining or discussing my plan with the others. We were standing right in front of the speakers so the music was *so* loud they wouldn't have heard me anyway. I decided to take a slow walk around the room to see if I could spot James. Gwen followed me while the guys stayed at the bar.

We began circling the dance floor, pushing through the thick crowd of adolescent boys and girls. The girls were dressed in their finest – or slutiest clothes hoping to attract a boys attention, while the boys stood in huddles leering at said girls. We stopped as a guy approached Gwen. Wearing a blue t-shirt with 'FCUK' written on and jeans which hung below his arse I couldn't see him being Gwen's type, let alone that he was obviously about 8 years younger than us both. I smirked, highly amused as he lifted her hand and pressed a kiss to the back.

"Does your mama know you're out?" she asked him in reply, snatching her hand back.

With a leer he said, "baby, don't blow me off so quick. I got what you need!"

She rolled her eyes as I stifled a laugh. "*You* got what I need? Well I need you to get your skinny white ass out of my way."

His jaw dropped and he looked instantly in love with her. She shoved past him, grabbing my arm on her way past. I giggled as we pushed our way through the crowd only stopping when I caught sight of James...with the skank.

I leaned close to Gwen. "That's him."

We stood together in the thick of the crowd until the opportunity presented itself. The skank left James and went to dance on the dance floor leaving him standing with his friends, an amused look on his face.

"Do it now!" Gwen urged, shoving me forward.

I bit my cheek, my heart pounding so much it ached. I took a deep breath and marched up to him, stopping when I was a couple of feet away. He stopped talking to his friend and looked at me. Of course that was the moment I went completely blank and forgot everything I was going to say. His friends started to snigger.

I sucked some air into my aching lungs. "Hi," I said, unsure if he would actually hear me over the music. Up close he was a little taller than me, but not by much. His brown hair had streaks of blonde running through it, and his brown eyes were not completely brown but had flecks of gold dotted through.

He lifted his eyebrows and gave me a look of pure distain. Though I immediately felt hurt and embarrassed I tried to look at it through his eyes. A random stranger walks up to him and barely says a word – *freak*!

I shook it off. "I need to speak to you," I said calmly.

"Do I know you?" he asked, frowning.

"No, well, kind of, I guess. We *should* know each other. Is there somewhere we can talk in private?" I stammered.

"Mate, she wants to jump you!" one of his friends crowed.

I flushed red, embarrassment followed by anger. God, I wanted to pound his face into the floor. But no, I needed to control myself, I was here for James.

He twisted his mouth in thought. "You know, seeing as I don't know you, and you're clearly a wack-job…I'm gonna go over here, and you can just go somewhere else," he drawled. He pushed past me and his friends sniggered as they trailed after him.

I could feel my anger already beginning to wake my power up. The churning mist was already creeping up through my stomach higher and higher. How *dare* he talk to me like that? He didn't even know me! When he realised who I was *then* he'd regret his words!

I stormed through them all, knocking his friends flying, barely restraining myself. I grabbed James by his elbow and swung him round to face me.

"What the fuck?" He knocked my arm off, and glared at me.

"I put my hands on my hips. "What the fuck? I'm you're fucking sister you dick head!" I yelled.

"You're a fucking psychopath!" he shouted back, twirling his fingers beside his head. He spun around and raced through the crowd. I quickly followed him. This wasn't going how I had hoped it would but I needed to get this sorted now. I ducked under arms and scooted around people as I followed him through the club to the very back of the room where he exited through a door. I ran through it and followed him into the back alleyway. I saw him take off, running pretty fast down the alleyway. Not fast enough though. I sucked in my power and pushed it through my legs sprinting until I over took him. I spun around and forced him to stop.

"Get away from me!" he shouted.

"What are you running from?" I asked, confused.

"You! You need to stay away from me. I don't know how you found out but if you come near me again I'll go to the police!" he bit out. He was so angry, his face red, his eyes glaring hatred at me.

"You're my brother! I came here to see you! I wanted to know you," I said, still in shock, my anger subsiding.

"You're nothing to me. I don't want anything to do with you. Stay away from me and stay out of my life!" he bellowed pushing past.

I was so confused. What was he talking about? It didn't make the slightest bit of sense, although he seemed to believe me which was kind of strange actually.

"James! You're in danger! I only just found out about you and I came to protect you!"

He stepped back away from me. "The only thing that is a danger to me is *you*. I know all about you and your kind. I'm nothing like you!"

"My kind?" I asked incredulously. What the hell?

He took a hesitant step closer. "Demons. I know about them. My parents told me about them, said that they'd come looking for me."

I huffed out a breath. "You know that's funny, because firstly, you're my brother and apparently our mother is dead and our father is somewhere else, secondly I'm not a demon I'm an angel!"

"You're talking shit." He looked me up and down. "As if *you're* an angel!"

I scowled, "I'm a Nephilim – half angel – just like you!"

He shook his head, "I'm nothing like you!"

"So what, you didn't know you're adopted?" I asked spitefully.

“I know I’m adopted. No one else knows...” he scowled at me. “My parents told me that my biological parents were Demons and one day they’d come for me. The thought of it used to scare me, but you...you’re not even remotely scary,” he sneered.

“Actually, you’re very wrong about that!” I growled.

My head snapped to the side with brutal force. Had he just hit me? My senses came to me too late and I felt something snap in my chest as I was kicked. I flew through the air landing on a parked car, my full weight smashing the windscreen. I groaned as I rolled off the bonnet and lay face down on the floor, my body in agony. I was dragged to my feet and a punch to the jaw sent me flying into the brick wall of the shop beside me, obliterating the bricks as I crumbled into a heap on the ground. I sat there dazed for a second then jumped to my feet and threw myself to the side as the parked car hit the brick wall, exploding into flames.

I flipped up to my feet fending off the next attack. This time I saw his face and I knew...Fallen Angel. I smiled wickedly and kicked out with my foot, snapping his neck. He screeched and fell to the side, clutching his neck. I retrieved my dagger and sliced his head off cleanly.

As I was congratulating myself on a fairly easy kill a groan made me look up. James was standing in peculiar position...no, he was being held in a peculiar position. His head fell back as another Fallen Angel sunk his teeth into neck. I pulled up my power and forced it through my body, allowed it to take over my body. I was instantly beside them. I pulled James away, dropping him to the floor. The angel snarled at me, blood pouring from his mouth.

“Did Asmodeus send you too?” I asked, smiling grimly.

The angel frowned. That was all I needed to know. I threw my fist up, dagger clenched. The angel leaned back quickly, my dagger slicing through thin air. A kick to my thigh had me crumbling to the ground. I gritted my teeth and dived forward, tackling him to the ground. I smashed his head off the ground, allowing my rage and regret to take over. Lifting his leg, he kicked me off. I thumped down on the ground, my head smacking on the gravel. I rolled over and jumped to my feet. As he ran towards me I leapt, clearing him by a meter. Landing behind him I spun around and buried my dagger in his neck. I wiggled it fiercely, smiling only when his head was ripped from his shoulders.

I spun around to find James. He was kneeling on the floor clutching his neck. I ran to him and knelt beside him.

"Shhh! It's okay!" I whispered. I lifted my hand and touched his shoulder, letting my mist flow through. The sparkles found the wound on his neck and began to knit the flesh back together, multiplying his blood cells to replace those he had lost.

"What are you doing?" he groaned.

"I'm healing you! I'm half angel, like you! We have abilities, like strength, and healing, some Nephilim can even fly."

He knocked my arm away and scrambled to his feet.

He glared at me with hatred. "Stay away from me! Don't come near me again!"

I remained where I was on the ground kneeling, as he staggered away into the dark.

17

Every man needs a woman when his life is a mess, because just like the game of chess, the queen protects the king.

Unknown.

"Jasmine!" I heard Sam shout. Someone pulled me up off the ground. Zach.

"What happened boo?" Gwen stroked my cheek. "Where's James?"

I drew in a shaky breath. "We were attacked. I killed them." I gestured to the body parts that were rapidly disintegrating on the ground.

"And James?" Gwen asked.

"He left," Sam answered for me.

"Let's just go," I said. I turned and walked towards the alleyway in the opposite direction to the way James had gone. I spun back. "Zach..."

"I'll make sure he gets home okay," Zach promised gravely. His wings unfolded behind him and he took off into the sky.

"Are you okay?" Gwen asked, her brown eyes melting into mine.

I shook my head. "No, not really."

As a group of people exited through the back door to the club, Gwen grabbed my hand and pulled me down the alleyway with Trev and Sam in tow. We began to jog down the road towards the house. It was important no one saw me, seeing as how I was covered in blood. God, the blood – I would have to appologise to Gwen when my brain functioned properly again.

We reached the house and barreled through the front door. Maion stood to attention as we came in.

"Trouble?" he questioned angrily.

"Nothing that *you* need to be concerned about," I replied snarkily.

I left them all and stomped upstairs to the room Gwen and I were sharing. I looked down at myself in the mirror and did and an about-turn. Entering the bathroom, I peeled off the beautiful, now ruined dress and stepped under the steaming hot water. I closed my eyes and let the water wash the makeup off my face. Who was I kidding? I wasn't that glamorous, beautiful girl I pretended to be tonight. I was me – the screw up, the disappointment, the miss-fit. Of course he wouldn't want to be related to me. After what happened tonight I didn't want to *be* me.

I looked down and watched the blood stained water swirl down the drain. I had thought I had it all figured out. I was strong physically. I could rip apart a Fallen Angel, I could gut a vampire. I was a Nephilim, a half-angel warrior. I was prophetic, I was even a Soulmate. But in reality, in the *real* world I was nothing. I was an orphan. My real parents hadn't wanted to know me, my brother didn't even want to know me. So that was that. That was the end of my dream. I wouldn't have a family.

I pulled on jogging pants and a t-shirt and wrapped my duvet around me. I sat outside on the balcony looking up at the stars, listening to the waves crash up the beach, smelling the salt in the air.

I felt someone sit beside me - the screech of the chair was also a giveaway.

“Are you okay?”

“I’m not, but I will be,” I replied.

There was a small silence, then I turned to look at Sam. He had an odd expression on his face.

“What?” I asked, frowning.

“I didn’t say anything,” he said quietly.

I frowned to myself then shrugged. “I knew you were going to say it though.”

He grunted and sat back in his chair. “So this James is a douche-bag?”

I smiled sadly. “He wasn’t what I expected. You know what the weirdest thing is? I was wondering if he would be like me, maybe in looks or in personality. And I realised when he was talking all sarcastic and just plain bitchy…that’s what we have in common.”

“You’re not a bitch,” Sam said softly.

I shrugged. “If the label fits. I know I can be. I know I *used* to be.”

“You’re *not* a bitch,” he repeated.

"Then why doesn't my father contact me?" Tears began to fill by eyes. I cursed myself. I refused to cry! "Trev's mother talks to him all of the time. So where's mine?"

Sam sighed. "If we're playing that game, then where's *mine*?"

I bit my lip. "Do you think they've completely abandoned us? Or do you think they're out there somewhere laughing as we fuck up again and again? Do you think..."

"What?" Sam asked as I trailed off.

"Do you think that they preferred James, and that's why they sent him here to a nice family?"

"How do you know they're nice?"

I shrugged. "I don't. But the chances are high; nice house, nice school. Apparently they warned him that 'Demons' would come after him." I turned to him. "I don't think he knew really what he was."

"He needed to know."

I shrugged again and shook my head slightly. "I don't know. Maybe I've come here and just screwed up his life. Haamiah didn't say anything about talking to him. He just said he was in trouble. Well, I killed those Fallen Angels and unless there are any more in the area I'm pretty sure he'll be safe now. So, I guess we should pack up and head back to the safe house."

"Home," Sam said.

"What?"

"Head back...*home*. You mightn't think you have a family, but we consider you part of ours, and we share a *home*, not just a safe house."

I turned to face him. He was so sweet. He was just a genuinely lovely guy.

"You're not too bad yourself," he whispered. He leaned over and kissed me on my forehead before disappearing back inside.

I was only alone for maybe thirty seconds before Gwen appeared, plonking a bottle of tequila down on the little metal table in front of me.

"If we're gonna sit out here all night, we're gonna need something to warm us up!" she laughed, unscrewing the lid.

Tilting the bottle she took a deep mouthful before grimacing. I smiled at her and snatched the bottle for myself, taking a big gulp. As the tang burned my throat I gasped out a breath.

I turned to her. "I'm sorry about your dress."

She waved her hand. "Don't worry about it. I can get another one."

"Can I ask you a question?"

She nodded for me to continue.

I worried with my lip for a second before taking the plunge. "Is having a father really so great?"

"No!" she exclaimed immediately. She sat silently for a second. I knew she wasn't finished. "Well, I guess it's not all bad. It's nice to have someone visit and take me out. I guess if I needed someone non-angelic then he would be there for me," she shrugged.

"Then why do you say you hate him?" I asked.

"I don't *hate* him...he gave me up. Rather than take care of me himself he handed me over to the first angel that came along."

"Was it really like that though?"

"Maybe not," she whispered. "But, it sure would have been nice if he'd wanted to keep me enough to put up a fight. He could have promised to send me in for lessons, or bargained with them that he had to move in too. But no...I was given to the angels, and he carried on living his life."

After a little silence I asked, "Do you love him?"

She smirked, "I suppose so. But I'm *really* pissed off at him!"

We smiled and chuckled together. Sitting watching the stars, was the most relaxed I'd felt all day. I was incredibly disappointed that things hadn't worked out with James, but I guess it took a lot of the stress off me. Now, the ball was in his court. He could stay here and carry on with his little life with his cheating girlfriend and pretend he never met me, or maybe one day he'd decide he wanted to meet his real family. Seeing as how he thought I was a Demon, that was a tad unlikely, but still, I'd be there and I'd give him an opportunity to make up for lost time if that's what he wanted. And if not, well I'd be here in the shadows looking out for him. I knew the Grigori watched over him already, so it wouldn't be hard to find out if he was ever in trouble again.

"Huh, that's my cue to leave," I heard Gwen mutter.

I snapped out of my reverie and watched as she stood up, taking the bottle of tequila with her. As she moved out of my line of vision I saw Zach. He stepped towards me slowly until he stood right in front of me, forcing me to crank my neck uncomfortably so that I could look up at his face.

He remained silent for a long minute, seeming to be choosing what he wanted to say carefully. “He got home safely. I presume the ‘trouble’ Haamiah had talked about is now gone.”

I nodded. “We should probably set off for the...for *home* in the morning.”

Zach nodded his agreement. “Probably. If that’s where you want to go.”

I smiled sadly. “I don’t *have* anywhere else to go.”

“You’re wrong. We could go to the Island...if you wanted.”

Hope fired up in my chest. *That* was home. The Island he spoke of was called Ujelang Atoll. It was in the Marshall Islands in the middle of the Pacific Ocean. Zach, Maion and the others had built themselves a small beach house on the deserted Island hundreds of years ago hoping to create a place of tranquility and safety that they could return to when they needed to recuperate. It was the most peaceful place I had ever been to. It was perfect.

I nodded. “I’d like that.”

Zach nodded solemnly and turned away. He jumped onto the railing surrounding the balcony, his wings outstretched. He paused for a second and turned his head just slightly so that I could just make out the profile of his face.

"Earlier you didn't give me a chance to finish what I was saying. You looked...*beautiful*."

And he leapt up, his wings pounding the air until he rose high above me, just a dot against the *beautiful* starry sky.

18

'The only time a woman is ever helpless is while her nails are drying.'

Unknown

The next week followed peacefully. After discussing our options we decided to stay in Meadowbrook for a week or two more to relax before Zach and I left for our Island, and the others went home with Maion. We figured we had been long overdue a holiday and technically Haamiah didn't know that we had already finished what we had set out to do. We decided to do everything that regular people did on their holidays...however as only Gwen had ever been on a regular holiday we decided to follow her suggestions.

As we were following Gwen's directions – a *lot* of shopping was done. We also ate a ton of ice cream, went to the cinema, rented a car and drove to The Twelve Apostles. Our time on the beach was hilarious – Sam and Trev rented surfboards and took to the water. Trev had surfed before and was pretty good, but Sam was terrible – which made for a lot of laughter. And we didn't see one single Fallen Angel.

I still followed James, as unobtrusively as I could. It had proved impossible to stay away completely. The Fallen Angels who had attacked him had been easily put down, so I didn't understand why Haamiah would send me here. It just didn't make any sense – of course knowing Haamiah, it would have some impact on events to come. Though if there were any huge changes *I* couldn't see them. James seemed to be continuing his life as he had been before I had appeared. He was still with that slut of a girlfriend, he continued hanging out at that club most evenings. He didn't seem bothered at all by anything that I had said. I couldn't help but compare it to when I had been told that Fallen Angels and demons were hunting me – my world had turned upside down! Admittedly it was already on its side...but still finding out that you were part angel and demons were trying to kill you wasn't exactly everyday news.

Who knew – perhaps his parents had counseled him and he felt better about the whole situation. I didn't have anyone to talk to when *I* had found out but James had a whole family, friends and a community to support him. Maybe that was why I had spiraled out of control and he had stayed sane.

After asking our permission, Sam invited Lilura to stay with us for a few days. I was apprehensive at first but when she came to stay Sam was ecstatic. Seeing him like that was an eye-opener for me. He was so...*happy*. I made myself a promise that if she ever hurt him I'd hunt her down and kick her ass.

Lilura turned out to be both sweet and sassy, and not at all intrusive which was perfect for our little gang. She and Sam tended to hang out on the beach alone for most of the day but during the evening we would all sit together on the decking and drink and laugh.

At first she had politely refused to tell us anything about the Sorceri, but one night over dinner she confided in us a little. We learned a little about her family – enough to keep my curiosity satisfied - but she was still quite guarded – as *we* were about the angels and Nephilim. She told us that the Sorceress of Ice was the Queen of Ice – meaning she was the most skilled of all the Sorceri in that particular area of expertise. She could control it in any form and she could freeze anything, which was quite a handy skill to have. The Sorceress of Ice was the head of their kind in Melbourne. If a Sorceress were to enter her territory they had to go before her and claim allegiance. Most would stay there during their stay, although some of the older Sorceri chose to live apart from the majority and live in their own homes. They were all made to return often however, to pool their strengths and abilities for various tasks.

Lilura was not the Queen of anything. She did have the same abilities as all Sorceri though. She could manipulate gold with her mind, she had strength and speed (though not as much as other creatures), and she had some other magical talents. She had shown skill in creating Illusions, but she said she was nowhere near good enough to take on the Queen of Illusions.

It was refreshing to hear about someone else's life. We all knew that vampires, demons, plus a hundred more, existed, but it was different to actually talk to one who wasn't trying to decapitate you. Her life was oddly similar to ours in many respects. When she was younger she had to attend classes, even now she had to complete drills and training. Their biological families never stayed close – giving their children over to the care of others in different countries. There was one area of difference which made us all gasp though. The elders in the Sorceri community both encouraged and actively participated in all kinds of illegal activity – car-jacking, stealing, blackmailing, some of the celebrated Sorceri were even for-hire killers. That peace of information had certainly taken our breath away. But when Sam compared our situations we could see the similarities despite that one major lifestyle choice. And it did make me look at Sam in a different way.

When dinner was over and everyone began to disappear to their rooms, Sam took me aside.

“Zach needs to speak to you,” he said quietly, seriously.

I frowned at him. “Where is he? He’s been gone all day.”

“Outside I think,” he replied. He turned away and left the room.

Frowning to myself I walked out through the back door. Zach was waiting for me on the decking. As I approached him he turned, his form in shadow against the moon behind him.

“What’s up?” I asked.

He reached out to me with one arm. I smiled, my heart melting, my soul beginning to burn. He pulled me closer into his body, his hands slipping around my waist. He slipped his fingers under my T-shirt, lightly caressing my skin.

“Mmmm,” I murmered, pulling myself closer to him. I leaned my cheek on his chest, breathing him in. “Why are you so quiet?”

He sighed against my ear. “I have to go.”

“What? Where?” I pulled away from him abruptly. Fantasies of his naked body were rapidly being replaced by cold dread.

The darkness made it difficult to fully see his expression but from what I could tell he seemed anxious. And if Zach was anxious, something was definitely wrong.

After a second he shook his head sadly. “A Nephilim Safe House in the Philippines has been found by the Fallen.”

I gasped, "Children?"

He nodded.

My hand flew to my mouth as my stomach heaved. I knew the damage the Fallen could do to the Safe Houses. I had heard the horror stories, both true and those made up by the kids at home to scare each other. They rarely left any alive, usually leaving only body parts.

"Did they leave any alive?"

He nodded grimly. "There was no warning from the Seers. They've taken hostages. They want something. I have to go and deal with this."

"Of course. Is Maion going with you?" I asked.

"Yes, and more will meet us there."

"Can I come? I want to help." I gripped his hand tightly. I knew what he would say.

"No, it's too dangerous. There will be plenty of angels there to do what we need to do," he replied.

"Okay. Good," I exhaled. I had the utmost confidence in Zach's abilities but I couldn't imagine losing him. Maion definitely wasn't my favourite person but he was an exceptionally good fighter and I knew he wouldn't let anything happen to Zach. Selfishly, another thought popped into my head. If the Fallen or Asmodeus' vampires found us without the protection of Maion or Zach, would they come in force? Would I be strong enough to keep Gwen, Sam and Trev safe?

Zach correctly guessed the turn my thoughts had taken. “Elijah has ordered you to go back to the safe house. You need to go to the airport tonight and get on the next flight. You’ll be safe when you get back. I would take you myself but there’s no time. We’re leaving now.”

I stepped back, pulling away from him. “I can’t go back now,” I said softly, anticipating his response. I turned away from him and leaned against the railings, looking out to the black sea. “I’ll just put everyone in danger if I go back now.”

“And *you’re* in danger if you stay here.” I could hear the anger running through his softly spoken words. He never did like it when I disobeyed him.

“Between the four of us I’m pretty sure we’ll be okay. We’ve also got Lilura and Trev’s mother on our side,” I smiled weakly.

“Great, an angel in another realm and a Sorceress. They’ll be a great help,” he said, his words dripping with sarcasm.

“I’m strong Zach. You know I can fight well. We’ve been here for over a week and only one vampire has found us. If they knew where we were they’d have come here. Are you sure *you’ll* be okay?

“I’ll be fine,” he disregarded my concern. “It’s you I’m worried about. Please go back to the safe house. I beg you.”

I bit my lip and turned to face him, tilting my head so that my hair fell over my shoulder. “You know I can’t.”

“Damn it Jasmine! This isn’t okay! You came here for your brother, he was saved from an attack, he doesn’t want to know you further so *go home*!” he yelled.

I flinched. "Don't try to provoke a fight with me just because you're mad you have to go! You *know* if I go back to the safe house I'm going to put everyone there in danger!"

"And you're putting people in danger by staying here alone," he growled.

"I'll tell them what's happening and give them the choice of going back or staying here," I replied angrily.

He snorted. "You know what they'll say! They won't leave without you! They're as stubborn as you are!"

"I know. But I can't leave yet! I just have this feeling that it isn't over." I walked away from him, trying to retain my calm but finding it increasingly difficult.

I was so mad at him. I was so beyond frustrated! He constantly dictated to me what I could and couldn't do, he had absolutely no faith in my abilities at all which was infuriating because he had *seen* what I could do. I had proven myself over and over again. He always thought that he was right. Well in this case, he was wrong. I was sure of it.

"I need to be here in case something happens to James," I said through gritted teeth.

"It already happened!" he shouted. "You saw it yourself and you killed it outside the club. Nothing else is going to happen!" He took a deep breath and grabbed my hands. "Please...please don't stay here alone. I'll be too far away to help you if something happens."

My eyes stung with tears and I could feel my face flushing with emotion. I reached up and trailed my fingers down his jaw. “I will be fine. You need to concentrate on keeping yourself safe.”

He shook his head slowly. “If I get back here and...I will be so pissed off at you.”

He dropped my hands and backed away only to turn around at the edge of the decking. He was instantly by my side. I found myself crushed in his embrace, his lips devouring mine, his tongue stroking mine with force. He dropped me suddenly and whirled around, launching into the sky with his huge wings outstretched, glowing in the moonlight.

19

The things that we love tell us what we are.

Thomas Aquinas

The next day I sat huddled in the kitchen wearing one of Trev's sweaters. I had tucked my knees inside so that I was completely encased, and I hunched over a cup of coffee. I hadn't returned to my room when Zach had left but instead had sat out on the decking reliving our argument. One key point that had never been said, now wouldn't leave me alone. What if the attack in the Philippines had been a diversion? What if all the Fallen were headed here now that Maion and Zach were gone? I was sure Zach must have considered it. Maybe he hadn't mentioned it because he was worried that I would be freaked out. Well...I had thought of it a tad late, and *was* freaked out.

I decided not to wake the others up, seeing as our holiday was probably going to end today. I would tell them when they woke up.

"So Maion and Zach took off," Sam's voice startled me, making me spill my coffee on Trev's sweater.

"Shit," I swore as I rubbed at the stain. I glared at him.

"Sorry," he smirked.

I sighed. "You already know the story, right?"

He gave me a lopsided grin. “Kind of hard not to, when you’ve been replaying it over and over and over...”

I grimaced. “Sorry. It’s just...” I made a face.

He shrugged. “Don’t be sorry. It’s not your fault I can read your mind.” He paused. “Are you really that worried for him? He’s been fighting the Fallen for thousands of years. I might not like him all of the time but the guy’s got skills.”

I smiled grimly in response.

“And don’t feel guilty about me, Gwen and Trev. We *want* to be here.”

“What if it’s a diversion? What if an army of Fallen Angels are headed here right now?” I asked, looking up into his eyes to gauge his reaction.

“It’s possible. It seems a little extreme though. And we’ll face it if it comes,” he replied.

“What about James being in danger? Do you think it's passed?”

“I don’t know. It would seem like that, I mean, you killed the angel that went after him...”

“Do you think we should go back?” I pestered.

“I don’t know. It’s up to you,” he replied, very non-committal.

“Well that’s really helpful advice Sam,” I said dryly.

He laughed. “Lilura’s leaving today.”

I perked up in surprise. “She is? Why?”

"Something's going on at home. She wouldn't tell me what exactly. Seems like a big deal though and she's pretty scared about it," he said gloomily.

"Is there anything we can do?" I wanted to show my support for him.

He shook his head. "Family business apparently."

"Huh," I grunted.

I stood up to make Sam a cup of coffee, mixing in two sugars. I sat back down on the kitchen stool and we sipped our coffee in silence.

Eventually the others woke up and made their way downstairs. I was on edge, knowing I had to tell them, but not knowing exactly how to say it.

"Where are Zach and Maion this morning? They've hardly been here for the past two days!" Gwen commented between bites of toast.

I grimaced. That was my cue. Sam lifted his eyebrow. "They're gone," I blurted out. Silence ensued, and my words had ensured that everyone's eyes were on me. "Something happened in the Philippines. A safe house was attacked by the Fallen and some of the kids have been taken hostage. Zach and Maion have gone to help out."

"Oh my God," Gwen murmured. Everyone else looked equally as shocked.

"I know. And apparently Elijah has said we have to go back home *now*. We're out here with no protection, Zach will be too far away to help us if something happens..."

"But the danger is over, right? I mean you killed the Fallen that were hunting James. So technically we're safe here," Gwen frowned.

I shrugged, unable to explain further.

Sam grasped my hand. "We think that *maybe*, the attack in the Philippines was a diversion, and that the Fallen are headed here...now."

Gwen's mouth dropped open. "Then what are we still doing here?"

"It's only a possibility. And if we leave, and something comes here, it's going to find James," Sam finished.

"Mother of..." Gwen gasped.

"Wait," Trev said loudly. He tilted his head to the side, his gaze distant. Lilura looked between us, confused by Trev's odd behavior. Only to us, it wasn't odd. "*Elijah* told Zach to send us back."

Sam looked to me for confirmation. "Yeah," I said.

"Not Haamiah," Trev said.

Realisation came to us all at the same time. Haamiah was the one who orchestrated the movements of angels and Nephilim. If it was Elijah not Haamiah who had told us to go back, then it was clear we had to stay put.

"The danger's not over," I said quietly. I stood up and looked at them all. "I want you to think about this really hard. We're out here without anyone else. I can take on a few of them, and you guys have all got your own abilities too, but if too many of them come here – we're screwed."

"Are you staying?" Gwen asked.

"I have to. If the danger's not over, then that means I need to be here to help James," I replied.

"Then I'm staying," she said.

"I'm staying," Trev said.

"So am I," Sam finished.

I felt my eyes sting again. These guys...they were my family - the only family that I would ever need.

Lilura cleared her throat. "I would totally stay, but I have to go home. If anything happens Sam's got my number and we'll be down here in a flash I promise."

I smiled at her. I didn't entirely believe her – it wasn't as if the other Sorceri had been particularly happy to see us. I glanced at Sam and could tell that he agreed with me.

She stood up. "I should really get going; it's a couple of hours drive back to Melbourne."

We all nodded and said our goodbyes as Sam walked her out to her car. When she was out of sight, he came back in. We all sat in tension filled silence for a minute.

"You need to tell her what your mother said," Sam grumbled to Trev.

I lifted my head from where I had been resting it on my knees. I glared at Trev, "she said something else?"

He blew out a breath of air. "There's a lot of drama going on somewhere. People are being kidnapped all over the place. She said something about a Tournament. She said we have to hide."

I froze and was pleased when Gwen spoke up.

"A tournament?"

"She didn't explain further. Just said that that people are being kidnapped and there's a tournament coming up."

"We can only presume that the kidnapped people will be entered into this tournament," Sam offered.

Trev nodded. "I think that's what she meant."

"Anyone we know?" Gwen asked.

He shook his head.

As I watched them a spark of dread filled my soul. We had suspected a diversion...but what if someone planned a trap? Zach would be the ultimate warrior in a tournament. He was the strongest angel I knew. Maion would make an excellent catch too.

"We have to warn them," Sam said.

I whipped my phone of the bench and typed in Zach's name. Lifting it to my ear I could hear my own heart pounding over the tone.

“He’s not answering!” I cried. I pressed redial and waited. Still no answer.

“Shit, call Haamiah,” Sam said.

“I’m on it.” Gwen stood up with her phone to her ear. She bit her lip as she hung up. “No answer.”

The anxious feeling in my stomach abruptly escalated into a full on attack. I threw myself into Gwen knocking her to the floor as a fireball soared through the house.

20

Beauty in things exists in the mind which contemplates them.

David Hume

I covered Gwen's mouth with my hand and glared at her as she screamed in my ear, almost deafening me. The room was dark with thick black smoke and I could feel the heat singeing my hair and skin. As I was about to crawl off her and look for Sam and Trev I was kicked viciously in the ribs. I flew to the side, crashing through the cupboards in the kitchen and falling to the floor. I winced as I felt my broken ribs press against the tender skin there.

Sensing someone near me I jumped to my feet. A blow to my jaw sent me reeling to the side. I jumped back onto the kitchen bench and kicked out with both feet sending my attacker across the room, through the wall. I ran to Gwen, stopping a few feet away as Sam pulled her to her feet. Trev appeared to our right, blood running down his face. We whirled around with our backs to each other, the way we had trained.

Two dark haired Fallen Angels came at me with swords as a vampire tackled Trev to the ground. Through my smoke filled vision I could see Sam and Gwen defending him. I let my power sweep over me, just enough to energize and vitalize my limbs, but I stopped it at my chest, making sure I could control it. I ducked as one with a large scar through his lips swung a blade at my neck. I kicked out, snapping his arm. He screamed in anger and dropped back as the other leaped at me. We traded blow for blow. I spat blood out as he scored a good hit to my chest. I threw a punch at his neck which he blocked easily. I dropped low and swept round with my foot smashing his ankle. I smiled as I felt the crunch of bones beneath my foot. He howled and kicked me in the face with his free foot. My head snapped back, a haze covering my vision. I fought for consciousness, sucking in air. The other Fallen Angel grabbed me by the hair, fending off my punches, while the scarred one jumped at me punching again and again into my stomach.

My body tried to convulse, and I instinctively tried to fold over but was held up by the angel behind me. I pulled at my power, allowing it to seep further through my body. I bent my knees and as soon as he came into range I belted him with my strength. He crashed through another wall. I flipped up backwards and over the top of the Fallen Angel behind me. I kicked him forwards as I swept down and picked up the blade he had dropped. I spun around and sliced his head off, watching as it slid messily to the floor.

I heard a whisper of sound. I spun, knocking away the blade aimed at my face. It clattered to the floor as a second embedded itself into my abdomen. I screamed as I fell to my knees. Watching the scarred Fallen Angel approach me, I ripped it out and clenched it in my shaking fist. I threw my body into the air, spinning as I sailed over the top of him landing behind. He kicked the blade I held into the nearest wall.

Feeling the blood soak through my shirt, the warmth trickling down my legs, I knew I needed to finish this. I sunk into my power and jumped at him. I felt rage wash over me, exhilarating anger soaked through my pores as I slid down next to him. Haze covered my eyes, heat blistering my skin as I sunk my teeth into his neck. I ripped and felt blood splash on my face. I gripped with my hands, pulling and turning. I felt his teeth bite into my wrist and I let go, agony shooting up my arm.

I rose above my power and punched with my right arm smacking his face to the side. He lost his balance and fell to the floor. I leapt on top of him with a large splinter of wood. I stabbed it straight through his heart. As he convulsed on the floor Sam shouted my name and threw me a kitchen knife. I hacked off his head fiercely and sat back on the floor.

Sam ran to me and pulled me up off the floor. He pulled me out of the house through the huge hole in the wall and onto the beach. I could hear the sounds of fire trucks nearby. I looked up through the smoke to see Trev and Gwen standing by.

"Shit Jasmine! You're hurt!" Sam yelled, pulling my T-shirt up.

I shook my head. I was so tired but I made myself concentrate on healing my wounds. I needed to be able to fight if we were attacked again. After a few seconds I felt a little better but my blistered skin was red raw and the smell of my burnt hair made me gag. I forced myself to close in on Trev and I touched his face, sending a glittery mass shooting through me to heal him. The wounds on his head and neck quickly closed over and I felt confident that any other wounds that I couldn't see were also healed.

"We have to go *now*!" Gwen urged.

I looked along the beach, my heart sinking as I saw people rushing towards us from all directions.

"We're not going to be able to get past them!" I cried. "Hold on to me!"

Gwen and Trev grabbed hold of my arm thinking I needed help standing but Sam paused. "Jasmine, you're exhausted, are you sure?"

"What?" Gwen asked.

I waved my hand in her face. "Do you trust me?" I shouted fiercely at them.

They nodded and touched me. I drew on my power viciously, pulling it over our heads, absorbing my friends in the mist, and felt the ground drop away.

We reappeared at the top of the hill I had my eyes set on. We were a good distance away now and though we could see the beach and the fire, they couldn't see us. The sound of vomiting drew my attention. I turned to see Sam spewing on the grass. Gwen too, had been affected and was dry heaving, her skin as pale as it could go.

"Girl, that is *nasty*!" she groaned, clutching her stomach.

"Sam, we need to get a hold of Lilura. She promised she'd help us if we were in trouble," I barked.

I thanked my lucky stars as he slid his phone out of his jeans pocket. I curled my lip in disgust as he vomited more breakfast onto the grass, handing me the phone.

I dialed her number which thankfully was saved under 'Lilura' and not some gross pet name he had for her. It rang and rang. Just when I thought it was going to cut out she answered.

“Sam?” she wailed.

If it were possible to be any more anxious, I now was. “Lilura it’s Jasmine. We’re in trouble and we need your help *now*.”

“I can’t! I’m in the tournament. I was picked and I have to do it, I have no choice...” she wailed.

She continued wailing into the phone until it was cut off.

“Fuck!” I screamed.

Sam looked up from his kneeling position on the grass. “What’s wrong?”

“She’s been entered into a tournament. It has to be the one Trev’s mother was talking about. She said she has no choice and she was picked at random, and a bunch of other stuff that I couldn’t understand.”

Sam was on his feet in a second and snatched the phone out of my hand. Holding it to his ear he waited and waited. There was no answer.

“Take us to her,” he demanded.

“I have to get James first,” I said. I knew he wanted to argue with me. I could almost hear the words in his mind. I didn’t bother to try to hug him or console him – I knew rage when I saw it and he was pretty close to it. “We’ll get James then we’ll go to her, I promise.”

He nodded stiffly.

I turned to face the lower end of Meadowbrook where I knew James lived. I held out my arms and let my power melt the ground away again when I felt three sets of hands on me.

This time the landing was a little off. We landed on a tilt and fell into a pile on the road.

Picking myself up I forced my eyes to remain level as I sprinted up the road and turned a corner. My angelic senses were almost on overload and I could *feel* the others following behind. I skidded to a halt outside James' house, uncertain what to do as I saw two police cars parked outside. As the others caught up, Trev beckoned me to follow him into the neighbor's garden. We cleared the fence and landed in the bushes at the back of James' house. Creeping closer onto the back porch I could see the French windows were completely smashed in, glass all over the floor. I leaned as close as I could, not chancing walking over the glass and alerting them to my presence.

I focused on the voices I could hear inside. There was a woman crying loudly. It was almost as bad as Lilura's wail down the phone. I filtered out the high pitched crying and concentrated on the man's voice inside - James' father.

"They flew away!" he was saying.

The policemen obviously had a hard time understanding. "What do you mean they *flew*?"

"They sprouted wings and flew away!" he said.

I could just imagine the policemen's expressions at *that*. As they began to confer with each other I lost my last shred of patience. I stormed into the house through the broken glass and glared at them.

"Where is James?" I demanded.

"Excuse me Miss this is a restricted area, we're going to have to ask-"

I silenced the policeman with my hand and turned to his father. "Did they take him?"

He glared at me. "You're one of them aren't you? I told you to stay away!"

"Where did they take him?" I screamed. The policeman surrounded me and tried to back me into a corner. "Where is he? I can help him but you have to tell me where he is!" I screamed again.

"The tournament!" his mother shouted. "They said they were taking him to a tournament!"

I nodded grimly. I leapt away from them, landing next to the shattered glass.

"Who *are* you?" The father gasped.

I turned to face him. I bit my lip. "I'm his big sister."

21

Falling in love and having a relationship are two different things.

Keanu Reeves

We landed at the back of a crowd of – at a guess – close to a thousand people. A second glance had me correcting myself - *beings*. Elves, vampires, werewolves and hundreds more coursed around, chatting and laughing, some crying and hugging each other. Our entrance hadn't disturbed anyone, as they probably came here in similar fashions.

Trev had had the excellent suggestion of me trying to open a portal to Lilura's destination. She had a strong connection to Sam so with Sam touching me I should be able to follow the thread and open the portal. There, we should find both James and Lilura. I couldn't help but feel admiration for him when it worked. I presumed that this crowd was here for the tournament. Many were carrying banners with symbols; most wore swords and bows and arrows strapped to their body.

Sam pushed past me, searching the crowd. I could see the intense look of concentration on his face and knew he was *listening* for Lilura. There were too many voices though and his face strained as he failed again and again to locate her.

I stepped forward and grabbed his arm. "Let me try."

I held on and pushed out with my mist, searching for her. I found her general direction but couldn't pick her out specifically. I turned and pushed through the crowd, the others following me. After a few minutes Sam let out a cry and pushed past me, sending me flying into a demon who didn't look too pleased. I backed away from him, determined not to start a fight. I let Trev guide me in the right direction.

As we neared the group of Sorceri I could have wept as I saw Lilura wrapped in Sam's arms.

"I have to go! I don't have a choice!" Lilura wrenched herself away from Sam.

"You do have a choice! Come back with us! Jasmine will open a portal and we'll go! Don't do this!" Sam raged at her.

I looked desperately at Gwen and Trev. They looked as shocked as I felt. My heart was breaking watching them being torn apart. Sam was my best friend and I'd support him through anything. Part of me wanted to just rip open a portal and take us all home right this second then it would be done. But how would I find my way back? I couldn't leave without James. I *wouldn't* leave without him. Where would that leave Sam? What would I say if she agreed to leave?

"The Soceri are contracted to this tournament. If I leave with you and no one takes my place in the competition the Soceri will be contracted to find and kill me! It doesn't matter where I go, they'll hunt me down!" she replied. I could tell she was close to tears. She was barely holding it together. I wanted to interfere and give her encouragement but I couldn't bring myself to say anything. Who was I to say that she'll be fine and she'll get out of there okay when the chances were unlikely?

I couldn't wait any longer. "Lilura, where's James?"

"Your brother?" she asked through sobs.

"He's been kidnapped. His parents said the things that took him spoke of a tournament. He has to be here somewhere."

As I readied myself to search for his essence, Lilura spoke.

"No, Jasmine. If he's been kidnapped then he'll be in the prison, only the volunteers are in the crowd."

I felt my eyes begin to burn. "Then I'll open a portal to get to him."

She shook her head. "It's protected. More than half of the competitors have been captured. They take great pains to protect their catch. It's impossible."

She fell into Sam's arms again, weeping uncontrollably as I stepped back and gazed unseeingly into the crowd. I had failed. The one thing I was supposed to do, and I had failed. My only family. The only person I could claim as my own had been captured. He wasn't trained, he couldn't fight; he had no chance in a tournament. He was going to die and it was all my fault. If I had kept watch on him like Haamiah had sent me to do then this wouldn't have happened.

My body was ice. My mind was numb, foggy. I knew Gwen was saying something to me but I couldn't hear her words. I didn't want to hear. All I could think about was James. How frightened he must be. How utterly terrified and alone he must feel, trapped in a prison, waiting to be entered into a tournament that had nothing to do with him. All he had wanted to do was to live his life. He didn't want anything to do with me or the angels. Our parents had obviously wanted him kept out of it and that's why they had sent him to a family.

It was all my fault. I had led them here. It had to have been me.

I couldn't think of anything I could do to change the course of things, not one single thing. I simply let Gwen's words wash over me as I stared at Lilura and Sam. He was still trying to convince her to leave and was getting angrier by the minute.

As they stared each other down I felt myself bumped and knocked forward into Trev. He steadied me, turning to look behind me only to find that we were all being ushered towards the main stage. We were knocked and jolted and when we finally stopped being pushed I realised I was still beside my friends. I would have felt lucky, except that I was incapable of feeling any emotion at all right then.

"Creatures of the Realms! I welcome you to the Tournament of Ascension!" A small round creature stood before us on the grey stone stage before the metal gates bellowing out to get our attention. It worked. The crowd fell so silent that even Sam had to hold his tongue. "The Tournament will begin today!" the creature exclaimed.

The crowd flew into a rapturous applause. I glanced at Gwen and Trev who like me, held their hands still. I knew we were all wondering how this could possibly work out okay.

"Who is that?" I hissed at Sam.

"The Scribe. He has no name. He exists only for these tournaments," Lilura whispered past Sam.

"As you are aware there will be twelve competitors and only one winner of the ultimate prize. Sponsors may put forward no more than two entrants, and all sponsors of the competitors must agree to the terms and conditions," he clapped his hands in glee. "Now! First our non-voluntary entrants!"

A screen flashed up over the metal gate behind him. He stepped casually to the side so that all of us in the crowd could see clearly. The picture was initially all black then it flashed to the picture of a young warrior.

"Derek, for the Wizards of Old!" The stomping of the crowd accompanied the angry, bitter expression of the Warrior. I couldn't tell what species he belonged to, but it didn't appear to be an animal based one. I hoped that the Scribe would announce it, but he didn't.

He moved on to the next competitor being forced to enter the competition; a demon of some kind named Deshek. Deshek understandably looked as angry and vengeful as Derek. He bared his teeth at the picture, no sound emerging, but I imagine growling fiercely. Apparently Deshek had been captured and forced into the competition by the House of Gargoyles.

The next picture made my heart ache. James' picture flashed up. I was surprised but incredibly proud to see that he was stoic, no tears, no look of fear or pleading. He simply stared angrily out at us. The feeling of pride and the ache running through me swiftly faded and was replaced with pure anger – fury seethed through my veins as I awaited the name of his capture. Who would dare to capture and enter a Nephilim into this competition knowing the full wrath of the angels would fall on them?

When the name was announced I could have kicked myself for not guessing sooner. James had been entered by Forneus the Fallen. As in Fallen Angel.

I knew my friends had turned and were gaping at me but I didn't acknowledge them. I continued to stare at the face of my brother, silently promising him I would save him. And I would rip off the head of that Fallen Angel.

As my brother was replaced by another I began to survey the room trying to *feel* out the Fallen Angel. A number of the other sponsors were here...was he? If so, I'd gut him here and now.

I continued to look for Forneus but couldn't locate him. I realized I'd also missed seeing the other competitors. As the picture faded and the Scribe was once more in the center of the stage. A rush of rage left me shooting sparks of glitter from my fingers. I imagined ripping that little beast open on the stage. Let him see what it was like to feel helpless.

"Jasmine. Not now." Trev's eyes caught mine. He had moved in front of me, his face inches from mine, his body blocking my sparkles. I bit my lip and nodded, stepping to the side so I could once again see the creature on the stage.

"Now the first of our voluntary competitors!" The creature gestured to a large muscular man dressed all in white at the left side of the stage that I hadn't even seen.

The man marched to the creature and knelt before him with a roll of parchment. The creature snatched it from him and cast his eyes over the words written there giggling audibly as the man in white disappeared in a puff of smoke.

In a deeper voice, the creature began. “Our first competitor is Anora the Black of the Lycans of Abernon!”

A black haired warrior strode out of the crowd and up the steps to stand before the creature. Female, muscular beyond belief she was kitted all in black. She stood at around 6 and a half foot – and had a dangerous aura seeping from every part of her. When she glanced at the crowd she showed a flash of teeth. They were white, yes, but so jagged they looked like shark teeth. One bite from her and she would rip you to shreds. But that wasn’t the most alarming thing about her. A thick, jagged scar ran diagonal across her face from her right temple down under her nose, through her lips and ended somewhere beneath her black studded collar. And accessorizing her horrificness I could see a spike, an Axe, knives and I even saw a mace hanging from her belt.

In a throaty growl Anora the Black turned to the crowd. “I will enter for the Lycans of Abernon!”

As a thunderous applause rocked the arena the metal gates behind the stage silently ran open and she strode through with confidence oozing from her. And rightly so. Who could think to defeat her?

The answer to that question was the next competitor.

“Our second competitor is Maβik Fury Demon!” Maβik – apparently pronounced Mavik certainly was a Fury Demon. I had encountered many a while back and though I was confident I could rip off a head or two I had serious doubts whether James or Lillura would survive if put up against one.

Fury Demons were monsters. Seven foot tall with skin like red leather, and a blue lower jaw and lips. They rarely did anything for their own sake. They worked for others. Those I had encountered, and destroyed, had been working for a Witch, but they have been known to work for Wizards and occasionally for the Soceri. His solid black eyes were focused on the Scribe as he reached the stage. Impressively the Scribe didn't flinch as the demon towered over him, horns protruding and black talons stretched out where his hands should have been. His mouth was open, two sets of yellow, blade-like teeth visible.

"And who is your sponsor Maβik?" the scribe oozed.

In response the demon growled and roared at the crowd. As my heart went into overdrive, the scribe smiled. "Ah yes! The Witches of Malasi!"

The demon stomped through the open gates at the cheering of the crowd.

Apparently this tournament was not very popular for volunteers. Only three others were announced. Two were centaurs – horse-like creatures with the upper body of a human. Like the werewolf they were adorned with weapons made for killing. This time the competitors were entering for the same sponsor; the God of Fright. At the name of this sponsor I turned to Trev, frowning.

Trev closed his eyes for a second then leaned towards me whispering. "The centaurs are ruled by different Gods, this one is particularly poor and lacking in power. Whatever the prize is - he wants it. And apparently he's a dick." Trev shrugged, as if asking for history lessons from the angels were an everyday thing. I guess for him it was. For a brief moment I wondered what it would be like to know whenever you needed to ask someone a question you could think it in your mind and an angel would whisper the answer to you. An intrusion of privacy? Sure. A handy talent? Definitely!

Apparently sponsors rarely entered two competitors because once in the tournament they were intrinsically linked. If one died during the competition, so did the other. Though it was handy working as team, it doubled their chances of being killed.

The centaurs had come and gone and now the Scribe turned back to his list. "The final voluntary competitor is Lilura for the Sorceress of Ice!"

As Lilura made to walk forward to her doom, Sam swung her back by her arms, caging her in. He began to push her back through the crowd.

"Where is Lilura?" the scribe screeched. The crowd began murmering, turning to look in our direction at the commotion. Noticing us, the creature ran down the steps, parting the crowd instantly.

Sam spun around pushing her behind him. My heart sinking into my stomach I raised up my power until it was running through my fingertips. If this mother-fucker tried anything with my Sam I'd eviscerate him. Or at least I'd try.

"She's not going," Sam bit out at the creature.

"What?" The shrill cry rang out, echoing around the arena as the crowd fell silent once more. "This is the final competitor. If there is no final competitor then the tournament is void!"

"Then its void!" Sam hissed. "You're not having her."

As the crowd began to roar in anger Lilura made a sound of protest. Sam pushed her back again.

The creature giggled. “Perhaps you don’t understand what it means if the competition is *void*. Should there be no competition *every* competitor dies. Including your precious Sorceress.”

The crowd went wild. Demonic wizards, black-clad witches, centaurs, goblins cried for our blood, demanding Lilura go forth. My own body cried out in pain. If Lilura didn’t enter then both James and Lilura would die anyway. At least if she entered they would be in with a shot. Sam looked at me, stricken. I knew he was thinking the same thing.

Lilura ducked under his arm and turned to him, taking his face in her hands.

“I love you. I have to do this. There’s no other way.” They kissed tenderly, even as the baying crowd continued.

I stepped closer, realizing belatedly that Gwen was holding my hand. I shook her off and approached the Scribe. “All you need is one more competitor? It doesn’t matter if it’s a Sorceress?”

The Scribe froze, then turned his head fraction by fraction until he was facing me. A demonic smile on his lips, his eyes lit up with excitement. “It matters not, which creature, or which sponsor, as long as I have the final twelfth entrant,” he whispered.

“I’ll do it.”

22

One loyal friend is worth ten thousand relatives.

Euripides

"I'll do it." The words jumped out of my mouth before I'd even considered saying them. There was no way I'd take them back though. This was the opportunity I'd been waiting for.

"Are you fucking crazy?" Sam shouted, going red in the face. The others protested just as loudly.

"Don't talk to me like that! This is perfect!" I retorted angrily.

"Perfect for what? For getting yourself killed? For getting *us* killed when Zach finds out what you've done?" Sam shook his head in exasperation.

"Honey, we know you want to help your brother, but have you been listening to *anything* Lilura has been saying?" Gwen squeezed my hand, her eyes pleading.

I turned to Sam. "Zach doesn't need to know." At his exclamation I pressed my hands together. "*Please*. I've just found my brother and this is the only way to save him." I drew a deep breath in. "Gwen, I know it sounds bleak but I have a real chance in there. A better chance than Lil, a hell of a better chance than James. How many times do I have to prove myself to you all? Believe in me!"

"We do believe in you Jaz, but you're going up against Fury Demons, Werewolves, Fallen Angels, vampires and more. You've got to understand where we're coming from," Trev paused. For an odd moment he froze as if listening. At length he exhaled and rubbed the base of his neck. "But if this is something you've got to do, then I'm behind you."

I frowned at him. The others hadn't seemed to notice the dazed look on his face during his pause. I was sure he had been listening to someone, I just wasn't sure who. Which angel would be encouraging him to get on board with this plan?

Gwen threw her arms around me, dragging me into a bear hug. After a moment I pulled back, looking into her tear filled eyes.

I sighed. "I'll be fine. You know what I can do."

She nodded and bit her lip, stepping back.

Sam took her place before me. "Is there any other reason you're doing this besides helping your brother? If there is, then it should be *me* doing this not you."

Though he was being cryptic I knew what he was talking about. He meant that if I was doing this to save Lilura then he should be the one volunteering in her place, not me. Admittedly I was mildly curious why he hadn't volunteered. Maybe if I hadn't then he would have. Maybe he thought that Lilura had a stronger chance of surviving it than him. She probably did.

"There's no other reason," I denied. I slipped my ring off my finger and handed it to him. It was too beautiful to be lost. "Give this back to Zach when you see him."

He closed his fingers around it and hung his head. “Shit. You’re really going to do this?”

I nodded grimly.

“Are you sure?” Lilura whispered. “Do you really think you can get out of there?”

What I really wanted to say was that if I couldn’t I’d die trying, but one look at Gwen’s tear stained face made me bite my tongue. “I do,” I said simply instead.

“We have a new contender then?” the Scribe rubbed his hands with glee. He scurried off towards the podium gesturing wildly for me to follow.

Not wanting awkward goodbyes or any more tears or hugs I set off earnestly after him. Pushing through the milling crowd, I dodged dwarves and ducked around Wizards until I could scramble up the steps. The crowd hushed as I reached the top, shocked that a last minute alteration had been made.

As I stood there beside the rather short, creepy looking Scribe – of undeterminable species, the first flutter of nerves began. What was I thinking. Well...I knew what I was thinking – I was in big sister mode, but could I really pull this off? I glanced quickly over at my friends, keeping my face straight as I saw their worried expressions. A cough drew my attention.

“What?” I asked, turning to the Scribe.

He frowned at me and huffed out a breath. “Of what Order are you entering? You clearly cannot enter under the Flag of Soceri! Whatever you are, I hope you have arranged a sponsor and are not wasting our time!" He turned to the observing crowd and gestured to me.

Panicked, my mind went blank. A sponsor? What was he talking about? I needed someone to sponsor me so I could enter the tournament?

"Well?" he growled at me.

"Of course I have a sponsor." I thought back to what the other entrants had said. "I enter for the House of Haamiah." I said the first name I could think of. Not for the first time I silently prayed that Haamiah would have foreseen this. After all, the meaning for his very existence was to guide angels and Nephilim, and though it was unconfirmed, the general consensus in the safe house was that he could predict the future.

The Scribe rubbed his chin, his eyes frowning in thought. "The House of Haamiah? The angels? Interesting." He turned towards the back of the stage where the metal gates were currently closed. "Our final competitor – Jasmine, of the House of Haamiah!" he announced.

As one metal gate creaked open the Scribe raised his eyes in surprise. Perhaps if I had given a made-up name it wouldn't have opened. Either way, the gate was open now and I bolted towards it, not looking back once as the crowd roared.

23

Never be bullied into silence. Never allow yourself to be made a victim; accept no one's definition of your life; define yourself.

Harvey Fierstein

Once I was through the gate I found myself in a brick wall tunnel. Without thinking I ran down to the other end and through the second metal doorway there. I was in a huge white room; large white tiles lining the walls and what appeared to be white marble on the floor. The other competitors were sitting on benches on opposite sides of the room. The volunteers were free to sit, stand or walk about. The forced competitors were sitting side by side with chains to their ankles and wrists attaching them to a bolt on the floor.

A little like the Big Brother house, they all turned to see who the latest entrant was. James mouth dropped open and for a second I saw a look of pure relief pass over his face. It was quickly replaced with anger.

I quickly ran over to him and stood before him hesitantly. I wanted to hug him, to run my hands over his face and reassure myself that he really was here, alive. I wanted to gush to him that I'd save him. But we hadn't gotten to that familiar stage with each other yet and I was pretty sure from his expression that he wouldn't appreciate a hug. I also considered that promising I'd save him was not something I should do in front of the others. Not that is wasn't true. I damn well *would* save him. But I didn't want them to think he was easy pickings if it came to fighting.

"What the hell are you doing here?" he hissed.

A little taken aback I frowned at him, "What do you think?"

He glanced at the demon next to him and back at me with a warning in his eyes. I gave him a look in return that assured him I wasn't an idiot I knew not to say that he was as weak as a baby and didn't have a hope of coming out of this thing alive if it wasn't for me.

I turned away from him to see the others. When I had been busy searching for the soon-to-be dead angel I had missed some of the introductions.

There were twelve competitors. There were five volunteers including myself – the werewolf and the Fury Demon were sitting on the bench opposite, the two centaurs were standing quietly talking to each other in the corner of the room. That left seven chained competitors. They sat in the order they had been announced, Derek the young, dark haired warrior sat on the end followed by Deshek the horned demon. James was the third. He was followed by four others. Next to James sat a tall, willowy female with ash-blonde hair. She was beautiful. She looked human to me, but after catching a glimpse of her pointed ears I wondered if she were Elven. Beside her sat a vampire. I didn't have to stop and think for a minute what species he was. Blonde and muscular, wearing modern jeans and a t-shirt, his fangs were revealed as he snarled, heaving against the chains. Beside him was another warrior, with blue eyes, and then what I could only presume was a Troll, or an Ogre; never having seen one before I was unsure on the details that would tell them apart.

This creature was huge though with a human-like body shape. Sitting down he was full head and shoulders above the tallest of the others. Thick, wrinkled skin coated his body like elephant hide. One completely white eye observed the others just as I was observing him. Thick black horns protruded from either side of his forehead, sharpened at the ends to a point. I shivered as I imagined being skewered by one of them. I presumed that was what they were for.

I looked down at James again and rolled my eyes when he leaned back against the wall refusing to meet my eyes. I turned and stomped over to the bench considering sitting down then quickly changing my mind as I realized I would have to sit next to the Fury Demon.

24

Be more concerned with your character than your reputation, because your character is what you really are, while your reputation is merely what others think you are.

John Wooden

As we waited, the room echoed with roars and cheers from the crowd. I didn't give myself a chance to feel afraid. Instead I spent the time studying the competitors, trying to remember what I could about their weaknesses and strengths.

A small door swung open in the side of a wall and a thickly built man marched into the room. He clicked his fingers and the chains binding the non-voluntary competitors fell to the floor.

As I stepped towards the burly man, I pulled James along behind me. We were here now and there was no getting out of this. We were competing in the competition now and we had to win. No, I corrected myself. *I* didn't have to win. But I had to make sure James did. He was innocent in all of this. It was my fault he had been dragged into it. If I hadn't been so obsessed with finding 'family' I would have realised that Sam, Trev and Gwen were my family. Zach was my family, and though I might not like him all of the time, Haamiah was also family.

If I hadn't been so short sighted and so determined to make some sort of relationship with James I would have realised that the most important and sisterly thing I could do would be to leave him alone. I could have asked Zach to request for the Grigori to watch over him in case the Fallen ever found him. Instead, despite everyone's warnings, I led them straight to him.

I glanced at him, feeling a breathtaking slam of regret and guilt batter at my insides. I tried to contain it, but though I knew feeling guilty was useless I couldn't push it away completely.

Feeling my power begin to swirl at my tumultuous emotions, I looked away from him and focused again on the man in front of us. I noted now that the group of competitors had formed a loose semi-circle around him, a respectful two meters or so back. I pushed my shoulders down, lifting my chin, and promised myself that even if I didn't survive the coming battle, I would ensure that James did. I wouldn't let him down again.

"Welcome Competitors," the man began, anchoring my concentration. He paused and turned very slowly to each one of us. To check we were listening? To see if this year's competitors were exciting enough to amuse those watching? To see if he could correctly guess the winner?

"I know the question burning on the tip of our tongue...those of you who *have* tongues that is," his eyes flicked over towards the two Reptile-like warriors across the room from me. "The prize you are all risking your life for is..." he paused dramatically. "Star Mist, gifted to the competition by the Sorceress of Mallabee."

Star Mist...I racked my brain, thinking back to the tedious lessons Haamiah had given back home, but I couldn't recollect anything about stars. If anything, he had been particularly guarded, bordering on snobbish about Astrology and Astronomy, deflecting any questions posed about stars, the Zodiac and anything related, from the younger, curious Nephilim. I had presumed it was because you didn't normally think of God and angels along the same lines as Astrology and Psychics. Maybe this was something that would have been of actual use to me, like a lot of things I hadn't been taught. Then again, Star Mist could be anything. There was no end to things about this mystical world that I didn't know.

The mention of Star Mist had had an impact on some of the others though. The instructor was waiting silently until the news had been fully absorbed and the pause was becoming uncomfortable and strained. The Reptilian warriors were snapping their teeth rapidly, inching closer and closer to the instructor. The Elf looked stunned. The vampire was smirking cruelly – I would make sure to keep out of his way. The Fallen Angel was frowning in concentration. Perhaps he had also never heard of Star Mist.

The other competitors who had clearly been forced into the competition, like James, looked bewildered. Some looked like they were wondering if it were morally right for them to win it and then hand it over to their captor, or whether it would serve them right not to win it at all. I frowned at the turn my thoughts had taken. As I looked at the competitors who had been forced I could almost visualize what each one was thinking. I must have become a good study of facial expressions. Not that James' had taken much contemplation. He was scowling at the Instructor, an angry look on his face.

I couldn't really care less about the Mist. My only goal in this competition was to keep James alive. And I *would* succeed. The Star Mist...if I won it by chance then I would hand it over to Haamiah, if not then it wasn't my problem anyway.

The instructor laughed, jolting me out of my thoughts. "I see most of you are stoked at the idea of winning the prize, and some of you...have absolutely no idea what it is." He turned his head, his ice blue ice piecing me. "Trust me when I say you *want* this prize. It is a highly sort after and most elusive gift that you will probably never have the opportunity to own again."

He walked to the warriors at the end of the line and began a slow walk past us all, staring each one of use down as he passed. Even the demon flinched and averted his eyes.

"For those of you who were less than voluntary in this competition do not fool yourselves into thinking that winning is of no concern to you. This is the most deadly competition known to our kind. Most, if not all of you, will die a painful death in this contest. Most of you will be killed by another competitor in this very room," he paused as shock seemed to slow time.

I earnestly searched the faces in the room. Who would try to kill me and James? The vampire? The demon? The Fallen Angel wouldn't get a chance as I would rip his head apart the first moment I got.

I grimaced at my gruesome thoughts as I suddenly pictured Aidan. Though he was a Fallen Angel, he was sweet, gentle and kind. He had loved me. I frowned and pushed the guilt away. I wouldn't even try to find out the nature of this one. I had to win, which meant he had to die. I needed to concentrate on getting James out of this alive, and if I had to kill someone then so be it. I'd be gunning for the angel first.

"You will form alliances," he continued. "You will suffer betrayals. You will make enemies. You will lose limbs, you will become manipulating, calculating and strong or you will die. And you *will* try to win the prize."

He had come a full circle and was once again standing at the front. "The rules. There aren't many. Firstly, you will obey all instructions given to you during the competition. If you don't, there will be consequences," he shrugged, smiling. "Secondly, you may not, until instructed, kill another competitor."

James' fingers found mine. The tips, barely touching, somehow gave me the strength to look the instructor in the eye as he turned to look at me.

"The competition starts now. Good luck."

Without turning his back to us – which was very sensible considering his audience – he left the room via a small black door at the back.

There was silence, as though it took twenty seconds or so for his words to fully sink in.

'Most of you will die.'

'Star Mist.'

'...lose limbs...'

His words crashed through my mind in a clamoring din. So loud I could barely make out the words. Other words and thoughts flew past me, catching me off guard, preventing me from thinking straight. My heart was echoing the commotion with a dizzying beat.

I turned to look at James, and was shocked out of my confusion instantly. I had expected him to be frightened, scared, crying even, but he looked in an uncontrollable rage. The kind of insane anger that I normally associated with the Fallen. His lip was raised in a snarl, his eyes almost closed in a scowl, his brow furrowed, his fists clenched so hard his knuckles were white.

I grabbed his shoulder and spun him to face me.

"It's going to be okay! I promise I'll get you out of this," I whispered hurriedly.

His angry eyes narrowed on my face and he wrenched his shoulder away. "It's *your* fault I'm here in the first place. Stay the fuck away from me. I don't need anything from you," he growled.

I froze, unable to do anything but watch as he stomped away from me.

25

Power is always dangerous. Power attracts the worst and corrupts the best.

Edward Abbey

Within seconds a portion of the wall at the front of the room slid to the side amid creaks and groans. I raised my eyebrow. They could have at least oiled the damn thing.

With no other option, we stepped through the opening into an equally inconspicuous room. Almost identical to the room we had just left, minus the small door and the metal gate at the back. White tiled walls, white marble floor…it was like being in a laboratory. I was almost waiting for the men in white suits to appear and lock me into a strait jacket. If a couple of years ago I had thought this would be my life now I would have had myself committed immediately.

Taking a deep breath, I stepped forward slowly, cautiously, apprehension thickening the air, as we milled around, seeing nothing but each other and the white background. My senses went into overdrive. I could hear every swallow, feel the sweat trickling down the crying boy. I could smell the fear permeating the room as though it were a living, breathing thing. I could even sense the excitement and aggression coiling, waiting to strike in the hearts of the Warriors here by choice. My mind was a launching pad for the thoughts winging across my eyes. Some were thoughts I hadn't realised I had until I heard them, some just moans and groans of fear. I guessed I was able to control my mouth, but I couldn't fool myself on the inside.

I stared at the white wall which appeared to be at the front. We all seemed to be waiting for it to slide open like the last, but whoever controlled it was keeping us in suspense. Probably enjoying the tension.

I could feel someone's eyes on me but I didn't dare look around. I needed to maintain a cool, calm façade. Though inside I was trembling in fear, screams echoing through my brain, I needed to appear aloof, in control, someone to be scared of. I couldn't make myself an easy target. I hoped James was doing the same. It would be too easy to be seen as the weakest one and be picked off first. No one here would help us. I was sure that the slightest weakness would set the more obviously aggressive warriors off. The Instructor had stated no one was to kill another competitor until we were told, but I was pretty sure it would take more than one threat to control the Reptilian Warriors and the Fallen Angel. If the angel saw an opportunity to murder me, he would take it. No rule was going to discourage him.

I spotted James on the far side of the room and averted my eyes quickly. I couldn't blame him for being pissed at me but I dreaded meeting his gaze and seeing the disgust and hatred on his face that I knew would be there. If only I could look up and see Zach's menacing scowl, have him yell at me for getting into this mess and promise to get me out of it. Haamiah could kill them all with a flick of his hand, even Maion wouldn't be entirely unwelcome in this situation. He would at least *try* to keep me alive out of his loyalty to Zach. Aidan...If Aidan was here he would have knelt before me and swore to the heavens that he'd give his life for mine.

I sighed, annoyed at myself and allowed my eyes to flick around the room in attempt to distract myself from my wayward thoughts. I couldn't allow myself to start wishing for someone else to come and save me. I could do this. I was just as strong and powerful as other Warriors in the room, if not more so.

I blew out my breath slowly. James was staring at the wall like the rest of us. In fact everyone in the room was staring blindly at the white wall. All except a demon I hadn't caught the name of. Tall and broad, darkened skin and piercing blue eyes, he carried himself with a certain grace that the others lacked. He seemed...*noble* somehow. He held himself straight, carrying a sword in his right hand. He appeared to me like a knight from olden times. Beside the curved grey horns protruding from his forehead of course.

And he was staring right at me.

I quickly averted my eyes as our gazes met. I stared at the ground, pretending I hadn't noticed him looking at me, trying not to let my emotions play across my face. After a suitable amount of time had passed – ten seconds or so – I looked up at the gate, pretending obliviousness.

Unable to look away any longer I glanced sideways at him. His blue stare was still focused on my face. I looked away quickly, scowling, determined not to look at him again.

As I positioned my body so that I could see the wall and James without being too obvious I felt the floor give way. One moment it was there, the next I was falling, gravity spinning around me every which way. My arms shot up automatically, trying to hold on to something, trying to stabilize my fall. Horror was surging through me, fear, terror at falling into the unknown threatening to choke me. Had I opened a portal accidentally? How would I find my way back? How would I get back here to save my brother?

Amid my terror, I realised to my confusion that I was lacking the mist that always accompanied my portals. I wrenched my head to the left to see the other competitors all falling beside me. Some had grabbed hold of each other, some were actually fighting with each other in midair – striking at each other with knives and swords. Some were screaming, spinning out of control. Thankfully I had been standing a little distance from everyone, as had James, so neither of us were within striking distance of one of the beasts.

There was little I could do besides allow myself to fall like the others. If I had been Gwen I could have flown to the bottom safely. If I were Trev I could have begged an angel to soften the fall. But as my abilities were healing and opening portals I would just have to fall, and pray there was a soft landing waiting at the bottom. I did consider opening a portal for a fleeting second, but I couldn't guarantee 100% that it would open at the bottom and not somewhere else completely, and I just couldn't risk leaving James here on his own.

With difficulty I swung my body a little more. I was unable to face upright but at least now I was falling down in a fairly straight line and not rolling through the air like some of the others. There was nothing to do now except hope that the fall didn't go on for too much longer, as we were picking up speed with each second.

26

Heaven has no rage like love to hatred turned, nor hell a fury like a woman scorned.

William Congreve

I sunk below the surface of the water when I reached the bottom, taking in a small mouthful of water. Amid the pounding of the water, I kicked my legs and reached up with my arms, desperately trying to find the surface. I coughed and spluttered when I finally broke the surface, vomiting water I had swallowed, gasping for air. After a few seconds I was able to take in a deep lungful of clean air, and calm my brain, pushing away the screams and shrieks clamoring for attention.

Thankfully I had fallen vertically and had slid into the water. The only damage being unfortunately taking a breath as I did so. The mixture of splashes and accompanying groans made it evident to me that some had belly-flopped into the water. I almost winced in sympathy until I remembered that they would probably try to slit my throat at the first chance they got.

As I shielded my face from the splashes of the panicked creatures surrounding me, I realised our figures were highlighted only by the light from the white room hundreds of meters above us. I anxiously searched the faces I could see around me, making out James treading water four or five meters away. Relief surged through me.

I was beginning to think that all of the Warriors appeared to have survived the fall when I felt something bump against my shoulder. Spinning in the water, I quickly pushed the face-down body away from me and swam backwards away from it. I tried desperately not to think of the blood that was probably mixing with the water I was swimming in, lapping against my face, all the while ridiculing myself for being so girly.

Eventually as time passed, the other competitors quietened down, the crying turning into silent tears, the angry growls and snarls only echoing every few minutes or so if one Warrior had come too close to another.

The intensive training I had received over the past few months had greatly strengthened my legs and core muscles and I found I could keep my head above water easily, but I worried for James. As he was a Nephilim he would have the additional strength and resilience all Nephilim had, but he hadn't been trained to use it, hadn't been tested and trained. I was only thankful that he was at least on the Football team and had *some* strength and stamina.

A surge of water sent me sailing into the wall of the tunnel. I pushed off from the wall, continuing to tread water. As another wave sent me careening into the wall, harder this time, I began to wonder what was causing the turbulence in the water. Was there a tunnel somewhere that we were supposed to find? An exit out of this dark, watery hole?

The waves seemed to be coming from the opposite side of the tunnel so I pushed against the wall, moving sideways. The tunnel was maybe five meters in diameter so it wouldn't take long to get around to the other side like this. I pushed again, sliding through the dark water.

Another wave smashed me against the wall. I sunk beneath the surface, kicking hard to get back up. This time the others had also noticed. A low bur of voices and growls echoed around the tunnel, making it sound as though there were a hundred of us down here. James was holding on to the wall a few meters away. He looked worried, anxious.

I lifted my feet and pushed off against the wall, sailing across the middle of the pool. I swam around the elf, who raised her lip and snarled at me as I passed close by her. I copied her look, flashing my teeth angrily at her to warn her off. It seemed to work. Or possibly she thought it was just amusing. Either way, I had managed to navigate my way past everyone until I had one hand on the wall beside James.

He was glaring at me again.

I rolled my eyes. “Quit it already!” I snapped. “You’ve made your point! You’re pissed off at me, you hate me...whatever! But did you even think for a second that this might have happened whether I found you or not?”

“No I didn’t! You bought them here! My life was perfectly fine until you wrecked it!” he shouted above the growling.

“Well the Fallen found me without any help! So the chances are that they would have found you whether it was now, or in a year from now! The only difference is that now, you have me and Zach and the others to help you.”

“Yeah well I would have been pretty happy not knowing about any of this crap!”

“It’s not crap! It’s us! It’s our life! Our destiny!” I shouted.

James leaned closer. “I don’t believe in any of that bullshit. My destiny-”

“Was what?” I interrupted. “Your destiny was to play pro-football, hang out with your friends, go clubbing on weekends? What if it’s more than that? What if your destiny is to fight…” I lowered my voice “Fight Fallen Angels, or vampires. To save the Nephilim being hunted by them? To save angels?”

“Why would I be meant to save angels? That’s such a load of crap and you know it!” he spat. “God I can’t believe I’m even having this conversation! I’m clearly insane and I’m in some deluded fantasy! I’m probably locked up in some asylum right now-”

“Shut up!” I silenced him. My power was surfacing, alerting me to danger. I was so in-tune with it now, I knew exactly what it was telling me. The way it was rolling through my stomach, rising up like a snake through my chest to my throat, told me that something was hunting me, or us.

“Don’t tell me to shut up!” James raged beside me, completely oblivious to our impending doom.

“Something’s wrong you Arsehole!” I was infuriated by him. How did I ever think that we would be best friends? That we would instantly have a brother-sister bond? He was an immature, arrogant little boy, and he was pissing me off!

“Yeah there *is* something wrong. *You*!”

I turned to him, feeling rage pour out of me in a glistening mass. “Shut the fuck up. Right. Now.”

I allowed the sparkling, tingling power to run through me. Previously, it would have taken over me completely, but now I was able to let it run through my veins, seep through every pore until it almost consumed me, but not quite. I was still in control, and could still see and feel through this sparkling mass around me. Though others had described it as a shadow surrounding me, and in the past I had been frightened by the haze that seemed to absorb me, I could see everything clearly, sparkling, crystal clear. And there was something in the water.

27

It takes courage to grow up and become who you really are.

E. E. Cummings

With my intuition I had known there was something wrong, but shooting my sparkling shadow through my eyes – like looking through glasses on the inside – I could see a circling shape beneath the dark water. It seemed to be rising through the water very slowly and every few seconds it would jerk its tail, sending a huge wave rocketing up towards us. As I stared down into the water I could just make out a second shape further down doing a similar motion.

I glanced at James. He was glaring at me in hatred. I debated telling him that there were giant creatures in the water beneath us – probably stage one in this competition. If I was honest with myself though, I just wanted to frighten him because he was irritating me so much.

I had been staring at him for too long.

"What?" he asked.

"Nothing," I said, looking away.

"What is it?" he pestered.

"Hmm?"

“You said there was something wrong...There’s something in the water isn’t there?” His voice, no longer angry and forceful was now trembling.

I blew out a long breath of air, ducking under the next wave. The others had obviously noticed the wave and knew something was happening, but hadn’t realised it was going to come from beneath them yet.

“Just stay against the wall and we’ll be fine,” I reassured him.

“What’s in the water Jasmine? If something’s in here with us, I want to know what it is,” he demanded.

“I don’t think you do,” I muttered.

I turned to face him, my heart melting at his expression. He was obviously terrified but was holding onto his strength by using his anger and hatred for me as his armour.

“I don’t know exactly what they are...”

“*They*?” he asked.

Oops. Wrong choice of words.

“You know what an eel looks like? Well there’s something like that in here with us...only bigger.” I told him honestly.

“How much bigger?” he asked after a second.

I looked down into the water then back up at him. “A lot bigger.”

“It’s okay. Honestly, we’re so tiny compared to the others that they’ll probably not even bother with us,” I tried to reassure him. “Just lift your legs up and pull them into your chest. Then there’s nothing hanging down there.”

Even in the darkness I could tell that James was pale. Admittedly I wasn't too keen on the thought of having my legs bitten off either, but shockingly, I felt fairly calm. Maybe it was the thought that if I lost control I would find myself in some other realm without James, maybe it was because if I freaked out then James would certainly lose his already fragile hold on his cool.

"The others don't know what's down there, only we know. So that gives us an advantage, see?"

"Shouldn't we tell them?" he asked innocently.

"Are you kidding?" I asked. I stopped suddenly. I was about to say that this would have the potential to knock out some of the other competitors. Which was entirely true. But looking at his face I could see the dilemma through his eyes. Were we murderers by default if we didn't tell them? There were others out there who had been forced into this too, just like James. Should we warn them and help them?

In *my* mind they were numbers to be knocked out. If only one person was going to survive the competition then I wanted the rest of them to be deader than dead so that I could ensure James' survival. If I said something now, would it just be to kill them later today? Or tomorrow?

"Well, well, what are we talking about over here?"

My blue eyed stalker had found us and had brought some friends. I panicked for a second wondering what he had heard until I realised that he had gathered the other competitors who had been forced to enter. Derek the young warrior who had been entered by the Wizards of Old seemed relatively calm. Deshek the demon with his blue skin was floating beside him, angry and menacing, growling loudly. Who knew, maybe demons weren't keen on water?

One other male was there, one I hadn't seen introduced earlier. He swam next to the others, looking equally angry and afraid.

I turned my back to James so I was facing the newcomers face on. This was it. The Instructor had spoken about allies – this was obviously the first gang to form and they meant to drown us or something. Well they weren't counting on me being strong. I had a feeling I would probably be the strongest and most powerful here, and that was my secret weapon. They would be expecting me to be weak, an easy one to pick off. I was prepared. My power was shooting through my very fingertips, pumping energy and strength through my muscles.

"We're not talking about anything," I denied, defiantly looking into his piercing blue eyes.

"Yeah sure," he laughed.

He and his followers continued to tread water beside us. This was totally the opposite of my plan. I had hoped if James and I kept still on our side of the tunnel that the eels would be attracted to the others wiggling around and fighting in the water in the middle.

"What do you want?" I huffed.

"We just thought we'd hang out over here," he smiled charmingly at me. If it hadn't been for my history with Aidan and Zach – the two most gorgeous men I had ever met, I probably would have fallen for his schmooze, now however, I just thought he was slimy. And he clearly wanted something. I just needed to know what it was.

"What do you want?" I repeated.

"For fuck sake Jasmine," James interrupted, splashing past me. "Guys, there's something in the water."

"James!" I exclaimed. That was so typical! I was so pissed off that he had just given up our one advantage, I could have kicked him. I had specifically told him *not* to say anything so what did he do? *Argh*!

"What's in the water kid?" the blue eyed demon asked seriously.

"Some eel thing," James replied.

"Well I guess we're better off sticking together then," he said, smirking at me again.

I scowled. "And why is that exactly?"

"Predators pick off the weaker members of the herd," he replied.

"And you think we're the weakest?" I asked, my eyebrows raised.

The demon smiled in a creepy, malevolent way. "Aren't you?"

I wanted to reply saying that I was probably the strongest here but bit my tongue, reminding myself sternly that my advantages were few and the element of surprise could come in handy. I ignored him and turned to glare at James instead.

"They deserved to know," he said, swimming to the other side of me, closest to them.

"What do you think you're doing?" I demanded, dragging him through the water away from them.

His reply was lost as a wave smashed me against the wall. Pain stabbed through my head, numbness spreading down my neck and shoulder. Sinking underneath the water I gulped down water over and over. I kicked my legs and stretched my arms, trying to reach the surface as fire burned through my lungs. Panic shot through me, taking over until I was screaming for air.

As one creature slithered towards me I wrapped my arms around my head and tucked my knees into my chest. The agony in my chest was unbearable but if I moved around they would head straight for me, I just knew it. I held on, peering through my water hazed eyes as they glanced at me then swam past, catching me in the wave that followed, smashing me against the wall once again. I gasped again, swallowing more water.

The lower down I sank the clearer the eels became. They were huge! At least four meters long each, they were thick and bulky. Thick black eyes with a red outline peered evilly up at the legs splashing around above us. I could almost imagine them salivating as they snapped their teeth hungrily at them. Their teeth...their teeth were huge. Like grey spears slicing through the water, they glinted, flashing as the eel circled past.

They didn't seem to take much notice of me at the moment, but that was because I was no longer struggling to rise through the water. As one, then the other glided past me, I allowed myself to sink lower and lower into the darkness, forcing my power to still my actions and calm my raging mind. Now that I saw the eels up close, I realised there was no way I could kill it on my own. They would slice me into shreds in seconds or drag me to the bottom of this tunnel and rip my limbs off.

Suddenly I was grabbed by something and dragged. I fought, slashing with my arms but was quickly restrained against something soft and dragged upwards. I slammed my head back catching something hard. My head rung from the pain, dizziness swirling around my head. I could feel myself beginning to pass out from lack of oxygen. I struggled, fighting against whatever had a grip on me. It was strong, unrelenting, impossible to shift. I kicked, catching something. I kicked harder, stronger wriggling and fighting. I managed to turn my whole body around and sunk my teeth into something soft, tasting blood. As a roar filled my ears, my word turned black.

LAURA PRIOR

28

Live as if you were to die tomorrow. Learn as if you were to live forever.

Mahatma Gandhi

As I came to I realised someone was holding me. Zach. It had to be. Or Aidan. I'd be happy with either at this stage. The body was hard, muscled and thick. I wrapped my arms around the mountainous shoulders and rested my head against the hard cheek.

"Is she okay?" I heard a voice. James. So he cared after all.

I sighed my contentedness and looked up into arctic blue eyes, grey horns jutting out above them. With all my force I pushed away, sinking in the process. I was instantly pulled back to the surface and against the demons hard body again.

"Get off me," I spluttered, choking on the water.

"Ha ha! You want to be fish food?"

"What?" I coughed.

"You were unconscious. You've lost your strength. You're weak. If I let you go, you'll sink," the demon seemed to take great delight in informing me.

“I am not weak!” I denied. I couldn’t have them think that. They would attack me immediately. As it was he could squeeze his arms and crush me. I pushed against him; more angry than anything.

“I think I’ll keep hold of you for the time being, all the same,” he laughed.

Another wave sent us into the wall, which the demon easily deflected, pushing off with one hand, while sheltering me with his other one. I didn’t know why he was helping me, or even if he *was* helping, but for now I was pleased to be above the surface with oxygen readily available. My head was still ringing from the bang against the tunnel wall, my vision still hazy.

A high pitched scream rang out, echoing over and over and over again in the tunnel. I clutched the demon tightly, lifting my legs up out of the way of any hungry eels circling below. I was ready for something to bite my legs at any second.

I could see James floating right next to us, fighting to stay calm. The two warriors and the demon also floated beside us, forming a tight pack. It would be easy to kill James and I off right now, I was useless, though I refused to admit it, and James was untrained and too…*human* to be of any help.

Screams and shouts for help, combined with snarls and growls grew louder and louder, surrounding us, almost deafening me. At least two of the other competitors had been bitten, or by the sounds of it ripped into. The splashing made me think that at least one had been dragged under, but I couldn’t be sure as the light above us had ceased, plunging us into darkness.

I felt the surge of the water as one of the beasts descended on us. The demon swung me behind him and as the monster neared us he instructed me to hang on. He surged forward with lightening speed and rammed it with his horns, slicing through the slippery skin. The eel shrieked; the most awful sound I had ever heard, so piercing that I lost my hearing for a few minutes afterwards. As the demon launched himself at the beast again I let go, slipping away through the water to James' side.

I watched through the gloom as the demon was knocked aside and thrown with force against the wall repeatedly. There was no way he would make it. It was impossible. Every time he tried to hit or kick the monster he just glided right off. His horns were the only thing that did any damage. His sword would have worked but I couldn't see it on him so I presumed he must have dropped it. The other three attempted to attack it but encountered the same trouble the demon had. I was the only one who hadn't tried. And I had no intention of doing so. I was going to stay out of the way, tucked up where my feet couldn't be bitten off. James had other ideas.

"You have to help them," he urged.

"What? I just drowned! I have concussion! That thing clearly can't be killed and you want *me* to go up against it?" I demanded, outraged.

"Everyone else has tried but you. You're always saying how powerful you are, so prove it!" he shouted.

Pain blossomed in my chest. He really didn't care about me. He truly didn't care if I died or not. All of my dreaming was for nothing. My whole life my one wish was to have a family, and here was real flesh and blood family, and he wanted nothing to do with me. In fact worse than that; he wished I'd never come into his life and was now baiting me, taunting me into a fight against an eel.

I stared into his brown eyes sadly. His belligerent, angry expression was all I was used to. He had never smiled at me, not even once. I shouldn't have presumed so much. I had put all of my eggs in one basket so to speak, had presumed we would be best friends, that he would be so excited and happy to have a real sister, that I hadn't foreseen this at all.

There was nothing I could do to change that. Nothing I could do to improve his opinion of me. I knew that now. The only way out of this was to literally find the way out. I wouldn't do this for him anymore. Yes I would help him if I could, but no, now I would focus on myself. Focus on winning the competition and getting home to my friends.

I turned away from him towards the center of the pool. My power had waned since falling unconscious but now I called on it, literally sucking it up through my body right through my blood and lungs until I was filled to the brim. The sensation was wonderful, like being high, only better. I was in control, I was hyper aware of everything, my very blood sizzled with wanting. My mist surrounded me, pouring out of my skin into the water, sparkling and glittering like a thousand stars. I dived under and located the nearest eel still attacking the demon. I felt like I sizzled through the water, every droplet kissing my sensitive skin.

My vision narrowed, seeing only the eel. As it turned, its red circled eye on me, I smiled and shot forward. I reached down for the knife I knew was strapped to my ankle inside my boot and rammed it straight into the eye nearest to me. The creature roared and shook, rearing through the water with me and the knife still attached. As it retreated lower in the water I swam to keep up, pulling myself alongside until I could wrap my legs around it to hold on.

With my lungs burning and my eyes losing sight in the darkness I held on tightly to the knife that was still buried in the eyes, and lay my left hand on its back. I allowed the power flow through me, feeling myself suck the energy out of it, draining it of its strength. I could feel my lungs begging me to take a breath but I wasn't quite finished. I had to hold on just a little longer. I pulled up my power to an extent I hadn't allowed for a long time, allowing it to completely take over my body; my vision, my limbs completely under the control of the angel instinct within me, that *was* me. I held on to the tiniest flare of life inside me only to stop myself from taking a breath. I could almost feel the strength flaring through me as my arms ripped the Eel apart completely, my teeth ripping out bones and savagely biting on flesh and spitting it out. The taste of rotting flesh and oil burned my tongue. I screamed in anger, feeling that out of every emotion rage was the strongest, the most complete. I felt so angry, so betrayed. I was gloriously furious. And I was so petrified of the beasts in the water with me, the flash of eyes in the dark as something else slithered towards me...the second monster coming to avenge its mate. The flash of teeth as they cut through the water beside my face.

The water was black, pitch black. I could barely see anything, I could only feel. And I was so angry. The lack of air was beginning to affect me now, my lungs had stretched beyond burning and were now on fire. The pain was excruciating. It was just as painful as the cuts and slices on my skin. I could feel the blood seep out of me, dissipating in the water along with my control.

There was nothing I could do. There was another monster here somewhere. I couldn't see it, but I could feel the water rising as it swam closer to me, darting away at the last second. I peered into the water, at the last second spinning around to see the enormous open jaw of the eel snapping at my head. I blasted my power through my body. I allowed it to not simply trickle out but pour into the water around me, turning it into a whirlpool of angel magic. The power was exhilarating, liberating, and didn't let go of its hold on me as it burned through the water. Instead, as I let go to oblivion, it took over me completely.

29

I am not afraid of storms for I am learning how to sail my ship.

Louisa May Alcott

Taking a huge breath I knelt up in the waist high water. My throat constricted, I sucked in gasps of air hoarsely. My legs had taken a beating; they throbbed all over. My knees in particular ached as I knelt on the rocks in the shallow water.

Unable to summon the strength to stand or even the interest to look around me, I concentrated on dragging my sorry-ass out of the water towards the nearest edge that I could see with blurry vision. It was covered in plenty of sharp rocks but it would do. As I groaned, half crawling half swimming I felt someone grab me under the arms and haul me out of the water, dumping me face first on the rocky embankment.

It must be James, I thought, relief coursing through my exhausted body. I lay still, allowing my blood time to rejuvenate my limbs. I healed quickly so I wasn't overly worried about any cuts and bruises getting infected.

"Is she even alive?" James' sullen tone reached me…from a good few meters away.

I immediately rolled onto my back and stared up at the *thing* that had pulled me from the water.

Blue Eyes. I snarled and flipped up to my feet, seeing James, and the young warrior and demon standing a little distance away. As I wobbled, he reached out to steady me. I quickly slapped his hand away.

"Don't touch me!"

"Woah easy! Just didn't want you to fall on your ass," he replied, smiling.

"I wasn't going to fall over. And I don't need your help," I denied.

"Jesus Jasmine, he was only trying to help. You should say thank you to him for pulling you out of the water in the first place," James muttered.

That was it. I'd had enough. How on earth could I be related to someone so callous, so mean, so unforgiving? I had thought I would finally meet someone I would have a connection with, someone I could have a bond with. I had thought that having a brother would truly mean something. I was wrong. Dead wrong. In fact, I couldn't have been more wrong.

This arrogant, argumentative little fucker was nothing like me! Yes I had my faults – I was indecisive, I had a tendency to over think things – clearly, I leaned a little more towards melancholy rather than happy 'angel-girl', and at times I could be a bitch – if the person deserved it. But this dear brother of mine was just a brat with no thought for anyone but himself, no perception of acceptance for the realities of life, or faith in our world. If there was even an ounce of angel in him I would be surprised. Demon, maybe, but certainly no angel.

I turned to face James. Anger made me shake. My skin was already shimmering lightly with my power.

“You...” I started, struggling to form the words. “You are nothing to me. I came here to help you, and you...” I stopped, shaking my head, my eyes conveying the anger that my words couldn’t. I took a breath. “Find your own way out of this mess. I’m done.”

I turned away from all of them and began to pick my way carefully along the edge of the water towards an area where a group of trees jutted out, hanging over the water. I seemed to be standing at the edge of a shallow but wide stream. All along the side I was on, was a thick stone wall with the trees jutting out just ahead. Across the other side there was a steep embankment with roots and bushes sticking out. I presumed that was probably the way everyone else had gone. If there was even anyone else left besides us five.

I looked ahead to the trees and hoped there were more behind it. After all, it was unlikely they would be sticking out of a stone wall. I had a lot of history with forests – both haunted and regular. It almost seemed a comforting thought; being hidden in a deep, dark forest. My good friend Valentina and I had travelled through one for weeks, hiding and tracking, so to me it seemed the best direction to be heading in.

As I hopped from rock to rock I noticed a large dark brown-grey object get washed up across the other side of the water. A larger piece emerged, then I spotted more pieces float through the water.

Was that...No it couldn’t be. I paused and frowned at it. It was the eel, possibly both of them. Somehow in my rage I had lost all control and had literally torn them into pieces.

After the initial stab of shock, I was unable to avoid the smug satisfaction that flooded through me. If he thought he was better off without me then I hoped he looked at this shredded carcass and thought again. I hoped he regretted every mean thing he had said. I hoped he was kicking himself for not trying to get to know what I could do. I hoped he was looking at my back right now, regretting not begging for me to help him, regretting not pleading with me to stay with him.

“Fuck this! If that’s what she can do, I’m with her,” an unfamiliar voice said.

I turned and gaped open mouthed as the young warrior and demon jumped over the rocks to reach my side.

“What are you doing?” I scowled.

They looked at each other. “We’re coming with you,” one said. The other nodded his agreement.

“I don’t need anyone to come with me,” I refused.

“The instructor said we were to form allies. Well out of everyone in the competition – you are the only one who took the beasts out, so you’re probably the most sought after ally here,” the Warrior said.

“Yeah. I might not be as strong as you, but I’m a Fire Demon. I can warm you up if you get cold,” the demon banged his clenched fists together. They instantly combusted, bright flames covering his hands, spreading up to his elbows. “Or if you’re truly cold, maybe we can make our own fire.”

What a geek. I just raised my eyebrows in reply. The demon shrugged and smiled. I glanced at the other warrior.

"I'm a warrior. I might not be able to do magic-" he frowned distastefully at the Fire Demon, "but I am strong and I can fight back."

I frowned at both of them, unsure of anything except the strong feeling that I wanted to be out of this conversation pronto. Having others want to be my friend was a totally new feeling. At school I had never been well liked – admittedly I had been a bitch, but still. In the Nephilim boarding house Sam had kind of taken me on as a pet project and Trev and Gwen had been foisted on me. Not that I didn't adore them now – I did, but I hadn't enjoyed the feeling of being shadowed constantly at first. Even Valentina had only befriended me because she had thought I was some prophecy...which I kind of had been. But this? These two...beings...wanted to be on my team because I was the strongest?

I rubbed my forehead in frustration. "Look, whatever, but don't get in my way." Aha! There was my inner bitch, I had turned a tad soppy over all this James shit, but now I was over it I could be myself again. If I was hoping that my bitchiness would scare them off I was wrong. The two of them nodded agreeably waiting for me to make a move.

I huffed and turned to continue my way towards the trees.

"Hold it Goldilocks."

I swirled around and glared at Blue Eyes. "Don't call me that!"

He held his hands up in mock surrender. "Just seems to me that if you're taking those two with you, me and the kid should get an invite too."

Irritation crawled through me, grating on my nerves, setting my teeth on edge.

“I didn’t invite anyone,” I growled.

“Okay, it’s a free for all then. Good,” he said cheerfully. He jumped over a couple of big rocks and waded through the water until he was standing beside me. “Hey congrats on the eel by the way, I would have jumped in there, but you looked like you were enjoying yourself.” He casually walked past me, heading towards the trees. My mouth was now open, gaping at his absurdness.

“Ugh!” I growled, stomping after him.

I continued making my way carefully over the rocks until I was underneath the trees. I could see a dark gap in the stone behind their trunks. I was sure there was a way out. Blue Eyes had stopped and was watching me, the others began to crowd around. I ignored them all and leapt up, catching hold of the trunk. I swung my body round until I was straddling it, then stood up and followed it to the large gap in the rock. Holding on to both sides of the wall I stepped over the jagged edges and sat down on the edge, dropping to my feet on the solid ground at the dark edge of a forest.

I hesitated for a second. Did I wait for them to climb over or just start walking? If I was planning on ditching them then I had definitely waited too long. I heard the thud of boots behind me, then a second thud. I rolled my eyes and marched off into the forest.

As far as forests go this one was pretty average. I didn’t know a lot about trees or foliage except for what Aidan had taught me, but the trees looked ancient, with thick, angry roots twirling above ground, ferns shooting up in all directions. Moss coated the tree trunks, running over fallen logs, while old leaves and shrubs created a crunchy, unstable carpet on the floor. There was no discernible track to follow, which meant I was continually coming upon new obstacles – fallen trees aplenty, a few boulders, even a sheer rock face, the latter of which I had decided to take as a sign I shouldn't head in that direction.

"Does she even know where she's going?" I heard James mutter.

Ugh, he was still with us. Part of me had both hoped and feared he would have sloped off on his own. I felt partly mollified when no one answered him.

I continued stomping through the woods, trying to ignore the sounds of feet and heavy breathing behind me. There was no end in sight. Every tree I passed seemed to look exactly the same as the last one. The only thing that changed was the light. Gradually, the sun was setting and the forest was growing dimmer and dimmer, and growing spookier by the minute. I began to look for somewhere to hide for the night. Valentina had always found our hiding places; caves had been her preference as they were usually dry and sheltered, but a few times she had found sheltered areas under trees or between tangled roots, so I started peering at the trees around me, moving on slowly, continuing to keep a look out.

I suspected that the other competitors had all left the stream via the obvious option – over the river bank and I prayed that was so. I didn't fancy taking on the Reptiles or the Elf when I was still recovering from my fight and near drowning. There would also be other creatures in the forest. Not necessarily all native creatures like wolves or foxes. I imagined some would be altogether more terrifying.

I slowed down, more determined than ever to find somewhere quickly. I ducked under branches and scrambled under roots, trying to find a space big enough to fit five people. Part of me just wanted to say 'screw them' and leave the others to find their own places, but the likelihood hood was that if they were found, I'd be somehow dragged into their fight too.

"What about here?" Blue Eyes called out.

I turned to face him. He was gesturing at a root maze nearby that I had already seen and disregarded as it looked far too small to fit five people in my opinion. I stepped closer and peered in, not seeing much except darkness.

"You think we're all gonna fit in there?" I muttered.

"Yes. I do," he replied smugly.

The others were all silent on the matter so I took a deep breath and slid myself feet first through the mass of roots. It was deeper than I thought and I dropped to the bottom with a thud, bending my knees slightly as I landed. Rocks scattered as I moved to the side to let the light in. I stepped forward, mapping it out in my mind. It would be tight but it was definitely a possibility. With the sun almost fully down now and the demons and vampires out there somewhere, it would be better to hide sooner than later. What was the chance of finding somewhere bigger or better in the next half an hour?

A thud behind me alerted me to Blue Eyes joining me in the pit.

"Seems big enough," he said nonchalantly.

"Fine," I replied. I sat myself down at the back, away from the draft, kicking rocks and stones out of my way. I prayed that I wasn't sitting on a nest of snakes or rats, or that a wolf pack would return from their hunt any time soon.

As the others slid in through the roots, I tried to completely ignore them and go to sleep. Unfortunately the ground was less than comfortable. I rolled onto my side, smacking my head on a particularly large stone in the process.

"You can snuggle against me, if you want," Blue Eyes whispered in my ear.

I scowled and shuffled away from him. "I'd rather lie on a rock."

I kept my back to him as I heard his stifled laughter. *Arrogant prick*. It was irritating that I could still hear them muttering amongst themselves as I tried to sleep. It did occur to me that perhaps one of us should be keeping watch, but I knew my angel instinct wouldn't let me down if something decided to come for me in the dead of night.

I heard James' voice asking questions of the others. Though I didn't want to care, I found myself listening to them. He had asked their names. The Fire Demon was Deshek – the angry guy with the blue skin. If I remembered correctly, he had been forced to compete by the House of Gargoyles. I grimaced to myself, that sounded particularly creepy. I had always thought of gargoyles as the ugly stone statues on top of old gothic buildings. I hadn't realised that they were real. Not for the last time, I cursed Haamiah for not teaching me more.

The other warrior was Derek. He didn't answer when James asked him what he was, he simply stated his name, and then remained quiet. The atmosphere was bordering on uncomfortable before it was interrupted by the demon next to me.

“You would not understand nor be able to repeat my true name as it is in Demonish,” he said. “Loosely translated, it is Blue Eyes. And that is what you can call me.”

Blue Eyes. I scoffed at the name. How typical! He couldn’t have a normal name, no. Not even a name we could pronounce. Instead he had to make up a name just to show how special he was. At least I wouldn’t forget it. Annoyed that my mind was becoming fixated on his name, I told myself to relax and shut the others out. I took deep, calming breaths and let myself drift off.

30

A sad soul can kill quicker than a germ.

John Steinbeck

My dreams were horrific. Dungeons, torture, Fallen Angels, gargoyles...they just continued one after the other. One dream in particular alarmed me the most.

In the haphazard, uncoordinated way dreams have, I found myself suddenly standing in a backstreet alleyway in the dead of night, unable to remember where I had been or what I had been doing. The alleyway was exactly how you would imagine a nightmare alleyway to be; tall non-descript buildings either side, two dumpsters side by side nearby, broken glass and soggy cardboard boxes littering the ground, and the smell of urine and rotten food permeating the air, almost making me gag. It was night, the sky was dark and I could hear police sirens in the distance as well as heavy traffic roaring by.

I followed the motions expected of me – I had no real control over my body. I turned my head to the right, seeing the alleyway continue into darkness, and then to the left – a repeat of nothingness. Just as I was beginning to feel that I should be doing *something* I was distracted by a buzz and crackle.

I looked up, noting for the first time a lamppost – the fluorescent yellow light casting its eerie glow on me and plunging everything else into darkness. It crackled again, dimming for a second before returning brightly. *Flies*, I thought to myself, seeing another black insect fly straight into the glow only to be zapped.

As I stood mesmerized by the hum and flicker of the light, a dark shadow obscured my vision for a second. My heart pounded as I spun around. Able to see once more, I noticed a figure standing further down the alleyway. Someone I had not noticed before. Slender, tall, dressed in a long floaty white dress that gathered at her feet, she was leaning back in an oddly uncomfortable-looking position.

I *knew* her. Somehow she was so familiar to me.

Zanaria. Her name was Zanaria. And I hadn't seen her for so long. My heart ached, my soul yearned for her. God how I missed her!

I pushed off, beginning to run for her, quickly building speed. I sprinted towards her, my arms outstretched. As I skidded to a halt beside her, she fell into my arms. Joy coursed through me, angels singing in my ears. She began to crumple to the floor with me, worry beginning to burn through my heart. What was wrong? Why wouldn't she stand?

Kneeling beside her, I turned her in my arms, gazing down at the face so familiar to me. White glassy eyes, full of horror stared up at me. My eyes took in her mutilated lips bloody and tense, the swollen wounds on her cheeks. I gasped and pressed my palm to her throat, desperately trying to stem the flow of blood seeping from the gaping wound there.

Anger. Hatred. Rage. My emotions were hot, fierce, burning through my soul. Revenge. I would destroy the monster that did this. He would beg for mercy but none would be given. I screamed – despair and raw rage echoing through the night, bouncing off the walls either side of me. Anger took over – my eyes turning black, my vision now only shades of grey. I was on fire. No; *I was on fire!*

The flames scorched my skin, smoke swirling around me in eddies. Fire licked at my clothes. A ball exploded behind me like a bomb. The world was heating up, hotter and hotter, smoke making me cough as the flames obscured my vision, searing my skin. Yet still I knelt, holding Zanaria.

Black eyes flashed before me. I screamed, wanting only to see the girl in my arms. They flashed again. Lips moved in my vision, a shadowy film imposed over the life I was in. An urgent voice whispered in my mind. I could hear my name repeated over and over.

"Wake up!" the lips shouted, louder this time.

I opened my eyes, coughing, choking. I rolled to my stomach, burying my mouth in the crook of my elbow, desperately trying to suck in oxygen.

Eyes flashed at me again.

"Quit it!" I shouted. "I got the message already!"

I kicked Blue Eyes awake and shouted at the others to wake up as I scrambled up out of the maze of roots and crawled to my feet, desperately looking around me.

Fire! There was fire everywhere. Which way did I go? My sparkling mist was everywhere now, coating my skin, acting like a balm to cool the areas that were scorched by the smoke and flames.

"This way!" Blue Eyes shouted hoarsely, tearing off through the trees. I followed him, in turn followed closely by the others – judging by the crashing sounds behind me.

"I can't stop it!" Deshek the Fire Demon yelled.

I should have thought of that. If Fire Demons could control fire then he should be able to put it out easily. Why couldn't he calm the flames? What did that mean? Had he started the fire?

I didn't have time to ask or answer any of my own questions, I simply ran, focusing on Blue Eyes' broad back as he leapt over a fallen tree in front of me.

An explosion behind us sent me flying through the air and crashing into the back of the demon. Smacking my limbs on rocks, I bounced along the floor as heat surged over us. He dragged me to my feet and continued running, pulling me behind him. I glanced back just to see James, Deshek and Derek picking themselves off the floor and running after us. I was so relieved. I hoped James could keep up with us. I made a mental note to keep an eye on him and ensure he didn't fall too far behind.

"Duck!" Blue Eyes yelled, pulling me forward under his arms.

Why was he shielding me?

A fire ball rocked past us, slamming into the tree next to us, ripping it apart. Flames reached for us, searing, scorching. I ran past Blue Eyes, sprinting forwards. Every tree around us was in flames. I sucked up my magic, using it to power my limbs as my feet pummeled the ground and I hurtled through the trees. Faster and faster I ran, avoiding the shooting flames, leaping over simmering bushes and sliding under trees so heavily laden with fire they were toppling in our path.

The shouts and yells behind me rang out as the others fought to keep up. I leaped over a thick log and sprinted up a small muddy hill, sliding and rolling down the following slope. Lying face down at the bottom, I groaned and looked up, watching as the others leapt down the hill much more gracefully than I had done.

Blue Eyes reached me first and grabbed my out-flung arm, dragging me up to my feet. Not letting go, he forced me to sprint to keep up with him. I groaned as we ran up the next slope, this one much steeper than the last. I slowed as I reached the top, beginning to feel faint. James, Derek and Deshek were only just beginning to climb the hill. I glanced down at them only to shriek as a fireball soared towards me. I turned and pushed off, finding myself freefalling from the top of the cliff.

For what seemed a lifetime, I fell. I was watching Blue Eyes fighting to stay upright, his arms spinning either side of him in an effort control his descent. The fireball sailed over our heads, smashing into the cliff opposite as we fell further and further through the air, down into the chasm towards the darkness waiting for us at the bottom.

I could see objects flying through the air at the other side. No, I could see the other competitors jumping off the cliff on the other side, fire chasing them.

My heart in my mouth, I plummeted into the darkness, screams and growls echoing from above.

31

No doubt exists that all women are crazy; it's only a question of degree.

W. C. Fields

I landed in the water feet first, immediately sinking a good few meters beneath the surface. I forced my aching legs to kick, and reached out to the surface, my lungs burning. I gasped as I reached the surface. I kicked strongly, powering through the water to get out of the way of the others falling from above.

"Get out of the way!" Blue Eyes hollered.

I didn't bother looking up but swept my way through the water as fast as I could, hearing loud crashes behind me. I treaded water, searching the faces of those falling into the canyon. Blue Eyes swam to my side.

"Are you hurt?" he shouted over the noise.

"No. You?"

He shook his head.

Blue skin fought through the water to our side – Deshek. Anxiety poured through me. Had James made it down? Would he even survive the fall? I bit my lip as Derek surged through the water. I turned to look at Blue Eyes, finding that he had disappeared. I sent my power downwards, seeking anything that might be lurking below our feet. I couldn't sense anything below us, but my angelic sense was warning me strongly about the other competitors who had fallen on the other side of the canyon.

As we waited, unsure what to do, a bright light appeared across the middle of the water. Our burly instructor appeared in the glow.

"Competitors you now have one minute to climb back to the top of this canyon. The last four will be destroyed. In this round you may kill anyone you like but don't forget to reach the top before at least four of your rivals. Begin." He disappeared in a flash.

We waited, frozen for a full two seconds before everyone erupted into action. We were the only people on our side of the water thankfully and we reached the edge easily. Growls and screams echoed on the other side as the others fought to reach the rock wall.

I reached across the rock above my head, searching for a finger hold. I gasped in relief when I felt a crevice I could use. I pressed the pads of three fingers into the crack and hoisted myself up, using the friction to walk up the wall. I reached up again, finding another and another, pulling myself up hand over hand until I was half way up. I paused. Derek and Deshek were a little lower down than me. Blue Eyes and James were nowhere to be seen. I could see someone on the opposite side nearing the top – it was the Lycan. The others were around the bottom still, fighting with each other.

"James!" I screamed. How could I keep climbing without him?

"Jasmine, climb!" Derek shouted as he neared me.

"Where's my brother?" I shouted.

"He definitely made it over the edge but I didn't see him when I got to the bottom!" he shouted back. He paused for a second, then as Deshek also leveled with us he continued to climb, shooting me a pitying look.

I searched the water desperately, looking for some sign that he was alive. The fact that Blue Eyes was also missing had me clinging to hope that he had found him, but I couldn't be sure. I let loose with my angelic power sending it into the water to seek him out. Nothing. There was only one other thing I could do.

Opening a portal when clinging to the side of a cliff was both difficult and dangerous. I felt it swirl around me, dizziness taking over, my sense of gravity shifting. I prayed that I was sending it to James. I let go of my grip and fell through in a swirl of sickness.

I felt my body slam into rock and begin to fall. I reached out with my fingers trying to catch hold of something – *anything* to save me from falling. I grasped nothing. But something grabbed me.

Blue Eyes had hold of my arm and was grimacing even as he was heaving me up to where he held James against the wall. I quickly found a crevice and was able to pull my own weight up. I glanced around, noticing that I was now on the opposite cliff, where the other competitors were. I couldn't be scared of that though, my heart was already in my mouth just seeing that James was alive.

"James!" I screeched searching his face for injuries. I could see blood running down his face, but otherwise he looked okay.

"Jasmine!" his voice shook, trembling and breaking.

"Lean in!" Blue Eyes roared.

I obeyed immediately, almost losing my grip on the wall as a body tumbled down past me.

Black eyes took over my vision. “Climb!” A voice roared through my head.

I obeyed immediately. I reached up and pulled myself higher and higher, building speed. I didn’t hold back on my angel power, letting it guide me to cracks I could use. Somehow I knew that Blue Eyes would pull James to safety. I just knew it. Now, I needed to concentrate on not being in the last four to reach the top.

I glanced across to guage where the other competitors were. A few were above and some about level with us. As I climbed I dared to look down, praying that there were at least four lower down than us. There were. I fought to climb to the top, my shoulders burning in agony, my fingertips bleeding. Scratches down my arms and knees were stinging and my boots were well and truly waterlogged.

I reached the top and hauled myself over, scrambling to my feet. I looked across, seeing that Derek and Deshek had reached the top on the other side. On my side I could see the horrific Lycan Anora, the blonde woman and the Troll. That left six places. I gasped and slid to the edge of the cliff. Blue Eyes was about equal with the vampire, the centaurs were lagging behind but the Fury Demon was ahead, almost at the top. I snarled, feeling rage wash over me. I *hated* Fury Demons.

As he neared the top, I felt a feeling akin to glee. I was actually excited to rip apart this beast. My eyes narrowed, all thoughts leaving my mind except the urge to rip and tear. As soon as I saw thick black talons appear over the edge I skidded over, ripping my knife out of my boot. I slashed immediately, laughing as blood sprayed out and the demon roared. He dug his talons in with his remaining arm trying to swing his leg over I hacked with my blade over and over, stabbing furiously.

When Blue Eyes reached the top I desperately wanted to help pull him over the edge. I could see he was struggling to haul James over, and I could see the vampire closing in on him. I screamed in fury. I was so infuriated. Everything was out of my control. I hated this! I just wanted to rip and rend and destroy everything in sight. I shrieked as I felt my power take over me completely, my eyes hazing over, mist everywhere. I felt my body going through the motions and I felt instant relief, instant pleasure at the destruction I caused. It was delicious.

Black eyes flashed. I raged against them before abruptly pulling back into myself. I stepped back falling to the ground. Blue Eyes stood, shock in his eyes as he shielded James' face from me. I took in deep breaths, finding my center, finding my calm.

“Did we make it?” I gasped.

Blue Eyes nodded as the screams began below.

32

Life could be wonderful if people would leave you alone.

Charlie Chaplin

No further instructions were given, which meant that up on the top it was a free for all. The two centaurs had never had a chance at climbing the cliff, and the only two that I had sworn to myself I would destroy had been eliminated. The vampire hadn't made it to the top and I'd shredded the Fury Demon in my fit of rage.

The blonde elven woman backed away into the still simmering trees and disappeared into the interior, the Troll roared and stomped and also seemed undecided whether to flee or destroy, but the Lycan had her gaze set on James.

It was as though she had scented the weak member of the herd and was narrowing in for the kill. She had lowered her head and crouched with one foot in front of the other, ready to spring into action. Blue Eyes was ready for her, his horns lowered, James behind him.

As soon as she moved I blasted her with my power. I no longer cared about staying in control. I was doing what I had to do to stay alive. I tackled her to the ground, slamming her head against the rock as I screamed. I felt myself flip over as she turned and knelt on me, her teeth snapping at my face like a rapid dog. I slammed my elbow into her nose, grinning as I heard a crack. She head butted me in return, sending black dots into my vision.

I shrieked as her teeth sunk into my shoulder and I returned the favour. I embedded my teeth in to her neck, literally chewing through her flesh. I could feel blood squirt into the back of my throat but I completely ignored it, continuing my feast of her throat. I stopped only when she lay still.

I was dragged backwards. I threw my leg up, kicking my assailant in the face.

"Shit!" Blue Eyes yelled.

I turned, still feeling caught up in the thrill of it all. I stood and faced the Troll. It growled at me then slowly backed away. I stood up straight, still anticipating an attack.

"When you think about coming near me with those teeth, remember I saved your brother," Blue Eyes words slurred through my mind, hazy and weak.

I snapped to, blinking repeatedly. I frowned at him. What was he talking about? I looked at James who was looking at me in an odd mixture of admiration and terror. Whatever.

"Jasmine...we have to go," the demon mumbled at me.

I forced myself to move past him, stomping into the bushes. I climbed over a fallen tree and stretched out my arms over my head. My shoulder ached but I just couldn't summon the energy to bother healing it. I could feel the blood dripping down my back slowly as it clotted off. My mind was a haze, I didn't feel myself at all. I felt sort of detached, as though I had felt so much emotion I could now feel nothing.

I could hear the sounds of the demon and James following me, so I forgot about them and concentrated on my own steps, through thick bushes. We walked and walked, no direction in mind, towards no specific destination until I heard the sounds of running water. In that instant revulsion washed over me. All I wanted to do was scrub the blood and gore off my skin.

I began to run, sprinting, leaping over rocks and boulders until I came to a screeching halt at the edge of a pond. It looked clean, with water falling into it from above and water trickling out at the far edge. There was a stone embankment, thick ledges jutting in and over. I ran my gaze across the far edge not seeing anyone else here. After a moment's hesitation I knelt by the edge and submerged my arms up to my shoulder.

The cold water seemed to soothe and massage my skin. Ice ran up to my shoulder to numb the wound there. I groaned as I began to wash the blood off my face, realizing it was coating my neck and chest too. I focused wholly on the task at hand, gargling the water and spitting it out. As I stared into the water at my rippling reflection I began to hear voices. I jumped to my feet and spun round.

Only Blue Eyes and James sat nearby. I stared at them, disturbed by their perplexed expressions.

I gulped. "I did what I had to do."

James said nothing but Blue Eyes acknowledged my hesitant statement with a nod.

"If I hadn't killed the Fury Demon you would both be dead by now. You heard the screams from the slowest four."

Blue Eyes nodded again. "I know, and I thank you for it."

I huffed out a breath. "And the Lycan would have killed you."

Blue Eyes snorted, "She would have tried."

"Then it doesn't matter which one of us killed her does it?" I retorted.

He shrugged and glanced at James. "I think you scared the kid half to death though."

I stared at him. He did look pale, but then it wasn't surprising with what had happened.

"I'm not a kid," he muttered.

I bit my lip. "I'm not sorry for what I did. I'm doing what I have to, to survive. That's all I've ever done."

I was met with silence. "I can feel you both judging me!"

"I'm not judging you," the demon replied calmly.

"I'm not...I'm not a bad person," I whispered, shaking my head.

Before I let myself go down that path, I stomped up to the rock I was sitting on. "We shouldn't stay here. I can hear someone coming."

The demon frowned. "You can?"

I sighed in exasperation. Why was he always questioning me? "Let's just go."

I jumped down from the rock ledge and led the way back through the forest, meandering as the light began to fade. Eventually we had no choice but to stop.

"Why's it dark?" James asked.

I rolled my eyes and was about to make some sarcastic comment about it being night before I realised...why *was* it dark? It couldn't be past midday. We had been woken with the fire in the very early morning, and it couldn't have been more than four or five hours later.

"Different realms, different time zones," Blue Eyes answered for me.

I nodded as James grunted in response. We found a small niche between some bushes where it wouldn't be easy to stumble upon us. James suggested lighting a fire but Blue Eyes adamantly refused and for good reason. The command to kill each other as we saw fit hadn't yet been lifted so it would be stupid to draw the others to us.

"So what kind of demon are you?" James asked.

I could see the glint of teeth as Blue Eyes smiled. "An honest one."

At that I snorted.

"Yes?" he asked me innocently.

"You'd be the first honest demon I've ever met," I replied snarkily. "How did they catch you? In fact, *who* caught you?"

"One of the Fallen," he said quietly.

I stared intently at him through the darkness. "Then I guess we *are* on the same side."

"How did they catch you?" I asked James.

"I was at home. I had taken the day off school. My parents and I were just in the house talking and something...something just smashed through the windows and grabbed me. It just took off with me." His voice wavered and I could see his eyes beginning to sparkle. "I have no idea what happened to my parents, if they're even..."

"They are," I whispered.

He lifted his head. "They're alive?"

I nodded. "Yeah. I came to see you, to speak to you and there were police cars outside your house. I snuck in the back and heard your dad talking to them."

He shook his head and rested his chin on his knees. "Why did you come looking for me?"

I gulped. "I couldn't leave things the way they were. You were so mad at me and I couldn't be sure the danger was over."

"No," he interrupted. "Why did you come *looking* for me? I was fine until you appeared."

Hurt began to thrum through my body. I tried to control it, though I could feel my power rising to defend me.

"I didn't know that. The angels at home told me that you were in danger. I didn't even know I had a brother until they told me that. I had to fight to find you, but I did it because I thought you were in trouble. And I was right because outside that club you were attacked!"

"Maybe you brought them..."

"I didn't," I bit out.

There was a short silence. “Are you really an angel? You don’t look like one.”

My eyes narrowed on him. “I’m a Nephilim. Half angel, half human…like you.”

“I don’t see how I can be that,” he said stubbornly.

“What, you didn’t know you were adopted?” I asked spitefully.

He glared at me. “I *knew* I was adopted. And I knew demons existed. I just didn’t know I was related to one.”

“I’m not a demon,” I spat.

“You sure look like one,” he replied sullenly.

“You know, you’re just angry that I happened to come here the same time that all this shit erupted in your life! You know, my life was also wrecked! I was hunted down and captured and I embraced the angels helping me.” I hissed, somewhat truthfully. He didn’t need to know that I thought Zach was insane when he first started talking about angels and demons.

He shot one last glare at me and then lay down and shut his eyes, whispering, “The difference is you probably didn’t have anything to lose.”

33

When I stand before God at the end of my life, I would hope that I would not have a single bit of talent left, and could say, 'I used everything you gave me'.

Erma Bombeck

I leapt across Blue Eyes to get to James and pulled him up from the ground, back handing him with an echoing slap. Blue Eyes jumped in between us and held James behind him.

"Jasmine, think about what you're doing!"

"You irritating little bell-end! I swear I want to rip you apart right now!" I was shaking, trembling with the need to do violence. "You know what? I *didn't* have anything to lose! Our parents sent *you* to a loving family who would protect you while I got landed with a rapist! When I was hunted down, I had *no one*...no big brother or sister or parent to look after me! When I was captured by a Fallen Angel and tortured for months no loving sister came to try to save me! No, I was alone! My whole life I have been alone! And when I was told that I had a brother who was in trouble, the first thing I thought wasn't to hide away and save myself, no...I rushed here as fast as I could to get to your side." I paced the ground, kicking at stones. "When I think of the agony I put myself through, wondering what to say to you, terrified I would say the wrong thing and you'd hate me, doing everything I could to find out if you knew about any of this or not...I really shouldn't have bothered." I leaned closer and peered around Blue Eyes. "And when I made the decision to enter this tournament to do everything I could to save you...well that was the biggest mistake I've ever made in my life."

I forced my clenched fists to my side and turned away, marching through the bushes at a steady speed.

"Jasmine!" Blue Eyes appeared in front of me. His piercing blue gaze impaled me. "What are you doing?"

"Leaving," I said calmly. "I want nothing to do with him. I'm done."

"You're not done," he said.

"I *said*...I'm done!" I turned to walk away from him.

"Aidan sent me!" he called.

I froze, my heart beginning to pound. "What?"

"I'm a friend of Aidan's. He sent me here to help you in any way I can. I owed him a favour and this is what he asked for."

"Why didn't he come himself?" I whispered.

He snorted. "Aidan isn't exactly a warrior. He wouldn't stand a chance in this tournament."

"So he *entered* you in the tournament?" I shrieked. That was it. I was finished! Why did the men in my life think they had a right to be there? Why did they think they could control me like this? I didn't need anyone!

I pushed past him, relieved when he didn't try to stop me. I was beyond infuriated. I actually despised him. I was nothing like him. I didn't want to be anything like him, and from this moment I decided that he was *not* my brother. I stormed through the forest, listening out for anyone else out here as well as continuing on a rant in my head.

I should have listened to Zach. I should have gone home like he'd asked me to. I closed my eyes in despair. If I ever saw him again I would tell him I love him and I would do everything he said from then on...maybe. God, I missed him.

What on earth was I going to do? How could I even survive this? I lifted my chin and mentally slapped myself. I *could* do this. Fuck James, and fuck Aidan. I would survive. I would win. I just needed to take one step at a time.

After a couple of hours of walking, I found a small cave to rest in. The entrance was pretty small and I wouldn't have seen it if I hadn't sent my angel sense out ahead of me to snoop for demons. It was small and a bit of a squeeze, it wasn't particularly comfortable either, but it was shelter from the wind and would definitely do for a bit of rest.

I found myself sucked into a nightmare.

I was standing at the edge of a field. I was just one person in a line of hundreds. Lifting up my bow I trained the arrow on the monsters before me. I began to tremble, sweat beading at my neck. Fury Demons, thousands of them were gathered before us, brandishing axes and swords, spine chilling roars shaking my soul.

I took a step back, turning to look for an escape.

"Eyes forward soldier!" a voice screamed at me.

I raised my bow again as a tall, lean man with loose black hair down to his waist marched past. He glared at me then continued on. My bow shook in my hands, my thighs spasming in fear. I was locked in position, I was doing as I was ordered, but I was utterly terrified.

The ground began to rumble as the army of demons stepped towards us, stomping over the ground. Weapons lifted, they ran for us, screeching.

"Fire!" the order sounded to shoot.

I pulled the string against my lip and let go with my rear hand, watching as my arrow embedded into the shoulder of a demon.

"Fire!"

I reached for another and sent it off in the next volley. And again and again. I held my ground even as the others broke and began to run. I dropped the bow to the ground and reached for my sword usually strapped to my back…only it wasn't there. I found an axe attached to my belt instead and I raised it, bracing myself for the impact.

The first demon reached me and nearly knocked me flat. I rolled across the ground and flipped to my feet, knocking his sword away with my axe. I swung again while he was regaining his balance and cut across his chest, blood spurting out in an arc. I was grabbed from behind and I sunk to the floor under the weight of a demon. Pummeled again and again, my face broken and bruised, I couldn't scream, I could barely see anymore. All I heard were screams.

I sat up with a start, hitting my head on the cave roof. I cursed, rubbing my forehead and the cut now there. My body ached initially from the dream, but then began to fade, replaced only by fatigue and hunger. I folded my body into my knees, resting my head as I shook in fear. What was happening to me? What did these dreams mean? Were they just nightmares or did they mean something? Was I seeing into the future?

I rubbed my face with my hands and tried damned hard not to cry. My whole body yearned for Zach. I wished with all my heart that he was here.

"I am," a voice whispered.

I lifted my head up immediately and looked around, tensed.

"Zach?" I whispered. There was no reply. Had I imagined it?

I blinked, jumping out of my skin when behind my eyelids I saw pitch black eyes watching me. I kept my eyes closed, trying not to hyperventilate. I'd communicated with him this way before. I knew I wasn't making it up – he was inside my head.

"Zach..." I whispered in my mind.

"Babe, why are you always in trouble?" His voice sounded tinny and weak.

I pulled my lips into a wobbly smile, *"I don't mean to be."*

I felt his hand caress my face, wiping the tears away from my cheeks. His fingers trailed down my jaw and smudged my lips.

"You're going to be fine. You've got skills and abilities that you don't know about."

I frowned, *"What do you mean?"*

"There's a lot we have to discuss when you get back, but for now, do you have your ring?"

Fear spiked in my mind.

"You gave it to Sam?" his angry voice echoed.

"I didn't want to lose it," I replied sadly.

I could feel him taking a deep breath, steadying himself.

"It's okay, it just means it going to be a little harder. You need to stay in control no matter what you do."

I nodded. "You'll stay with me?"

"Of course I will. I'll be with you throughout the rest of this, I promise."

I smiled, feeling warm again. I knew I could count on him.

"Stay away from the demon," his voice sounded hard, stern.

I frowned. I considered Blue Eyes. He said he had been entered by a Fallen Angel. Didn't that make us allies? Did he have another motive? *"Why?"* I whispered.

"I think he likes you," came the reply.

I grinned and let my body finally drift into a healing sleep.

34

Never be bullied into silence. Never allow yourself to be made a victim. Accept no one's definition of your life; define yourself.

Harvey Fierstein

I was shaken awake. Actually I was almost shaken unconscious as my body was thrown against the rock wall. The ground was vibrating with such force I struggled to slide out of the entrance to the cave. I stood unsteadily, bending my knees to keep my balance. All around me trees collapsed as the ground below my feet pulsated. I looked up into the sky, noticing to my horror a dark grey tornado building up in the distance above the tree line.

I ran.

I sprinted down through the trees sliding and skidding over the leaves as I pounded my feet into the ground, pouring my power into my legs and arms. At the top of an incline I leapt, narrowly missing the trees flying at me, to land on the opposite bank. I pushed my feet into the earth reaching the top. As I attempted to clambour down the next slope a tree was uprooted, and roared straight towards me. I dived onto the floor, falling and rolling to the bottom of the hill.

I dragged myself to my feet again and continued to run. Thankfully the ground had evened out and as I found myself running in a fairly straight line I was able to pick up speed. I glanced back, horrified as the tornado seemed blacker...and closer.

I saw a wisp of movement in between the trees beside me. I continued running, alternating my gaze between the movement and what was in front of me. As I narrowly missed running into a tree I heard a hiss in my mind. My body warmed instantly. Zach was still with me, he hadn't left me alone.

"Never," his voice echoed.

I pumped my arms and jumped over a fallen tree. I had to shield my face as leaves were swept up into the air around me, pulled at by the winds building above me. I ran through a thicker patch of trees, struggling to fit between the branches until I practically fell out of the forest.

The forest had ended, and before me were wide plains, sandy, rocky ground beneath my feet. I spun around, my hope disappearing as the tornado continued to sweep on towards me. I turned to my left, just now seeing the other competitors fleeing the forest, sprinting as fast as they could away from the oncoming disaster. I pushed off and began to run, clearing rocks, jumping over boulders that were unnoticeable until you were upon them.

As I rounded a particularly large rock I noticed the Elf running a few meters to the side of me. She kept glancing back fearfully. I looked straight ahead, concentrating on my own survival.

I screamed as a crack shot through the ground, throwing me to my knees. As the crack widened I scrambled away on all fours, the ground giving way beneath me. I panted as I reached the edge, the ground seeming to stop giving way. That was when I heard a scream.

I walked to the edge, peering down, not sure what to expect. The blonde haired elf was hanging by her fingertips.

"Help me!" she shrieked.

I paused, staring at her. Thoughts began to swirl in my mind. If she fell that would mean one less competitor. I would be one step closer to winning. If she died now, then I wouldn't need to kill her later. I could feel my power surge, mist beginning to hiss in the air around me as I contemplated ways to fully push her in the cavity. My eyes began to haze, a glittering mass covering everything.

"Control it!" a deep voice boomed in my brain. *"This isn't you! Control your power!"*

I began to smile, concentrating on the fingertips gripping ever so tightly. It would be so easy to just loosen one...

Black eyes took over my vision. I gasped, falling back to the ground. What was I thinking? What was I doing? Zach was right. This wasn't me! I slid forward to the edge and hung my arm down to the Elf.

"Grab hold! I'll pull you up!" I shouted.

"No you won't! You'll drop me!" she screamed back.

"I won't! I swear it!" I pleaded.

She stared at me for a long second before leaping and grabbing hold of my wrist. I closed my fingers around hers and began to haul her up over the edge. We fell in a heap on the ground, panting, completely breathless.

"Thank you!" she sobbed. "We're never going to get out of here alive!"

"We will," I whispered.

I stood and held out my hand to her. She grabbed it and pulled herself up. We began running again, this time shouting out to each other when obstacles appeared before us, to give the other some warning. The wind whipped at us. My hair stung as it slashed at my face. I could feel the sand abrading my skin as it was sent flying through the air. It seemed to go on for hours, time dragged second by second, my life flashing before my eyes, my heart pounding painfully with each new rock that was thrown my way, with each ripple of the earth.

The competitors seemed to all be heading in the same direction. I chose not to look at who remained, instead concentrating on speed and strength. I saw it as a race, as surely it was. This was all a way to weed out the weak – a tournament, after all what tournament was complete without a test of speed?

The elf seemed to be keeping up with me, though I knew I set a punishing pace. I was doing nothing less than sprinting as fast as I could, my entire body leaning forward, yearning to win.

The ground dipped, sending us into a funnel with the other competitors. We were now running along a makeshift road no more than a couple of meters across, making it treacherous to be within reach of any other competitor. The ground shook with each step, undulating. I turned my head to see the Troll bearing down on me.

I panicked and veered as far to the side as I could, praying it didn't squash me on the way past. He stomped in my direction, missing me by inches. I skidded to a stop, letting him overtake.

My heart in my mouth I continued behind him, knowing at some point I'd have to overtake. I had to stay ahead of the others who were a little distance behind me, far enough away from the tornado so that I wasn't swept up, yet I couldn't let myself get trampled by the beast in front of me either.

I was hit in the face by something. At first I thought some debris had hit me, only it didn't hurt...and it was wet. I lifted my hand to my face, slowing somewhat. It was red. It was blood. I fell to the side, vomiting. Only there was nothing in my stomach so only water and bile came up. My stomach heaved of its own accord, strangling me. I curled into a ball as the other competitors thundered past, their feet shaking the ground. Through their feet I could see a shape, distorted and broken.

I hobbled over and fell to my knees before the Elf. Her face had been obliterated, bones crumbled into pieces, blood staining the sand and rock. Her hand was completely detatched, lying beside her on the ground. I bit my lip as I cried, knowing I needed to get up, knowing I needed to keep running. There had to be a way out of this tournament or I was going to watch everyone die.

"Get up! Get moving!" a voice shouted at me angrily.

I wanted to rage. I wanted to rebel and shout at him to shut up but I couldn't. I focused on the strength he imbued with his words and forced myself to stand. I felt a haze begin to cover my eyes and I held tightly onto Zach in my mind and began to run.

35

The truth is you don't know what is going to happen tomorrow. Life is a crazy ride, and nothing is guaranteed.

Eminem

I struggled to catch up with the others. I could just see them rounding another corner further ahead. Somehow the majority had managed to get ahead of the Troll and were speeding off leaving him between us.

When the Troll screeched to a halt, bellowing, I had my opportunity to catch up. The road widened dramatically and I could see the problem we both now faced. The rock ended abruptly and hanging over the gap was a metal cage. I looked up, unable to see what it was hanging from. Some mystical wire, no doubt. If I took a run up I would be able to leap over to it. I could see some of the others had already made it and were clinging to the inside for safety.

Only the Troll and I remained. Somehow I couldn't imagine his great hulking body fitting inside so unless he planned on hanging on to the roof he had to know he was out of this one. Was I out too? No one else was running toward us. No one had specified if it was a case of last over first to die.

The ground shook. I turned fiercly to the Troll who was pawing at the ground, snarling at me. I thought of the Elf lying broken and battered on the floor. Remembered her cries for help, her pleading eyes, the way she had sobbed that we would never escape.

I built up the mist around me, letting the mass begin to swirl and sway around me. The nearing tornado had swept my hair up around my head, my clothes were being tugged at, the very ground seemed to be sliding closer and closer to the whirling pool of wind. Even so, I smiled. I felt no fear, only rage, only anger and determination, only the need to shred it from limb to limb.

I let my glitter explode over me, turning them into shards of ice and firing them into the Troll. He roared in agony as a thousand pieces pierced his thick hide, stabbing into his eyes. He ran for me. I skidded under his legs slashing my blade, across the inside of his knee. Howling he spun and kicked out at me. I ducked to the side and leapt above him, spinning as I sliced his shoulder.

Catching me in the face I flew to the side landing roughly on the ground. I flipped to my feet, ignoring the pound of pain in my cheek that was surely broken. I still had hold of my blade so I was ready when he came at me again. He punched out and I ducked, stabbing my knife deep into his thigh. As he snarled I used his body for leverage to jump up to his face. I stabbed my blade through his eye with a yell. He ripped me off and threw me to the ground with so much force I almost passed out.

"Get up!" Zach raged at me.

As the Troll ran for me I turned to the edge. I had barely any room but still I took two huge steps and leaped, feeling the air forced past my ankles as the Troll leapt for me, missing me by centimeters. I caught hold of a metal bar and looked down while the rumble of the Troll faded away as he fell to the bottom of the pit.

I reached up and grabbed another bar pulling myself up hand over hand. A demon reached out to touch me.

"Do not help me!" I snarled inhumanely. I barely recognized my own voice, but I couldn't have cared less.

I swung my legs up over the side and pulled my body into the cage, shutting the door behind me. I refused to look at the others. I didn't care who was there, only that I would win. That's all that mattered. That's all I could allow myself to think about.

The tornado swept closer, swinging the cage from side to side, batting us like a cat would with a toy. I held onto a bar and forced my body as close to it as possible, melding with it. The others seemed to do the same, though at times they were shaken loose and thrown around the inside of the cage. At times the air seemed to be sucked out of the cage, leaving me fighting for breath, and at other times there seemed so much of it I thought my head would explode right between the bars. Sand and rocks were whipped up at us, scratches and scrapes forming instantly, stinging as they were filled with dirt and the skin stripped away by the wind.

The sound was deafening. A hum like the sound of a giant vacuum cleaner bore through my head until I could feel blood leaking from my ears, dripping down my neck. We spun faster and faster, now unable to see anything but grey and black. I could make out nothing and no one and I could no longer hear Zach's calm whispered words.

Eventually it began to weaken, to fade away. When it was no longer necessary to keep hold of the bars, I sunk to the floor in the corner and rested my head. I could feel Zach's presence, could almost hear the steady beat of his heart and I let it lull me into sleep.

When I was shaken awake I heard Zach's voice shouting in my ear. My eyes snapped open and I shoved him away.

"Tell him to get his hands off you!" Zach demanded.

Perhaps I was just doing what I was told or maybe I was still angry, but I shoved Blue Eyes across the other side of the cage and snapped Zach's order at him. He sunk to his bottom across from me, not saying a word.

I glanced around at the remaining competitors, those who had made it this far in the tournament. James was cowering beside Blue Eyes, crying and dry-heaving against the metal bars. *Pathetic.* I looked to the other end of the cage to see Deshek and Derek still clinging on for dear life.

So it was just the five of us left. We had been allies at the beginning and now what? Would they pit us against each other? Although technically we hadn't been instructed not to kill each other yet and it would be so easy to just stand up and throw them out one by one.

"Jasmine..." Zach's voice soothed me, *"Come back to me."*

I frowned. I *was* coming back to him, but the only way to do it was to kill everyone else.

"I love you. Come back to me. Open your eyes and see," he whispered.

I felt the grey haze drop. My mist drew back, evaporating, revealing everything. I looked at James, sobbing, terrified, his whole body trembling. Tears instantly filled my eyes and I crawled across the metal floor to him. He fell into my arms, gripping me tightly, sobbing for all he was worth. It almost broke my heart. His face was cut and bleeding but he held it into my neck, refusing to let go of me. Tears began to pour from my own eyes as I squeezed him closer. After a while I looked up at the others noticing that they too all had tears.

The cage began to descend, slowly at first then faster and faster until it became imperative that we hang on to the bars in case it stopped suddenly. Which it did.

Deshek pulled the cage door open and slithered out to his feet. Derek followed. I stood and dragged James out with me, with Blue Eyes following.

We were standing at the bottom of a canyon, the cliffs either side ridiculously high. The dry valley seemed to wind round a corner.

A flash of light had us all jumping. The Instructor appeared in the light.

“Competitors…you are no longer permitted to kill each other. Your next test begins now,” he disappeared.

“I hate that guy,” I muttered.

My body froze and I stiffened in shock as our next test rounded the corner. An army of demons, fully kitted out with weapons, roared as they stampeded towards us.

LAURA PRIOR

36

Victory is always possible for the person who refuses to stop fighting.

Napoleon Hill

I screamed. Terror or anger – I had no idea. I ducked as a sword flew at me, rolling to the side as a whip cracked in my face. I glanced up as blood sprayed over me, coating my mouth. I gasped as Derek's head flew past me, hitting Deshek in the chest. He froze and met my gaze. We were screwed, and we both knew it. As I stared at him, the tip of a sword appeared through the center of his chest. He fell to his knees reaching out to me.

Deshek...Derek...I looked to where James cowered behind Blue Eyes. I pictured the Elf, the Fury Demon as I had ripped him apart, the screams as the others had fallen to the bottom of the canyon.

I screamed, mist shooting out and covering us all. Sparks exploded, deafening me. I could feel heat, burning scorching. My skin was blistering up. It was so hot I could barely breathe. I felt *charged* as though I were full of electricity. My hair whipped around me, slashing at my skin.

Everything was grey and white. Time seemed to cease if just for a moment, though I couldn't be sure – perhaps an hour had passed or a day. I could hear nothing but the crackle of static as it arched and flowed.

After some time I felt myself move. I felt the familiar feel of a sword in my hands as I hefted the weight up and swung. For a long time after, I remained in a haze of nothingness. I felt no emotion, no purpose...just fire and sword. Eventually I could hear wisps of sound, meaningless at first, then words, names...*my* name.

I opened my eyes to a sight so horrific I would be scared for the rest of my life. It was the nightmare of all nightmares. Bodies upon bodies lay before me, some whole, some in pieces – all charred to ash. Blood would have run in rivers around my feet if it hadn't been for the fact I had set it alight – so now only blackened dust trails remained, like a peculiar pattern on the rock.

I covered my stinging eyes as a flash of light appeared. As the ground dropped away beneath us I gave up. It was no use fighting any more.

My stomach rolled as I fell the short drop. I landed with a bang on a hard white floor hearing similar noises as the others landed nearby. I groaned and rose to my knees, swaying as I looked around me. My stomach heaved at the sight around me. I was in a white room with Blue Eyes, Deshek and James...and the bodies of all of the other competitors.

I covered my mouth as my stomach continued to protest as I recognized parts of the Lycan and the Elf. Derek's headless body lay just a few feet from me.

"Am I in Hell?" I asked in a small, wavering voice.

I crouched on the ground, as small as I could be. I could see the traumatised look in Deshek's eyes as he lay on the ground, groaning in agony, and the angry, bitter snarl on James' face. I looked at Blue Eyes expecting much of the same. Instead grim determination marked his face, a fierce expression tugging his eyebrows into a frown as he stared at me.

He had heard my words, I could tell by the way he tilted his head at me. He felt sorry for me. I paused, my mind frozen, the world dropping away. He felt sorry for me? For me? Had I become a creature of such misery that now demons felt sorry for me?

The thought felt like acid in my mind. I couldn't abide it. It was like a poison trying to erode my self-worth. I was strong and powerful. How could he think to be so condescending as to feel sorry for me?

I forced my legs to straighten and ordered my spine to hold my body up. I felt every bone creek, every muscle scream, as they contracted, pulling into place with a groan. I pushed my shoulders down and dragged my head up to glare at him.

"I asked a question." I snarled, not recognizing the animalistic voice growling out of my throat.

Blue Eyes took a step back, his eyes wary. I smiled, feeling victorious. This was what I wanted. I wanted them to be afraid of me. I wanted them to know that I was the strongest.

"You're not in Hell. I swear it." He said quietly.

I took a deep breath, feeling the now very familiar rage wash up over me. It was hot, almost spicy. I turned to James, my eyes narrowing on him of their own accord. I felt my hatred contract, a black smoky vision appearing before my eyes.

There was something peculiar about him, something I couldn't quite recognize. I felt the urge to go to him and search his aura. I restrained myself with difficulty. What was it about him? There was something so familiar and so wrong....

I caught a whiff of something from him. It was almost a scent but a tangible one, perhaps something I could touch. It was almost green, perhaps with a shade of blue, with red streaks lying dormant. The streaks were hot, burning, almost on fire.

I looked down and realised the room was beginning to fill with smoke. I didn't care. I watched as James' eyes narrowed on me with hatred. I began to pull myself back together. This was it. This was how he would kill me. The smoke was his doing.

I stepped forward, fists clenched when a buzz of whispering made me duck to the side. It was like a bee had gotten into my ear and was flying around in a panic – it's little wings clicking away in a desperate madness. I shook it off, refusing to give in to whatever trick he was playing. The voices persisted, louder now, shouting, conversation over conversations, a blue of words that I would never be able to understand.

My head began to feel thick, fuzzy and heavy. My eyes were in agony, a pain behind them stabbing at my brain. I forced my eyes open, tears beginning to stream down my cheeks. I grasped my forehead, moaning. What was happening? What was this madness taking over me?

I heard my name called loudly. I knew it was Blue Eyes, but I couldn't trust him. He could be in league with James. I couldn't trust anyone here. There was no one but me.

I felt him touch my arm and I lashed out, barely able to stay conscious under the onslaught of voices. I turned and kicked, the full force of my strength through my leg causing something to snap as I felt him fly away from me.

I leapt closer to James, knowing I had to kill him if I wanted to survive this. I felt utterly trapped in the madness he was causing. I felt as though I would explode like a volcano any second now. I focused on the colour swirling around him, on the red streaks. I concentrated on turning the noise down in my head. Drowning it out.

A blast of cold washed over me. Recognition…realization…he was part of this. Of everything. The voices told me of the lies and deceit that I could now see so easily swimming around him like sharks. The red flashes representing every treacherous deed against me.

"You knew." I whispered, frozen in place.

He scowled. "Knew what?"

"About us. About this. You knew all along."

Now he began to look cautious. A sly look crossed his face and left just as quickly. "I don't know what you're talking about."

That irked me. I could feel the irritation at his denial begin to raise the hairs on my arms. "You pretended to be frightened, to be shocked about what I told you about Angels and the Nephilim. You already knew."

I felt Blue Eyes presence and saw the movement of him in my peripheral vision. "What do you mean?"

Keeping James in my line of sight, I answered him. "He's working with them. I can't believe I didn't realize this straight away. It's so obvious now." I laughed, feeling almost euphoric now that I had worked it out and it all finally made sense. "The fact that it's taken me this long to work it out is insane!"

Blue Eyes raised his eyebrows at me. "I think you're approaching the insanity mark right about now."

"Confess it." I hissed at James. "You're working with the Fallen. You're on their side."

Black thunder covered James' face as Blue Eyes swung around to face him, his shock apparent.

James paused, clearly trying to decide what to say. In the end he just smiled broadly, beginning to chuckle. He shrugged. "I've got nothing to hide. What have the Angels ever done for me? Besides abandoning me as soon as I was born? I owe them no allegiance. I owe you nothing."

"This was some kind of trick...you being in the tournament was all some sort of plot, wasn't it?" I asked.

He laughed in response.

Raw fury took over, white clouding my eyes, the ground tilting and shaking. I felt the air move around me and my fist hit flesh. I tore and ripped everything I could touch. I felt free and gloriously furious. I felt as though I were the wind, a living breathing tornado bent only on destruction. All thoughts dropped away, all awareness gone in an instant, replaced by white clouds and shaking floors.

When something grabbed hold of me from behind I threw my head back, grinning at the loud crack I heard. I spun around and sunk my teeth into the flesh waiting for me, reveling in the very scent of fear and pain.

I stopped only when I found myself gasping for breath. I scratched at the hands clenching my throat desperately trying to loosen the grip. Along with the disappearing oxygen, the white haze lifted from my eyes and I found myself facing Blue Eyes, anxiety and stress wracking his face. I could see blood pouring from his eyes where I had tried to scratch them out. Three deep furrows on his cheek were gushing blood. I felt my barriers life, unable to sustain them any longer, unable to summon the energy to force anger into action. All I could see was his soul, soft and kind, warm and lonely in those beautiful blue eyes.

I crashed, melting into his arms, unable to stand. I grabbed hold of his shoulders, holding on to his hard muscles, letting him hold me. He lowered me to the floor, allowing me to breathe again. I felt safe. Even knowing James had betrayed not only me but our entire species, I knew Blue Eyes would protect me. I felt myself falling into his eyes just before I was abruptly pulled out of them with a snap of black, angry eyes.

I leapt out of his arms and stood up, once again in control, once again...me.

37

It is better to die on your feet than to live on your knees.

Dolores Ibarruri

The Instructor appeared before us.

"We have a clear winner," he announced. "You are a true deserver of the Star Mist."

I felt myself fall as something akin to a portal opened beneath my feet – something not of my own making. I fell, landing a few seconds later on the stage where it had all begun, to raucous applause and cheering.

The small rotund scribe handed me a glass and gestured for me to drink the contents. I did as he instructed before turning to where the other survivors stood. Blue Eyes held up Deshek who was miraculously still breathing, while James stood beside him, staring at me in horror.

"I'm sorry," I mouthed to him.

I turned to jump off the stage, finding myself instantly picked up against a hard chest. I dared to open my eyes and instantly met deep black, soulful eyes framed with thick black eyelashes. A silver bolt through the eyebrow above.

"Zach..." my voice cracked.

His eyes flashed angrily at me. "Don't worry babe, I'm going to kill them all."

I looked around me, noting the powerful creatures staring at us. Some had heard what he had said and were already prepared with raised weapons. I sighed and with what energy I had left I pulled up a portal. With a whir of motion we disappeared from the stage and arrived back at the Nephilim safe house. I said nothing as Zach carried me to Elijah's rooms for medical attention. I stayed perfectly still as they stripped me and Elijah lay his hands on my wounds; healing them with magic. There was apparently too much damage done to heal me in one sitting, as he told Zach to bring me back in a few hours.

Zach gently picked me up and took me to my room. He lay me under the covers and slid in next to me. He tucked me close in to his side and stroked my hair as I drifted off into an exhausted sleep.

When someone knocked at the door I opened my eyes, startled. It was still light. I could hear voices outside – it was Sam and the others. For a moment I wondered how they had managed to get back here so quickly. I soon remembered Sam's Sorceress – of course she would have helped them to get back. If I could have felt any worse than I already did, I would have berated myself for leaving them there. Instead I closed my eyes again, remaining still as I felt Zach leave the bed. I heard him order them to leave, almost smiling when they argued with him. As they bickered angrily, Zach closed the door on them and locked it. Silence resumed.

Hours later, I felt him stir. I could sense he was looking at me.

"Babe, I know you're awake. Talk to me," he whispered.

I shook my head and pulled him closer.

"Jasmine," he whispered in my head.

I lifted my hand to my mouth and met his eyes.

"I'm a monster," my voice cracked.

He shook his head. "You're not. You did what was natural."

I shook my head, tears falling. "How was *that* natural?"

"You did what you had to do to survive. It's part of you. It's a natural instinct to defend yourself. Your strength and abilities are yours to use," he said softly.

"No," I whispered. "There's something wrong with me. No other Nephilim could do that. I lose myself. My power takes over and I do terrible things."

He sighed, "You're right."

I looked up sharply.

"No. Not about you doing terrible things," he corrected. "About other Nephilim not being able to do the things you can do. Even a*ngels* can't do some of the things you can do. The portals, for example. I thought you had inherited that gift from your angel parent, and *that* still may be true but it doesn't explain the others."

I sat up and stared at him, wide eyed, afraid of what he was going to say next. "What others?"

He shrugged and blew out a breath. "Dream walking. Angel communication. Your strength and speed far surpasses the oldest and strongest of any Nephilim before you. You can wield Heavenly

Fire. You've shown signs of telepathy and you can heal as well as Elijah – an angel as old as time."

"What are you saying? Spell it out for me Zach!" I cried. "What am I?"

Zach took my hand and lifted it. "Your ring."

I looked down, noticing for the first time that Zach had retrieved it from Sam and had replaced it on my finger.

"What about it?" I asked, spinning the silver band around my finger. I rubbed the opal with the pad of my thumb.

"I was given it by an oracle...a seer," he answered. "He said it was yours. That it had been passed down through your family for generations." He stood up and paced the length of the room.

I slipped to the edge of the bed and sat, my hands braced on either side of me, waiting for him to drop the bomb.

He turned to face me. "Only Jasmine, baby, this ring isn't angelic."

I frowned, "It's from my human side?"

He froze and stared at me, pity in his eyes.

"My other side isn't human, is it?" I guessed.

He shook his head. I stood up, also feeling an intense desire to pace the room.

"Then what am I?"

He bit his lip. "We're not one hundred percent certain. It's still speculation at this point and I don't even want to suggest-"

"Cut the crap and tell me!" I demanded.

"Haamiah, Maion, Elijah and I have discussed it and judging by your abilities and temperament-"

At *that* I scowled.

"We think there's a likely chance that one of your parents is valkyrie."

I stared up at him. "valkyrie...I don't even know what that is."

Zach perched on the edge of the desk. "Valkyrie are ruled by the God Odin."

"I thought you didn't believe in any God other than your own," I interrupted.

He scowled. "They exist, I am just not ruled by any others. As I was saying, the God Odin rules the Valkyrie. They are warriors, the fiercest you could ever imagine. They follow battles across the realms, and choose only the deadliest and strongest of soldiers to save. They are described as battle-maidens who ride in the ranks of the gods. According to our Intel, Odin gathers warriors in preparation for the final battle of the realms– Ragnarök. The Valkyrie are Demi-Goddesses and have *many* abilities which explains why you can do so much and what makes you so powerful."

I nodded and sat down again on the edge of the bed. "So I'm half angel, half Valkyrie," I mumbled. "Are they evil?"

"No! God, no." Zach knelt before me, gripping my knees tightly. "Valkyrie are mischievous, and cunning and incredibly powerful, but they're not evil. I promise," he stroked his fingers down my jaw.

I tried to smile at him. I tried to show him I was okay, that I felt reassured I wasn't a monster, but I couldn't.

"Do Valkyrie do the things that I do?" I whispered.

"The mist? The explosions and sparks? Absolutely," he confirmed.

"What about the part where I haze over? Where I can barely see? Where I feel nothing, no pain, no emotion? When I am taken over completely? What about when I am completely controlled by the desire to kill? To rip, and shred and destroy everything in sight...the rage that takes over everything – do Valkyrie do that?" I waited, already knowing the answer, theories forming in my already petrified brain.

Zach crawled closer and took my face in both hands. "Jasmine, please don't make me answer that. You're not ready. You're still injured. Please give me time to confirm this."

"Zach..." I whispered, fresh tears burning in my eyes. "Valkyrie don't do that because you said they're not evil. And what I do *is* evil, I can feel it. I can tell the difference." I bit my lip hard to center myself and stood up, moving away from him. "I'm not half angel, half Valkyrie...I'm half *Fallen Angel,* half Valkyrie. Aren't I?"

38

It's not enough to know your truth, you must live it.

Stephen C. Paul

Zach nodded, so tense I was surprised he didn't break apart. I nodded in turn, and stepped carefully around the bed to the window which looked out over the garden.

"So my father is a Fallen Angel?" I spun around suddenly, eyes wide. "He's not..."

"No!" Zach denied. "It's not Asmodeus. Fallen Angels are evil but they would recruit you, not...*that*. Chances are that they don't know about you. If they did, they would try to get you to join them. And Jasmine, you don't know that it's your father."

"Aren't Valkyrie usually female? You called them battle *maidens,*" I asked, rubbing my pounding head with one hand.

Zach took over, tugging me to him as he massaged my temples with his thumb and forefinger.

"The majority are yes, but there are still some male Valkyrie."

"Well, whoever my parent is on the Fallen Angel side, it has to be someone pretty powerful, right? And the portals are from the angel side?" I continued when I felt him nod against me. "So tell me, which powerful Fallen Angel can open portals?"

“Lilith can open portals,” Haamiah’s voice boomed from the doorway.

Zach shot past me and gripped Haamiah by the throat, holding him up against the wall. As a second angel entered the room I found myself entranced, incapable of saying or doing anything.

Aidan stood there in the doorway. He looked the same – young and powerful. He was lean and toned; much slimmer than Zach, probably half the size though the same height. His face held a look of softness and caring unlike Zach who exuded strength and anger. His blonde hair fell in a shaggy mop around his face, and his grey-green eyes looked at me as though I were a princess. To compare them you would never think that Aidan was the Fallen Angel. But he was. He had rebelled with the others and hadn’t yet begged for forgiveness otherwise he would have the duties of the Grigori.

In a split second Zach noticed him and snarled. He gripped Haamiah’s throat tighter, crushing his windpipe.

“Zach!” I cried. I stood between them and shoved Zach away. He didn’t budge an inch. As Haamiah choked and coughed, Zach’s gaze dropped to mine. He slowly let him slide to the ground. He took a step towards Aidan, his eyes boring into his.

“What are you doing here?” he snarled.

“I wanted to see that Jasmine was okay,” Aidan answered shakily.

“I’m fine,” I answered. I almost took a step closer then thought better of it, instead taking a sidestep towards Zach. “Thank you for sending Blue Eyes. He saved my life.”

He inclined his head, “It was the least I could do.”

A low growl came from Zach's throat. I jerked my head up and turned to him with a scowl. I knew they had rivalry going on but this was ridiculous.

"Why?" he spat at Haamiah bitterly. It took me a second to realize he was asking why Haamiah had told me about Lilith not why he had let Aidan in the house.

"Because you weren't going to tell her," Haamiah replied calmly.

"I was going to tell her when the time was right," he snarled.

"She needs to know *now*, not when *you* think the time is right!" Haamiah said.

I replayed the conversation in my head and began to feel faint as I came to their conclusion. "My mother is Lilith?" I asked in shock. "The Queen of the Damned? The murderer of children?"

"There is more to it than that," Haamiah sighed.

I laughed hysterically. "Then please *do* tell me how evil my mother is."

Haamiah huffed out his breath and crossed his arms. "Lilith was not always evil. She wanted equality. She wanted to be respected. She wanted the attention of God. She was sent to Adam - an incredibly powerful being created to populate this realm. She escaped the Heavenly realm and fled to Earth before Adam to make it her own. She wanted to take control before he was sent there. Three angels – Senoi, Sansenoi and Sammangelof were sent to bring her back. It took years to find her and when they did she threatened to murder every human child created if she was returned to the Heavenly realm. Only, the angels had orders and they returned her as they were supposed to do."

“What happened?” I asked, breathless.

Zach stepped forward and with a glare in Aidan’s direction he continued the story. “When the war began and some angels fell, Lilith hid herself among them. She returned to earth and hid amongst the humans and Fallen Angels. She consulted an Oracle who told her that the three angels continued to look for her. The angels had devised a plan – distributing amulets with their names engraved. If any child wearing that amulet was stalked by her, they would know and would be able to track her instantly.”

I turned away from him and stared out of the window, no longer seeing the beautiful gardens or the Nephilim lounging on the grass.

“So my mother is evil. My mother is Queen of the Damned,” I whispered.

Haamiah nodded as Zach swore.

“It’s not definite! Your father could be the Fallen Angel!” Zach argued.

“Are there any male Fallen Angels who can open portals?” I asked knowing the answer. Haamiah wouldn’t have brought up the subject if he wasn’t certain of it. Zach wouldn’t purposely lie to me but he loved me and if he thought that thinking I was half *pure evil* was going to harm me then he would certainly avoid the subject or offer false hope.

Zach and Haamiah looked at each other silently. I could feel the hostility coming off Zach in waves.

“It could be Vassago,” Aidan suggested.

Zach snarled at the mere sound of his voice.

"It wouldn't be," Haamiah growled. "Vassago is the discoverer of the lost and hidden – he would know if he had a daughter!"

"Anyone else?" I pleaded, looking at Aidan.

"Lamia," Haamiah offered.

Zach swore and stepped towards him with murder in his eyes.

"Who's Lamia?" I jumped at the chance of *not* being part evil. Who was Lamia? I searched my memory for any trace of her name, coming up blank. It appeared Zach knew who she was and even if he wasn't pleased at that suggestion either, surely she had to be better than Lilith.

Zach turned away from Haamiah, stalking across the room to lean against the wall, glaring at Haamiah.

He sighed and answered my question. I wished he hadn't.

"Lamia is also a Fallen Angel, but one who identifies with serpents."

I didn't like where this was going. Surely nothing serpent related could be good mother material.

"Lamia is beautiful, perhaps more beautiful than Lilith. Lamia is also known as the night monster. She is the seducer of young men and the most sexually powerful of all angels," Haamiah said.

I glanced at Zach, flushing red. I didn't think that was really possible.

"Men have no defenses against her. She is the personification of female sexuality. She was never at home in Heaven; causing disruption and destruction everywhere she went. She had no aspirations for good, she never did anything worthwhile, only using her sexuality to seduce human men. It was frowned upon but at the time we thought there were many more important issues to attend rather than curb her wild behavior. When she began to seduce angels we could no longer let her go unchecked. The intervention was unsuccessful and she was one of the first to be cast out."

"Before the War? Before Lucifer tried to take over?" I interrupted.

Haamiah nodded. "She was cast out among humans where she would be harmless. Only she grew stronger and stronger, developing from a femme fatale to a calculating, evil, seductress – luring men to their deaths, drinking their blood. vampires worship her. The Succubae sacrifice virgins for her. The Nymphs and Siren model their behavior on her. She represents female sexuality to a deep and dark level."

They were silent. So that was it. I wasn't a Nephilim at all. I was the daughter of the most evil Fallen Angel of all – the Queen of the Damned *or* an evil angel slut. I wasn't sure which one I preferred. I had only just begun to find my identity. Things were just beginning to make sense and here the carpet was ripped from under my feet yet again.

I closed my eyes and counted to ten. I felt as though I were drifting, floating through the room. My choices of mother were limited to either the murderer of children or an evil seductress – the role model for all Succubae.

"We should contact the Valkyrie. If we can discover who her father is then we will find out who her mother is," Haamiah spoke to Zach. They were mumbling to each other.

I shook my head, “No.”

“What?” Zach asked.

“No!” I screamed. “I need a break! I need a vacation from all of this! I feel like I’m just being thrown from one drama into the next!”

“You want to go on holiday?” Zach asked, uncertainly.

“Yes! You promised me you would take me back to the Island! I can’t deal with this right now! I’ve been through too much to do this with you.” I could feel my legs shaking. I felt close to a melt down.

“This is not the time to leave the security of the safe house,” Haamiah admonished with a disapproving look.

“I will take you somewhere safe Jasmine, if you’ll let me,” Aidan whispered. His soft grey-green eyes beseeched me.

Zach glared at him and stomped over to me. He reached down and took hold of my chin.

“Baby, I’ll take you anywhere you want.”

39

Never stop. Never stop fighting. Never stop dreaming.

Tom Hiddleston

I smiled tiredly at him and pulled up my power, enclosing us within it. Instantly I felt gravity shift and I held Zach tightly to me. I felt his chin rest on my shoulder as he pulled me closer into his chest, and I entwined my fingers around his neck.

A sharp jolt told me that we had landed. Zach placed me back down on the ground and I let my fingers run down his neck to catch his hand. Without opening my eyes I took in a deep, soothing breath and blew it out slowly, like the first breath of a free man. It was heaven. The tinge of salt, the warmth on my skin, the slight spray on the breeze...I was in heaven.

I opened my eyes and looked around, feeling instantly relaxed. I had missed this place. I still remembered the first time I had opened my eyes to this vision of beauty. Zach had found me and had rescued me again and again from the Fallen Angels who hunted me. We had fled across the world, hiding only to be found once more. Zach had told me that the angels were following the scent of my emotions and that the only way to hide our trail was for me to be at peace. So he had brought me to the only place in the world where *he* found peace.

We were on the most beautiful island called Ujelang Atoll, one of many in the Pacific Ocean that made up the Marshall Islands. Most of the Islands were uninhabited, a couple of the larger ones had some tribes and fishermen occasionally visited some of the smaller ones, but our Island was on the far north corner and remained secluded. Most of the Islands were covered in coral beaches but one edge of Ujelang Atoll hid a beautiful soft, white sandy beach and that was where Zach, Elijah and the others had decided to build their retreat. They didn't use it often, only using it as a sanctuary when it was necessary. It was a place of innocence and beauty, somewhere to hole up when the world was crashing down around them.

When I was last here I had certainly found peace, as well as love and lust with my handsome warrior. Unfortunate circumstances had led to my capture by Asmodeus and my eventual arrival at the safe house where I had stayed...but this...well, *this* was home.

I had managed to get us pretty close to the house – on the soft beach in front of it. The house was a double story wooden building with a large wooden decking running around the outside and out onto the beach. One whole side – the side facing the sea was entirely made of glass, meaning that whether we were relaxing in the open plan kitchen-living area or upstairs in bed we could gaze out to the never ending sea.

Lining the beach and surrounding the house were thick trees and bushes, and though you couldn't see it from where I stood, a mud road led from the house through the trees to the south where another beach lay.

We were a few meters away from the sea, lapping up at the sand. It was crystal clear and I couldn't stop myself from wading into the water in my bare feet, letting it wash up my calves, soothing the burning muscles there. I turned and smiled at Zach as he remained still on the beach. I felt the familiar burning of lust as I watched the sun caress his face. *God*, he was hot.

I remained staring, my eyes riveted to his chest as he shrugged out of his swords and pulled his t-shirt over his head, throwing them to the sand. He sauntered towards me, gliding through the water until he towered above me. I was eye level with his nipples and couldn't do anything other than reach forward and enclose my mouth around one.

He hissed in a breath and growled at me. I pulled my head back, my lips curling as he lifted me up, his arms encircling my lower back as he crushed me to him. Rising above him, I descended on his lips, licking and biting, inhaling as much of him as I could. I threw my head back as he bit down my neck to my collar bone, sucking hard on the tender flesh there.

He marched out of the water with me and threw me to the sand, covering my body with his. He ripped my legs apart and slammed his hand down between my legs, pressing and rubbing, all the while staring fiercely into my eyes.

I knew he was marking his territory. I knew that most of the fierceness of this came from seeing Aidan in the safe house. I could sense the possessiveness and need to control seeping into me.

The pressure was building, the lust washing over me in a wave of need as I undulated beneath him. I needed more, I needed everything he had. As if he knew it, with two hands he ripped the t-shirt from my body and began to feast on my breasts, laving them with his tongue, biting hard on my nipples until I wasn't sure if I was coming from pain or pleasure. Meanwhile, his thick fingers continued to probe me through the trousers I wore.

Soon I couldn't bear to feel anything between us. I reached down and tried to shimmy out of them only to have him spin me to my front and rip them down to my thighs. I heard the wisp of sound as he freed himself and I felt the probe of his thick, hard knob as he caressed my buttocks. He probed deeper until he reached my inner core and rammed me to the hilt, filling me with hot, thick, hardness. Lying as I was I couldn't move, but could only accept his pounding, as it pushed me higher and higher, making me scream in need.

I soon pulsed around him, my muscles milking him for every drop. He rolled me to my back and stripped my trousers and panties from my body, lifting me up with him until I wrapped my legs around his waist. He seated me on him, filling me up completely, pulling me down onto him until I stretched impossibly. He began to walk up the beach to the house, each step jolting me, sending his cock deeper. With each step he rubbed different nerves, touching different places, even as his arms held me close, tenderly.

I lay my head on his shoulder as he sauntered up the beach.

"You know that I'll always pick you, right?" I whispered.

I felt him drop his lips to my shoulder and kiss the skin there.

"I do now."

Zach jumped upon the decking with me still in his arms and slid the large glass doors apart. They were never locked because no one else lived on the Island, and in fact, no one else knew it was even here. It was well sheltered by the trees so that even looking up from the beach you couldn't see it unless you knew what you were looking for.

The downstairs of the house was very minimalistic. The kitchen was white with a breakfast bar and stools. A small dining table stood in the corner and a sofa and coffee table faced the glass windows leading to the decking.

Zach carried me through the door at the far end and almost ran up the stairs leading to the second floor.

My heart almost melted as I looked around - the second story was beautiful. All one room with brightly coloured mattresses and cushions everywhere, coloured drapes separating them, it was a truly serene place to be.

Zach picked one closest to the window that ran floor to ceiling and lay me down on it, following closely. I stretched my arms above my head, caressing the bright pink material, the diamantes and beads sewn in. I closed my eyes, my lips curling happily as he rocked into me again and again, building a slow tempo, while feasting on my neck. I ran my hands down the thick muscles of his back, digging in my nails to encourage him to pick up the pace. He began to slide in quicker, his hips rocking, his balls smacking against my bottom with each thrust until I came. Then he gave himself his release with some quick, short thrusts, falling to the side and pulling me close.

I was exhausted and the tranquility of the room and the peace of the island had begun to soak into me, but still, I felt traumatised by the recent revelation.

"Zach?" I whispered, turning my face up. "What are Valkyrie really like? I want to know the truth."

He sighed and kissed my forehead. "I told you the truth earlier. They are creatures ruled by the God Odin. They save the spirits of soldiers to fight in the final war."

I shook my head. "No. You told me what they *are*, but I want to know what they're *like*."

"They are fierce, among the strongest and deadliest of all creatures of the realms. They have many foes because they take no allies."

"None?" I exclaimed. Even a*ngels* were allies with other beings.

Zach shook his head in reply. "They think themselves above all other creatures. They believe themselves to be demi-goddesses. They are deadly warriors who offer no mercy to their opponents."

I bit my lip. That didn't sound like something I wanted to be, but perhaps the rage I often felt came from them. I rolled my eyes. Or it could come from my other evil half.

Zach shifted on the mattress and stroked my hair while looking into my eyes. "They're not evil. They are incredibly cunning and calculating. They are a deadly force to reckon with. They win all battles they enter, and they destroy any foes easily."

"Is there anything good about them?" I whispered.

Zach smiled. "They are beautiful, and they value individuality."

I sat up, staring down at him earnestly. "They do?" This was what I had been most worried about. I had finally been accepted by the angels only to find that I wasn't one. I had no plans to associate with any Fallen Angels, but would the Valkyrie accept me as their own? Would they actually *want* me to be part of their family? Or was I orphaned again?

He nodded, his lips curling handsomely. "They do. All Valkyrie are known for their individuality. They are even named according to their strongest attributes. I remember Helen the Temptress and I believe one is called Sheree the Seducer for her ability to seduce her foes to their death." He looked away from me and laughed.

I narrowed my eyes. "Those *would* be the only two you remember."

He chuckled, "some angels are partial to a Valkyrie."

I rolled my eyes as he ran his fingers down the side of my face. I sighed and pressed my face into his palm.

"Are *you* partial to a Valkyrie?" I whispered.

He leaned closer until his lips were almost touching mine, "I'm partial to one particular Valkyrie."

He closed the gap between us and tugged my body closer to his. His lips were like a taste of heaven; soft and sweet, yet at the same time hard and sensuous. He nibbled at my bottom lip and when I opened my mouth he took advantage, sweeping his tongue inside.

We kissed for what seemed like hours, touching and stroking, until he turned me and pulled my back into his chest so that I faced out to the sea. I stared out, watching the waves washing up the beach. I began to feel Zach's presence soothe me. I concentrated on relaxing every muscle of my body, starting from my toes. After a while I began to feel oddly peaceful. I let my eyes close and I continued to listen to the sound of the waves and the smell of the sea.

I felt Zach move away from me and I rolled into the warm space he had left, continuing to drift off.

40

We cannot pass our guardian angel's bounds, resigned or sullen, he will hear our sighs.

Saint Augustine

We entered the house and he sat me on the soft chairs as he poured out cold water into two glasses. He handed it to me then sat down next to me, facing the glass window, looking out to the beach. I pulled a blanket over me, feeling a little too nude.

I took a big gulp then shook my head. "I still can't believe it."

"That's you're not what you thought you were?" Zach murmured.

I shrugged. "Everything. I just got used to being one thing, I just got *over* Asmodeus and the Wolf realm…and I find myself smack bang in the middle of something else." I turned to face him fully. "What about James? Is he…what I am? Or is he still a Nephilim?"

I watched as Zach shrugged and put his glass down on the table in front of us. "I don't know. That's something we'll have to find out from the Valkyrie."

I sighed. "Do we have to go there?"

"Don't you want to? Don't you want to try to find your father?"

I turned away from him and stared out the window. Did I want to meet him? The way everything else was going it was fairly likely he would be a disappointment. What about James? I had presumed we were both Nephilim with the same parents, but what if he was only my half-brother? It would be typical if he was half Valkyrie and half Angel whereas I was half Valkyrie and half evil. That would suit him just fine.

“Why didn’t he like me?” I asked in a small voice. I felt ridiculous for even asking. I had told myself that I didn’t care. He hated me and I should be okay with that, not whining about it.

“I don’t know.” Zach replied softly.

I stood up and walked towards the glass. I pressed my face against it and felt the coolness from the other side. “That isn’t a very good answer.” I whispered.

I felt the rustle of material and knew he had stood up. I soon felt his arms wrapped around me.

“Perhaps he didn’t want to acknowledge his heritage. Maybe he was happy pretending to be human.” He whispered.

Tears pooled in my eyes. “But he was being hunted. I didn’t have any choice but to tell him...did I?”

“I can’t tell you what might have happened if we had done things differently. Everything happened the way it was supposed to happen.”

I spun around and wrenched myself free of his arms. “You can’t say that! I was supposed to kill all of those creatures? The Elf was *supposed* to be trampled to death? If that is in God’s plan, I don’t want any part in it!”

Zach groaned. “Ah Jasmine, you frustrate me! I was trying to be comforting! James would have been taken for the tournament whether he was aware of his abilities or not. The way it happened, at least he was semi-aware of what was happening."

I shook my head. "No! I could have done things differently. I could have just watched him and protected him. I could have been there to stop them from taking him."

He snorted. "Oh yeah that would have worked just fine! What about when they crashed through the windows into his house and attacked him in front of his family – how would you have stayed hidden then?"

"I would have disappeared again afterwards." I answered. Why hadn't I thought of this at the time? I really screwed up.

"They would have come after him again and again! They wouldn't have stopped just because you got them the first time. Would you have stayed here for the rest of your life, watching him from the shadows?" He asked sarcastically.

I shrugged. "Maybe, if I had to."

He stepped up close to me, crowding me. I refused to back away. I stared up at him, scowling.

"It isn't you. I swear it. He's a fool to not appreciate you. He's a moron to not accept what he is and see that he is lucky to have family. Speaking as someone who no longer has *any* family...he should have embraced you and never let you go."

The tone of the argument had altered. I frowned at Zach, noting for just a second that his guard had slipped. He was always so careful not to allow his softer emotions to surface. He was always so stoic and guarded with his emotions. Somehow this talk of family meant something to him. What did he mean by it?

“You do have family.” I stated, still frowning.

He shook his head and began to turn away. I grabbed his arm and forced him to turn back to me.

“You have Haamiah and Maion and all of the other Angels out there.” I said, clutching tightly to his arm.

He raised his eyebrow, his mask back in place. “That is like saying the whole of the human race is *your* family.”

“You mean you have actual family?”

“Had.” He pulled away from me and pulled open the glass doors, stepping out onto the wooden porch. I followed him of course, there was no way I was letting this conversation slip through my fingers.

“Where are you family now? I didn’t think Angels died...” I frowned at my own words. Obviously Angels died; I had killed Fallen Angels myself. “What happens to them? Do they go to Heaven?”

He paused for so long I didn’t think he would answer. Eventually he said, “They don’t go to Heaven, no one does. They go somewhere else.”

“Woah! Hold on a second! There’s no Heaven?” I exclaimed.

He tutted, obviously annoyed. “Of course there is a Heaven – also known as the Heavenly realm – which you knew already! But that is not where the dead go. They go somewhere else. And before you ask me where – I don’t know!”

I frowned in complete amazement. I hadn’t known this. All along I thought people went to Heaven or Hell. Now that I thought about it, it made sense. I had been taught over and over that the universe existed in realms. The Heavenly realm was where the Angels were, where the Heavenly army waited. The Hell realms were where the evil creatures lurked, where they dragged captives to torture...where Asmodeus' army waited. But the dead went somewhere else? Another realm? Would it be possible to go there? To bring someone back if necessary?

"We're getting off track. What happened to your family?" I persisted.

"I don't want to discuss it." He turned to face me, his eyes black, his face stony. "Don't bring this up again. One day, when it is the right time I will tell you. That time is not now."

I gulped and fought against my curiosity. It wasn't my place to demand that he tell me. It was his story, his memories, his family.

"Do you think I should forget about him? I told myself I would." I leaned in against him and wrapped my arms around his thick waist.

After a second he leaned down and kissed my hair. "I do. I don't think he is worthy of you. Forget about him. Leave him to his life. One day he will think back and regret his actions. You saved his life over and over. That is a debt that should be repaid, I will not hesitate to remind him if that time ever comes."

I nodded, feeling the truth in his words. He was right. I knew it, and hopefully one day I would be able to accept it and move on. For now, I would lie to myself, and pretend he didn't exist.

41

It is during our darkest moments that we must focus to see the light.

Aristotle Onassis

A few hours later when the tension had dissipated Zach questioned me about the tournament. With only a few tears and one fist through a wall on Zach's part he was clued in. He was still furious that Aidan had interfered but had begrudgingly accepted – or I so I liked to think – that Blue Eyes had certainly come in handy.

"I was furious when I heard you had entered in place of the Sorceress." He grumbled.

"I knew you would be." I said. "I didn't have any other option. I had to get James out, and the look on Sam's face when Lilura was told she had to enter…it broke my heart."

Zach rolled his eyes and I glared at him in response.

"You were very brave to do that…don't do it again." He ordered.

I grinned. He was so macho and so bossy. I couldn't help who I was. I knew I was impulsive and continually got myself into trouble, but I all I could do was learn from it and hope next time I wouldn't make the same mistake. Though, if I was honest, even if I went back in time, I would still do the exact same thing. Besides

James, Sam was the closest thing I had to a brother. There was no way I would let him down.

“What happened in the Philippines?” I asked. “We thought it might have been a diversion and the Fallen were headed for us.”

Zach looked away.

“Zach what happened?” I grabbed his chin and turned his face to mine. I searched his eyes for any clue.

“Hundreds of Nephilim were killed. The Angels guarding them were also destroyed. In place of the hostages they wanted the Falchion of Tabbris.”

“The what?” I interrupted.

Zach spread his hands and took on his familiar teaching expression. “A Falchion is a sword. It is slightly curved, one handed and has magic imbued inside. Tabbris was an Angel. He was of the Throne class – the keepers of justice. He presided over free will, self-determination, choice and alternatives. He was very important and gave perspective when it came to judging the crimes of Angels and humans alike. He embedded his Angel magick into his sword so that the bearer is capable of seeing and choosing alternatives to whichever goal he seeks. Tabbris gave his sword to his Nephilim child to protect him…and brought about his own downfall. The sword is kept safe in the Heavenly realm along with others.

It was unclear whether the Fallen who attacked the safe house were in league with Asmodeus, but we must presume that they were and that his aim is to use the Falchion to find a way into the Heavenly realm or to capture you.”

"So what happened?" I had a sickening feeling in the pit of my stomach.

Zach clenched his jaw. "We were unable to make the trade and there was nothing else they wanted."

"They killed the hostages?" I guessed.

Zach nodded once.

My heart sank. I felt as though I could cry for him. My poor warrior – unable to save the Nephilim, unable to do his duty; it would eat at him, whether he admitted to it or not. I span my ring around my finger repeatedly as I stared at the brave warrior beside me.

I crawled across the chair to him and sat on his lap, my legs on either side of his. I leaned forward and stared deep into his eyes, startling him. "I will kill him for you. I will kill every single one of them." I remained there for a second, unsure what had just come over me. I slid back and stepped away from him. He remained where he was, staring at me in shock and confusion. I was unable to answer the question in his eyes but I felt it ring in my own head. What had happened to me? Where had meek, soft, scared Jasmine go? What was this creature stood before him who promised death to all who threatened them?

I turned fully and swept upstairs to bed. I felt exhausted, drained of all of my energy. I curled up on the bed closest to the window and closed my eyes.

When I woke up it was dark. I sat up and crawled to the glass panel, pressing my hands to it. With the moonlight shining down brightly, and a million stars twinkling, I could still see the whites of the waves sliding across the sand, reaching towards the beach house. I could see the glow of the light below me, highlighting the sand around the decking. I couldn't hear Zach but I could sense him nearby.

I stood up and stepped off the mattress, ducking under the hanging drapes to make my way to the door at the edge of the room. I ran down the stairs quickly and peered around the kitchen, looking for Zach. I could still feel him but I couldn't see him. I slid the glass doors open and looked out, reaching into the air with my power, seeking him.

I could feel him ahead of me, an odd mixture of happiness and worry emanating from him. Frowning, I jogged down the sand to see his incredible form swimming through the water. I watched each splash signaling a kick from his powerful legs, each stroke cutting through the water.

I knew the instant he realised I was watching him. His aura changed, the worry dissipating and excitement and desire taking over. I smiled broadly as he stood up and began to surge through the water towards me.

The water dropped away leaving him standing in nothing but shorts. The black of his tattoo swirled around his chest in inky black lines, the metal in his eyebrow glinted sharply in the dark. The muscles rippled as he stalked towards me, his lips curving into a heart stopping grin. He stopped in front of me and cupped my face with his hands, kissing me deeply.

He dropped to his knees on the sand and held out a diamond and emerald ring on a silver band.

"Jasmine...will you marry me?"

I froze. Was he serious? Did this *angel* actually want to marry me? Was he asking me this because he felt sorry for me? Because I belonged nowhere? Was it because of what I had said earlier?

"Why?"

He grasped my hands and held them tightly. The ring glinted in the moonlight.

"Because you are strength. You are power and fire. You astound me every day. I never want to live a single day without you in my life. I want to spend the rest of eternity proving my love for you, showing you with every part of me how much I adore you. I need you."

He paused and stared up at me with soulful black eyes.

I dropped to my knees before him. "Yes! I'll marry you!"

The next few days passed blissfully. I was ecstatic, all memories of death and anger were completely eradicated and replaced with a new sense of peace. Zach and I did nothing other than play, laugh and make love. My world was complete, my life now perfect. I could forget about everything and everyone else if I wanted to.

I had initially wanted to tell Sam, Gwen and Trev our news and Zach had laughed and handed me his phone but I had changed my mind at the last minute. I wanted to just enjoy this time with Zach. I wanted to revel in the thrill of our engagement. I was officially betrothed to Zach – *my* Zach, my Guardian Angel. He'd promised to love me forever, promised to protect me for all time.

Every time I thought about it, I would laugh; every day I would see his smile, see the glint in his eyes as he joked with me, see his breathtakingly beautiful body. I'd be devoured by his body for the rest of my life, I'd travel the world with him, experiencing everything it had to offer, everything *Zach* had to offer.

My happiness continued until one day Haamiah showed up unexpectedly. Zach and I were sitting in the kitchen talking, when Haamiah appeared upon the decking and let himself in through the glass doors. Zach leaned over the counter and frowned at him.

"Come to enjoy the sunshine?" Zach raised his eyebrow.

Haamiah nodded in greeting and turned to me, "there is something we didn't discuss before you left."

I sighed, "and that would be?"

"What happened to the Star Mist?" Haamiah asked.

It took me a second to realize what he was talking about. "I drank it," I whispered. I looked up at him as he stared at me in shock. I laughed. "What? What's it going to do...kill me?"

He took a deep breath, "possibly."

Everything seemed to fly into action then. I was whisked back to Elijah who examined me head to toe and concluded that he couldn't see anything wrong. All of them refusing to answer my questions.

"Will you please explain what it does?" I bellowed for about the hundredth time.

"Star Mist increases...everything!" Haamiah said somewhat ambiguously.

"And that means what?" I spat.

"Your abilities, your strength, your emotions...they are all heightened," he stated.

"I don't feel any different," I said, beginning to panic.

"The ring!" Zach cried. At first I thought he meant my engagement ring but then he lifted my hand with the opal ring and showed it to Haamiah. "The ring has to be dampening it, holding it back."

"Maybe," Haamiah shrugged, clearly not committing to that theory. "The only thing we can do now is to contact the Valkyrie. We need to know if the ring is theirs and what it can do. She's a ticking time bomb! We need to find out what is stopping her from exploding, what is stopping it from taking over. Otherwise-"

"Otherwise what?" I asked coldly, daring him to say it. I couldn't believe this was happening! Just seconds ago I was living in bliss and now I was back, smack bang in the middle of all of this supernatural crap.

"Otherwise you will have to be put down," Maion's thickly accented voice came from the doorway.

I jumped up off the bench, ready to face the angel. His words resonated through my mind, echoing, each word getting louder and louder until I could barely hear anything but the sound of his voice. I felt red. I felt as though my anger were alive, literally burning through my veins leaving a trail of black ash behind. I felt it seep up to my eyes, burning, scorching. Anger gave way to pure rage and it surged through me, picking up momentum fueling my power. I bent my knees just slightly and leaned forward, focused on Maion's arrogant face. As I was about to leap and claw his eyes out, Zach pulled me away.

“Contain her!” I heard Haamiah shout as Zach held me by my throat.

“Contain this!” I snarled, shooting white fire out in all directions.

The room flashed in a blinding white light and I felt my body fly through the air. As I landed against the wall, obliterating it, I slid to the ground, panting for breath. Everything was all consuming. I could hear voices, screams. I could see visions in my head of murders and battles. It was all horror, all terrifying and soul destroying. I screamed – the sound so loud I could feel the flames in my throat.

I clenched my teeth and clasped my hands to my head, trying to pull myself together. What the hell was happening to me? And then I knew. As I ran my fingers over my bare hand where my ring should have been, I knew it was all true. It had fallen off when I had hit the wall and revealed its secret. It was a mask. It hid my true self...the killer that lurked inside of me.

That was when I knew it was no use fighting the inevitable. My eyes rolled back and my body began to convulse as the power took over.

To be continued...

LAURA PRIOR

ABOUT THE AUTHOR

Laura Prior grew up in the North East of England, and has travelled the world while working as a Nurse. She is currently living and working in Melbourne, Australia with her partner. She enjoys snowboarding, long walks, shoe shopping and cocktails. She loves reading passionate novels with strong female characters.

Find me:

www.facebook.com/fallingforanangel

Twitter @falling4anangel

www.lauraprior books.com

Made in the USA
Charleston, SC
05 October 2013